Dan Jacobson was born in South Africa to Lithuanian Jewish parents. He has worked as a schoolteacher in London, as a journalist in South Africa and also spent some time on a kibbutz in Israel. He moved to England in 1955 where for many years he pursued a career as a freelance writer of fiction and essays. He then entered academic life and eventually became professor of English Literature at University College London. He also held visiting professorships and fellowships at universities in the United States and Australia. Since his retirement from University College he has resumed working as a full-time writer. His novels and stories are strikingly various in nature and set in many countries – among them South Africa, England, ancient Palestine and the Republic of Sarmeda, a country of his own invention.

GW00645144

THE PRICE OF DIAMONDS

A novel by Dan Jacobson

HOUSE OF
STRATUS

Copyright © 1957 Dan Jacobson

All rights reserved. No part of this publication may be reproduced, stored in a retrieval system, or transmitted, in any form, or by any means (electronic, mechanical, photocopying, recording, or otherwise), without the prior permission of the publisher. Any person who does any unauthorised act in relation to this publication may be liable to criminal prosecution and civil claims for damages.

The right of Dan Jacobson to be identified as the author of this work has been asserted in accordance with sections 77 and 78 of the Copyright, Designs and Patents Act 1988.

This edition published in 2001 by House of Stratus, an imprint of Stratus Holdings plc, 24c Old Burlington Street, London, W1X 1RL, UK.

www.houseofstratus.com

Typeset, printed and bound by House of Stratus.

A catalogue record for this book is available from the British Library.

ISBN 1-84232-138-2

This book is sold subject to the condition that it shall not be lent, resold, hired out, or otherwise circulated without the publisher's express prior consent in any form of binding, or cover, other than the original as herein published and without a similar condition being imposed on any subsequent purchaser, or bona fide possessor.

This is a fictional work and all characters are drawn from the author's imagination. Any resemblance or similarities are entirely coincidental.

Author's Note

The Price of Diamonds is a work of fiction. It does not portray any existing person, town, or institution in the Union of South Africa.

1

When the white beggars – the poor whites – came to the office, their faces were dusty from veld roads, their skins were bronzed, tanned, hardened by exposure to a sun from which there had been no buildings to flee into, and their palms were open. They never came back, for they were always on their way to more distant destinations. All that they came for was a helping hand, mate.

The helping hand was a shilling. From Fink or from Gottlieb they took their shillings and made off hastily, some limping, some staggering, others walking with a purposeful stride to the nearest bar. A few of them gathered together could make the shade near the public lavatories in the Market Square hideous with vomit and caterwauling; but in journeys to customers in the country Fink and Gottlieb saw the brothers of these same men sitting alone like philosophers in the empty, silent veld. To the office in Old Mine Street, Lyndhurst, these migrant poor whites brought an intimation (though the knowledge was almost inescapable in Lyndhurst, from every street's end) of the veld, the dust, the heat, the untilled and unpeopled spaces that lay for so many hundreds of miles north, east, west and south of the town. But the intimation was without grandeur, and could be invested with no romance: dust was dust, thorn was thorn, squalid and abject poverty remained squalid and abject for all the space which it unendingly traversed.

For the man who introduced himself as 'Peter', Gottlieb went immediately for a shilling to the cash box kept in the office of Miss Scholtz, who was out at the time. Gottlieb paid no more attention to the man's announcement of his name than he had paid in the past to other things said by other men who looked like this one. Sometimes they were garrulous: one said that his wife was in Johannesburg and as true as God he was going to see her; another that he had been offered a good job and as true as God he was going to start working again; a third that a kaffir had stolen all his clothes; a fourth and a fifth that as true as God it was too bloody hot (or too bloody cold) these days. They said these things and they received their shillings, for whether it arose from discomfort at seeing his own caste degraded, or whether because he feared their wildness, the possibility of meaningless and irrational violence that a great many seemed to carry half-disclosed with them, Gottlieb, who was usually ready enough to pass the time of day with a stranger, never engaged them in conversation and had as little to do with them as he possibly could.

'Don't you know me?' the man asked.

Gottlieb ignored the question as he had ignored the introduction. He took a shilling out of the box. 'Here,' Gottlieb said.

The man looked at the shilling in Gottlieb's hand. Then he shrugged his shoulders a little. 'Well, I'll take it,' he said. But he hesitated a moment further before stretching forward and taking the shilling carefully between his thumb and forefinger. He turned it this way and that, polished it against his thigh, and dropped it sideways into the pocket of his shirt. Then he smiled at Gottlieb.

But he did not look at Gottlieb as he smiled. His eyes were to one side, cast towards the corner of the office, as if he were looking to see if there were anyone else in the room, who might spoil his amusement – which, his glance suggested, was

2

innocent, quiet, shared between himself and Gottlieb only. He showed his teeth as he smiled; they were remarkably white and even, and when he saw this Gottlieb saw too that the stranger was really a light-coloured, blond man, though his skin had been beaten by the sun into that coppery hue which was one of the marks of the poor whites – an alien, half-savage colour, like a Red Indian's in a technicolour film. Slowly the stranger's eyes moved their gaze from the corner of the office towards Gottlieb, and as they did so his smile grew broader. Then the one side of his mouth lifted acutely towards the eye above it, as he winked at Gottlieb. When the wink was over, he looked gravely at Gottlieb's feet.

'My name's Peter,' he said to Gottlieb's feet.

'So?'

The man nodded, showing Gottlieb the top of his skull. His hair was thin, blond, and disordered. He carried his body to the side, leaning on one arm akimbo.

'Peter,' he said.

'I heard you. What do you want?'

'I've done what they told me to do. I've come here to see you.'

'But I don't know you.'

He had listened intently for Gottlieb's answer. He stood in the posture of listening for a moment after Gottlieb had ended, then prepared himself for speech by rearranging his body, so that he leaned now on the other side. When he had done this he said cautiously, 'I don't know you.'

He smiled tentatively at the far corner of the office, and waited again.

'But what do you want?'

'I came here to see you. They told me to come, so I've come. Right?'

3

'No,' Gottlieb said. 'I don't know what you're talking about.' A possible explanation of the man's behaviour occurred to him. 'Are you looking for work?'

'Work?' the man said. 'Work?' He considered this carefully, his head bowed to the corner of the room. Finally he shook his head. 'I can't say that's why I came here, really.'

'Then you must go,' Gottlieb said abruptly.

He came close to looking directly at Gottlieb, but his gaze fled from Gottlieb's own after barely a moment's meeting. He stared above Gottlieb's head. 'Just now,' he said. His face was flat, with wide-spaced cheekbones protruding delicately through the hardened red skin. His hands too were delicately boned, hanging to the sides of his crooked body. He seemed frail and distant as he announced above Gottlieb's head, 'When we've done our business.'

'What business? I've got no business with you.'

'I've come to visit you.'

Gottlieb made an angry gesture, but the man did not seem to see it. He did not budge. He asked quietly, conversationally, 'You doing a lot of business?'

'Quite a lot,' Gottlieb responded in surprise.

'Lots of people doing a lot of business these days. What's your business?' He paused, returning his gaze to the corner of the office in which it seemed most comfortable, and asked, 'Your real business?'

'We are manufacturers' representatives,' Gottlieb replied with a politeness which he thought even the man before him would realise was sarcastic.

But the man gave nothing away. He nodded merely, then put one hand in the pocket of his ragged, stained flannel trousers, and took out a small box, the size of a matchbox, wrapped in brown paper. 'Here you are,' he said. He put the box on the desk in front of him.

'There you are,' he said. 'That's business.'

4

Gottlieb had decided that the man was mad; and had decided too that the best thing to do was to humour him. 'What business is it?' he asked.

The stranger smiled. 'You're asking me? You should know. I come here, like they tell me, and then I go away again. That's all I do.'

'I see. So now that you've come here and done your business, you'll be going?' Gottlieb asked heartily, moving his shoulders in an invitation to the other to leave.

The man nodded, but made no move to go. He looked carefully at the papers on the desk, then at the waste-paper basket, then at the cupboard against the wall. 'That's the way it is,' he said. 'It's a hell of a life. Sometimes I wonder what goes on, but most of the time I just do what they say. And this bloke gave me your address, and this.' The man gestured towards the box on the table. 'Eleven, Old Mine Street – right? Right. And here I am, and now I've done my business, and now I must go. And that's just what they want.' The more the man spoke the more agitated his movements became, though the agitation was small: a twitching of his dangling hands, a quiver about the lips.

'They use me,' he said. 'I don't talk to anyone. Except like now, when I'm talking to you. But when other people ask me where I'm going, then I always tell them Bloemfontein, so they won't know I'm really coming here. That's how I am, and that's why I get jobs like this one. And tonight I'll have a drink in the bar, and they'll ask me what I'm doing here, and I'll say I'm going to Bloemfontein. And maybe I will go to Bloemfontein – I don't know yet. Because when I've finished a job I can go wherever I like, isn't that so? Who cares where I go? Do you?' His gaze slid towards Gottlieb, but again hastened away before it could be met.

'No,' Gottlieb said.

'You don't care *now*, you mean. Christ, I don't think there's anyone who cares. But when I've got a job, then they all care. If they told me to go to Lyndhurst and I didn't go to Lyndhurst, then they'd worry all right. But it worries me like hell too, all those people caring about what I'm doing. I'm more used to no one caring.' With difficulty the man had picked his way among these thoughts. 'Christ,' he said, and turned his head slowly from one side to the other. 'Each time I begin I like to think of all those people worrying what I'm doing. It makes me happy. I think that I'm all by myself – maybe I'm sleeping in the veld or in a shed somewhere, and there's no one to talk to, and I think about you waiting here in Lyndhurst for me –'

'Me!' Gottlieb protested.

But the stranger ignored the interjection. 'And I think of the bloke who sent me, and I think he's also worrying where I am.' The man seemed to swell for a moment: he looked firmly at Gottlieb, from the light eyes in his sun-darkened face. 'It seems nice the first night.' He gestured, first to one side, then to the other. 'People on this side, and people on that side – and me – me, joining them together. Like,' he added uncertainly. His eyes swam away from Gottlieb, flickered back, but could not stay, and found their place to the side of Gottlieb's head. 'But the second night it's bad. Even in the day it starts. Perhaps it's hot, and there's the sun, and there's the veld. Maybe someone gives me a lift, and then he drops me and I stand by the side of the road. And then it starts. Then I start thinking of you, and Moolman, perhaps, or Aprahamyan – I do jobs for him too – or Baker, and then it starts to worry me. I think of you watching me, and I don't like that. It's like I can see you watching me, and I start thinking mad things. I see a cloud of dust on the veld, and I know it's a car, and I think perhaps it's Baker come to see what I'm doing, and I wait for the car, and I see the dust growing bigger and nearer, and then suddenly it's all around me. It wasn't Baker in the car, it's some bloke I've never seen

6

before. But I've been thinking what Baker will look like when he comes out of the car, and what his voice will sound like, and the way he wears his suit like this,' the man said, plucking at his shirt, pulling it across his breast. With his hand hanging from the cloth and his eyes staring above Gottlieb's head he cried: 'Then I can't stand being joined on to so many people. It's being joined on to them, and knowing that they think of me that starts these mad things. Why do they think of me? Why don't they leave me alone? Do I want to be joined on to anyone?'

He dropped his voice and answered his own question. 'I do. That's the trouble. I'm always so bloody glad to have a job finished. But give me two months, give me just two months, and I'll be going back to Slykersdorp and Klipdraai and those places and I'll be looking for a job again, all over again.'

'That's very interesting,' Gottlieb said with a politeness that was not at all sarcastic. He had been so busy listening to the stranger's tale that he had forgotten what he was supposed to be doing with him. When Gottlieb remembered he could only say again, 'That's very interesting' – but humouringly, this time.

The man was silent. Gottlieb ventured to say: 'Don't you think you'd better be going now? You've finished your business, so there's nothing to keep you here, is there? You can go just where you like. If you like you can go to Bloemfontein, anywhere. The people in Bloemfontein will probably be glad to see you –'

Gottlieb came closer to the stranger, to hustle him out of the office. 'And you've got a shilling. And I'll say goodbye. And thanks for doing that business for me. I'm glad you did it. I was wondering what had happened to you. But now I've stopped, and I promise you,' Gottlieb said sincerely and reassuringly, 'you won't have to worry about me. I won't be thinking about you, ever again.' And though Gottlieb did not touch him, the stranger allowed himself to be pushed towards the door, then down the corridor between the small offices, into the large front office, and so to the door that opened on the pavement. As he went he turned his head from side to side, trying to take in everything that fell within the sight of his light, sudden gaze. Only when he was at the door did he stop and take Gottlieb by the arm in a grip from which Gottlieb shrank, but to which, thinking it safer to do so, he then yielded himself, close to the man's khaki shirt, the sun-reddened patch at his neck.

'If that bloke ever asks you, you tell him that I did my job. That's one thing I've always done. That's why they're always ready to give me another job, whenever I ask for one.'

'I'm sure they are.'

The man released Gottlieb's arm. 'I have always done my job. They all know it.' He pointed at Gottlieb with his finger as if Gottlieb were one among a group of people in front of him. 'Your friend – I'd never done a job for him, but he came straight to me, and asked me, and I said yes. And now it's over, thank Christ. You think I'm going to Bloemfontein because I said so.' The hard red skin contorted shallowly about his pale eye as he winked at Gottlieb. 'You don't know where I'm going. There's no one in the whole world who does. Because now I'm finished my job I'm joined on to no one. Not to you. Not any more.'

The door rattled behind the stranger as he closed it, and Gottlieb did not open it until some minutes had passed, lest the sight of himself should bring the man back into the office. When Gottlieb did at last peep into the almost empty street the man was already at the bottom of the block, about to cross the street in the direction of the Market Square. He walked busily, his head thrust forward and his elbows coming in points behind him. Then a building cut him from Gottlieb's sight.

When Gottlieb stepped back into the office he felt acutely the fluttering of apprehension in his bowels. 'One of the worst,'

Gottlieb said aloud to the silent room, 'one of the very worst I have ever met.' He shook his head. 'Poor fellow,' he said aloud. 'What a life.'

The room made no answer. Gottlieb would have liked it to make an answer. If Fink had been there, there would most certainly have been an answer, and Gottlieb wished for at least the fifth time that day that Fink's holiday was over and Fink was back in the office – instead of only being due back the very next day. And then Gottlieb thought of Fink's scorn at Fink's hearing of the event, the way Fink would ask him how he could have let the fellow talk so much in the office, as if he owned it and not Fink and Gottlieb between them. If he had been there, Gottlieb could clearly imagine Fink saying, with perhaps a flourish of the arm, he would have thrown the fellow out before two words had passed. A shilling, yes – but a speech? – no, never, not from one of those fellows. So Gottlieb tried to pitch into the key of compassion the scene that had just passed, and mentally reproached Fink for having no heart, for being a kind of socialist without a heart for his fellow men. And what kind of socialist was that? Gottlieb asked, silently, this time, of the silent room. The worst kind of socialist of all, the room replied silently. So Gottlieb was encouraged to address the room aloud. 'Poor fellow. What else could I do? I had to let him talk. Only a heart of stone would have refused to listen to such a poor, crazy fellow.'

But the compassion would have been stronger if the apprehension had not been so slow to fall into inactivity in Gottlieb's bowels. Gottlieb stood in the attitude of one waiting for guidance; and his bowels gave it to him.

'You are quite right, Fink,' Gottlieb said aloud. 'With such fellows there's nothing to do but throw them out. They come disturbing a man from his work, taking up time, talking rubbish. Throw them out!' Gottlieb said, waving his arm with an imitation of one of Fink's flourishes. 'Their lives are their concern. My life is my concern. I give them a shilling because I have a shilling to give them, and that's enough. Throw them out!'

To this the walls of the office were silent. So Gottlieb muttered the rest of his sentiments. 'Giving a fellow a fright. It's not nice to get a fright like that in the middle of the day. Strange lives, thoughts all over the place, loafers, people who can't make a living.' The mutter had found its audience in Riva, Gottlieb's wife. 'Don't tell me that I've got a hard heart,' he told her angrily. 'I've got worries of my own. Plenty of them. Without organization, where would I be? The same place as that fellow. In the street. Joined on to nothing.'

Gottlieb was struck that he had used more or less the same phrase as the stranger. He stopped, shook his head, then made his way into the office. Even the mutter had died away by the time he sat himself behind his desk and began going through the letters that he had cleared from the post-office box after lunch.

'Oh, Mr Gottlieb,' Miss Scholtz said from the door. 'I found this funny little parcel on my desk. What is it?'

'Parcel?' Gottlieb looked up from his work.

'Is it yours, Mr Gottlieb? I've never seen it before.'

Gottlieb shook his head. 'It isn't mine.'

'Perhaps it's Amos's.' Miss Scholtz laughed at the thought of Amos, the native driver-cum-office-boy, having a parcel of any sort. 'Perhaps he wants me to post it for him.' The thought that Amos might want to *post* his parcel made Miss Scholtz laugh again.

'Amos is capable of posting his own parcels,' Gottlieb said, looking over his glasses.

'He's clever all right,' Miss Scholtz agreed immediately in an aggrieved tone. She leaned against the doorframe: whenever she did this Gottlieb feared that the frame, which was made of not much more than lath, would collapse under her weight. So far it had not, in the seven years that Miss Scholtz had worked in the office, but Gottlieb's anxiety remained. He watched her, while she complained on the grounds of 'cheekiness' of what Amos had said to her in the morning and what he had said the previous day. Now Amos's having a parcel became a source of irritation, not amusement. 'What should I do with it?' she asked. 'He shouldn't go leaving his messy little parcels all over my desk. It's cheek.' Miss Scholtz looked at the parcel with a grimace. 'I don't even know what's in it. It might be anything. Something dirty. You know what they're like. It might be … medicine, *their* medicine. Teeth, and other things like that,' Miss Scholtz said darkly, 'for medicine.'

'Is Amos sick?'

Miss Scholtz gave a little cry of laughter. 'Oh, Mr Gottlieb, you do think of funny things.'

Gottlieb shrugged. 'It doesn't seem so funny to me. You were talking of medicines.'

Miss Scholtz did not seem to know quite how to take this. She straightened herself from the doorframe. 'Well. I'm going to talk to him. I'm going to put him in his place right now.'

'Don't make a big noise about it,' Gottlieb called after her, for the numerous occasions when Miss Scholtz had gone to put Amos in his place had all been noisy occasions hitherto. And unsuccessful ones – to judge from the spots of colour which burned in Miss Scholtz's usually sallow cheeks, and the heavy breathing that she found necessary to pump the air into her large body when she retired to the privacy of her office, after each.

Gottlieb heard her footsteps retreating; then suddenly he called to her: 'Miss Scholtz!'

The footsteps halted, then came back. Miss Scholtz appeared at the door and leaned against the frame. 'Yes,' she said shortly.

Gottlieb had been about to tell her at length of the visit from the stranger, but the abruptness of her answer discouraged him. 'I've remembered about the parcel,' he said. 'It doesn't belong to Amos. A fellow came in and left it.'

11

'For me?'

Miss Scholtz had a large and easily-stimulated capacity for hope, and Gottlieb was sorry to disappoint her. He said gently, 'I'm afraid not,' and Miss Scholtz slumped more heavily than before against the frame. So Gottlieb did his best to cheer her up. 'It's nothing very exciting. He was a crazy fellow. I've never seen him before. He said he had to leave it for me, and he left it. And I forgot all about it.'

'Oh,' Miss Scholtz said, and came forward and laid the box on Gottlieb's desk. There it remained, until Gottlieb was about to lock up at the end of the afternoon. Then it caught his eye, and for a moment he played with it in his hand, wondering what might be in it. For some reason his mind ran on locusts. A dead locust that the crazy fellow had picked up in the veld – that was what the parcel was most likely to contain.

Gottlieb tore open the brown sticky paper in which the box was practically embedded. Inside the sticky paper was a box for paper clips. Inside the box for paper clips were a few small stones, some of them very light, almost translucent brown in colour, others a little darker. Well, it wasn't a dead locust, but it wasn't much better than that. A crazy fellow, Gottlieb thought, bringing a box of little stones and talking for half an hour, talking only crazy stuff. Gottlieb emptied the tiny, crystal-like stones into the palm of his hand. He pushed at them with his finger. When he recognized them for what they were his finger gave another push, a jerk without volition, and half the stones fell on the floor with a noise like beads scattering, and when these fell Gottlieb's hand jerked up and the rest fell too.

Gottlieb spent the next fifteen minutes on his hands and knees. He peered in corners, he scraped with a ruler in the narrow space under the safe, he shifted the desk backwards and forwards to look beneath it, he burned his fingertips with the matches he struck to help him look in the wide cracks between the floorboards, he went through the papers in the waste-paper basket one by one. When he stood up his face was grey, and there were large beads of sweat on his bald, light brown forehead.

Then Gottlieb spent another fifteen minutes looking for a place where he could hide the little box of diamonds in such a way that no one but he could ever find it. His method of seeking such a place was to put the box in, for example, a drawer of his desk or a compartment of the safe; and then to stand back with his arms folded, and to gaze first casually and then keenly about the room, imagining himself to be a man who was looking for the most likely spot in which a little box would be hidden. Invariably the man's attention was drawn just to the place where Gottlieb had last hidden the box, and with a stride or two, a jerk of his arm, the box would be revealed. In this way, and to his own dissatisfaction, Gottlieb tried the drawers of his own desk and the safe, of Fink's desk, of Miss Scholtz's desk, even the drawers of the battered, high late-Victorian affair at which on a high stool Amos occasionally performed his labours. Gottlieb tried to balance the box on the picture railing that ran around his office, but either the box fell off or when it didn't that imaginary observer with the folded arms noticed it in his very first glance about the room. Gottlieb put the box in the waste-paper basket, but the observer in passing gave the basket a little kick, casually, and the box came tumbling out. The filing cabinets were no good; the ready reckoner looked strange with the box thrust absentmindedly between its pages; the box fell out of the lightshade right on to the imaginary observer's head. There was nothing for Gottlieb to do but to put it in his pocket and to take it away with him.

And yet, despite these anxieties and exertions, Gottlieb was almost in high spirits as he drove home. A turn at a corner took him away from the town's commercial centre, and he had a broad, tarred road to himself, passing on one side the Lyndhurst Mining School – a sprawling, shabby, single-

storeyed building of old brick and a roof of corrugated iron –
and then a row of houses, every house like a smaller version of
the school, having the same brick, the same corrugated iron
roofing. But at the end of the road there was the glisten of a
bright iron fence, behind which, giant-like, there rose the
girders and the struts and the wheel of a mine conning tower;
and when he saw it Gottlieb exclaimed aloud, 'Fink! You
should know what is happening to me!' He slowed down,
almost as a mark of respect for the mining company, and then
accelerated, coming out on a road which gave a good view of
the sort of veld that lay all around the town. It sloped away, the
veld, behind a barbed-wire fence, to the sudden great pit of an
abandoned open mine, and rose again on the other side to the
haggard, greenish mound of sand that had been gouged out of
the mine. Behind that mine dump there was another, and to the
right and the left of it, nearer and farther across the otherwise
flat surface of the veld, the mine dumps rose again. There were
a few black thorn-trees, a few dark-green pepper-trees, but for
the rest – where the veld was not scarred by the pits of the
mines, the mine dumps, and the barbed wire – there grew only
the low, whitish, stalk-like grass. The road ran between this
veld on one side and a row of houses on the other: most of the
houses had their backs to the veld and the mine workings, and
presented only their back fences of corrugated iron, and their
rubbish bins. Then the mines and the mine dumps receded far
across the veld, to become indistinguishable from the veld
koppies on the horizon; and the suburb improved accordingly,
and the houses were able to turn around and face the veld
again.

Gottlieb turned to the right, and there were houses now on
both sides of the street, and other streets of houses running off
to the left and right. The suburb was not new, but it was still
good: the houses were big, each with a wide stoep and pillars
supporting the inevitable corrugated iron roof over the stoep,

and there were trees and lawns before each house. The house-owners, back from work, were watering their lawns, or watching their native servants water their lawns; the setting sun flashed between the rooftops, and some of the bigger trees were tall enough to cut it off momentarily too. Gottlieb parked his car in front of his own house, which, like the others, had been built spaciously of good brick, and was kept in trim by the servants, and had a garden in front of it, where a man could sit in the evenings. The sight of his house always gave Gottlieb satisfaction, for it was, in his word, a *solid* house. Against the gleaming arch of the sky Gottlieb could see a wisp of smoke from the kitchen chimney, which showed that the preparation of his supper was proceeding. There were trees in the garden, houses as respectable as his own all the way down the street – until on the horizon there was a rough yellow brush-stroke of light, where the veld lay as it had once done where Gottlieb's house now stood.

But in front of his solid house Gottlieb could afford to boast about the little parcel that the crazy fellow had left at the office: he could afford to say, as he did aloud, to Fink, who was due back tomorrow, 'Fink, you are the boaster and the talker, but I am the man to whom things happen, I am the man of action.' And Gottlieb thrust his hand into his pocket and fingered the little box. 'What do you think of that, Mr Fink?'

2

If it had not been for Fink, indeed, Gottlieb would have gone straight to the police after his first sight of the stones in the packet that the stranger had left with him, for Gottlieb was well aware that according to the laws of the land the possession of uncut diamonds by one who was not an officially registered diamond digger, dealer, or cutter, was a very serious criminal offence, punishable with a prison sentence of considerable length. But Fink was due back from Johannesburg the very next day, and while Gottlieb would have enjoyed telling Fink about the day's encounter and his visit to the police station, he expected far more to enjoy showing Fink the little box and its contents, and with that remarkable, dangerous box in his hand, impressing Fink with his coolness in keeping it with him overnight, in saving it to show Fink, and only then taking it to the police station. For Gottlieb did intend taking it to the police station as soon as Fink had seen it; he had no wish to become involved in the Illicit Diamond Buying which (under the familiar and simple title of its initials – I.D.B.) flourished in a secretive kind of way in the town of Lyndhurst, and about which Fink, the rebel, was always talking. Fink talked; but Gottlieb was silent, cool, a man to whom things happened; Fink would see the very next morning what kind of a man Manfred Gottlieb was.

And on the present evening Riva Gottlieb would see. Fink was away, and Gottlieb had to tell someone.

Riva, however, had something to tell Gottlieb, and before Gottlieb could tell her his story, he had to listen to hers. He did so with little patience, for he could not see that her story was of any importance. It was about Sylvia, the native cook-girl, and Sylvia's son Arthur, and a native who worked in one of the houses down the street, who had insulted Sylvia, and had been insulted by Sylvia, until these mutual recriminations had brought many of the neighbours and all of their servants into the back lane behind the house. 'It was terrible,' Riva said, and Gottlieb tried to establish who had started the trouble. But Riva was devotedly on Sylvia's side, and said so, as though that settled once and for all the question of responsibility. 'She's a good girl,' Riva said, 'she's been with us a long time, and that's what I told the neighbours.'

'I'm sure,' Gottlieb said.

'And then this native boy took Arthur, and knocked him over, and rubbed him in the sand up and down, and tore his shirt!'

'Well I suppose he didn't like Sylvia calling him a lazy kraal kaffir,' Gottlieb said.

'But that's all he is.'

'And you would like people to tell you exactly what you are?'

Riva thought this over for a moment. 'I'd like it if they said nice things.'

'Does lazy kraal kaffir sound to you like a nice thing?'

'No,' Riva admitted.

'Well that explains why he didn't like it.'

'But his crossness was nothing against Sylvia's,' Riva said, with scorn for the crossness of the other and admiration for that of Sylvia. 'Sylvia said that she was going to kill him.'

'And did she?'

17

'Manfred! Of course she didn't. But she gave him a fright and he ran away.'

'And is that the end of the story?'

'Except for poor little Arthur. He cried for perhaps a whole hour afterwards, even though I gave him sweets.'

'It couldn't have been very nice for him,' Gottlieb said. 'That girl – the way she carries on you'd think she was the Queen of England. At least the Queen of England. She's a coloured woman, she's got no business going around calling other people kaffirs, and kaffirs, and again kaffirs.'

'But she's educated.'

'And that's changed the colour of her skin?'

'No.'

'Well then.'

Riva said distantly: 'I don't think that's very kind of you, Manfred.'

'Look, Sylvia's been with us a long time, I'm happy with her, she cooks well, everything. But also I like people to be what they are, not to try to be what they aren't.'

This upset Riva; and even Gottlieb could not help thinking that he had not done so badly out of Sylvia's wish to be what she wasn't, for it was undoubtedly that that made Sylvia serve them so devotedly. Sylvia would have liked to have been a well-dressed, idle, white woman; but being coloured, poor, and a cook-girl, she had to take pride in the idleness and the dresses of her white mistress, in the size of her master's house, in how well-run, shiny, modern and generally impressive everything that appertained to her master and mistress was. Sylvia was a 'girl' of thirty-five – a plump, light-brown woman with generous flesh at her hips and bosom and the incongruous face of a prize-fighter above, her nose and forehead and chin being all square, each feature truncated. Throughout Riva's story Sylvia had been coming in and out of the room, bringing the dishes, and each time she came in Riva dropped elaborately into silence, waiting until Sylvia had left the room before continuing the tale. While Sylvia, Gottlieb was sure, stood and listened in the passage for as long as she safely could each time.

Yet Riva's story, and what he himself had said about it, had made Gottlieb uneasy about telling his own story – there had formed in his mind some kind of a connection between the two that he did not like but that he could not undo. So when Sylvia took from the table the last plate, Gottlieb prefaced his story with the stern warning, 'Now you mustn't worry about what I am going to tell you.'

'Worry?' Riva asked. 'What about?'

'I have also a story to tell you. But I can tell it to you only if you promise that you will not worry.'

'Why should I worry?'

Gottlieb reminded her: 'You haven't heard the story yet.'

'Oh,' Riva said, 'you mean that I'll worry after I've heard it?'

'That is exactly *not* what I mean. That is the opposite of what I mean.'

'I'm sorry, Manfred.'

'That's all right.'

Gottlieb waited for his irritation to pass, and then patiently he said: 'I know what I'm doing, and I tell you that there is absolutely no reason for you to worry.'

'Yes, Manfred,' Riva said obediently. As if it were a lesson she said: 'There is no need for me to worry.'

'Because I am not going to jail,' Gottlieb took up the lesson. 'Other people go to jail, but not me. Not Manfred Gottlieb, never.'

'Jail?'

'That's what I said. I'm not worried about jail, so on no account do I want you to worry about it. I am not the sort of man who lives the kind of life that sends him to prison. Everybody knows that. You do –' Gottlieb said, touching the

19

bulge in his trousers pocket where the little box was. 'Even now –'

'Manfred, I've never thought about jail.'

'Then don't begin now. There is absolutely no need for you to start thinking of such things as prisons.'

'For God's sake, Manfred, tell me what has happened. Why are you talking about things like this?'

Gottlieb banged his hand on the table. 'I *told* you not to worry! And now look at you! Take your hand out of your mouth – there's nothing to make you start biting, biting. I am not going to jail,' Gottlieb said slowly and emphatically, his hands flat on the table. 'Don't you believe me?'

'I don't know what to believe,' Riva replied, her teeth still tugging at her fingernail. Riva hadn't been a nail biter until Gottlieb had one day remarked that if there was one thing he could not stand it was a woman who bit her fingernails. He had happened to say the same thing the next day; the day after he had had to say it in particular reproof of his wife and not merely as a general observation about the state of his feelings.

'You must believe what I tell you,' Gottlieb shouted at her now; and Riva said immediately: 'Yes, Manfred.'

'Good. Then listen to me.'

When Gottlieb had finished his story he put his hand in his pocket and brought out the box, and placed it proudly on the tablecloth. Keeping the box covered with his hand for the moment, he told Riva, 'These are the things for which the I.D.B. laws send people to jail. These are the things for which the I.D.B. smugglers are ready to go to jail. These little stones are what people all over the world spend thousands of pounds on, so that women can wear them on their fingers, so that people can put them in their safes for an investment, so that kings and queens can wear them in their crowns. And now, Riva, you can look at them.'

Some minutes passed before Riva could bring herself to do it. She covered her eyes, she turned her head away, she cried, 'I don't want to see them, take them away ... Why do you want to go to jail? ... Manfred, I'm so worried, please ...' And Gottlieb asked rhetorically of the ceiling: 'What can you do with a woman like this? Her husband tells her not to worry, so *punkt*, she worries.'

But when Riva did at last look at them, her reaction was one of disappointment. 'Those?' she asked disbelievingly. 'Those little things?'

'These,' Gottlieb said proudly.

Riva's large brown eyes protruded a little. So did her teeth, which were large and white and seemed to lean against one another for support. Her face was forward-going, mobile, hopeful, under the red straight hair, heavily streaked with grey, that she wore cut short over the nape of her neck. Gottlieb stared into her greying hair, as she leaned over the table to have a closer look at the diamonds.

'Are you sure?' she asked; when she had looked close enough.

Gottlieb settled her doubt, and her hope, at once. 'Quite sure,' he said. 'An uncut diamond is not a thing that a man can make a mistake about. I've seen them often before, in the Legemco exhibitions. These, for sure, are diamonds, the most valuable stones in the world. And there they are, a boxful.' Gottlieb emptied the box on to the tablecloth.

'They're rubbish,' Riva said helplessly, leaning back in her chair. 'I've seen little stones like these a thousand times, anywhere, in the garden, on the pavement, in the veld. Who would want to spend so much money on them?' She turned to her husband, 'Who would want to go to jail for them?'

'Not me,' Gottlieb said firmly. 'But there's a thousand fellows who would.' And he began brushing the stones together, across the tablecloth. Despite his own words about them, the few

21

stones had seemed less remarkable on the table than he had hoped they would be: they had reflected little light, they had hardly sparkled at all, they had looked merely like stones from the veld – tiny, yellow, anonymous, valueless crystals.

'But what are you going to do with them, Manfred?'

'I'm taking them to the police tomorrow. First I want to show them to Fink.'

'Why to Fink?'

'Because he is such a big talker. He is always talking about the Legemco, and the heroes in the I.D.B., and the injustice, and the barbed wire, and the diamonds down the river that lie so thick that when you walk you crush them under your boots like sand. Fink will be interested,' Gottlieb said, unwilling to explain further, unwilling to say how much he hoped that Fink would be not merely interested, but impressed – impressed above all with Manfred Gottlieb, who had not gone running to the police with the stones, but had casually kept them with him overnight, though for all he knew all kinds of roughnecks might have been looking for them, the police might have been looking for them, the crazy stranger who had brought them might have been looking for them. They lay in their little box on his tablecloth, the dull, illegal little stones – never had such things lain on any table of Fink's, the big talker. 'He's a big talker, Fink,' Gottlieb said. 'I don't talk so much, but I do things.'

'What things?' Riva asked, unable to follow the train of her husband's thought.

'Things like running risks with the diamonds. How do you know that terrible fellows aren't looking for me, to chop me up to get the diamonds?'

Riva's eyes opened wide. 'I don't know, Manfred.'

'And the police,' Gottlieb went on. 'For all you know, when I go there tomorrow they might say to me: we don't believe a word of your story, we were watching you last night and you are a well-known smuggler and I.D.B. man who must go to jail for at least six years.'

'They won't say such a thing!'

'They might. You never can tell with such things. These are dangerous things, not toys, tricks, talk like Fink's. These are the real things.'

'Then I don't want them!'

'But you've got them. You are also involved, because you are an accomplice.'

'Me?'

'For sure. Anyone who knows that something illegal is happening and does not go straight to the police with his story is an accomplice, which is as bad as being the criminal himself. Either he is an accomplice before the fact or an accomplice after the fact – I'm not sure what kind of an accomplice you are, but you are one of the two, at least. So if they put me in jail then they'll put you in jail too.'

But after a pause Gottlieb added dutifully: 'But there is nothing for you to worry about.'

'If they put you in jail,' Riva said, 'then I'll go there too. I don't want to stay outside when you are in jail.'

'No one's going to jail!' Gottlieb shouted. 'Don't say such things to me. I don't want to hear them.'

'But, Manfred, you were saying them a minute ago.'

'I don't remember,' Gottlieb lied promptly.

To every marriage there is a strategy: in Gottlieb's case, having decided sadly, early in his marriage, that his wife was a foolish woman, he had soon got into the habit of fairly cheerfully projecting upon her those desires, ideas, and anxieties of his own which he could not but occasionally feel even when he had no intention of letting them become a guide to his actions. So he let them act as a guide to his wife's; and she, for her part, had got into the habit of letting her husband suggest by his denials, dismissals, and prohibitions, what she should do. The thought of the roughnecks, or the police, who might be looking for the diamonds that had miscarried into his hands had given Gottlieb more than a moment's uneasiness since he had decided that the diamonds must be kept for Fink to see; so now he poured scorn on Riva as he saw her bolting the windows, locking the doors, and starting at every sound which occasionally broke the early-evening peace of the street outside the house. Riva said that they should not sit on the stoep later in the evening, because anyone would be able to see them under the light; she swore that she would not have a moment's sleep until Gottlieb had handed the diamonds to the police; she shook her hands when she remembered that the police might not believe Gottlieb's story – a fear which Gottlieb himself had known, which he had told her of, and which made him pull a face at the foolishness of all women when he heard it coming from her.

'How do you know it wasn't a police trap?' Gottlieb asked. 'I have heard that they do such things sometimes to respectable people.'

'It was a trap,' Riva moaned. 'Throw the stones away, then they won't be able to catch you.'

'They'll never believe that I have thrown them away,' Gottlieb said. 'They'll think I have hidden them, and then it will be worse.'

'Oh, Manfred, what can we do?'

'We mustn't worry,' Gottlieb replied. 'I'm not worrying, so why are you? Do you think I don't know my own business?'

But Riva's alarm was so great, and was expressed so vehemently, that Gottlieb began to think how much better it would have been if he hadn't told her anything about the stones. 'And there's one other thing,' he said, and held up one finger warningly. 'On no account do I want you to say a word about these diamonds to anyone in the whole world.'

The idea of telling anyone in the whole world about the diamonds had not entered Riva Gottlieb's head, but now, hearing her husband, she said: 'It would be good. We must ask the lawyers, they'll be able to tell us what to do. I'll do it if you don't want to go.'

'No one!' Gottlieb commanded.

'No one,' Riva repeated; but as Gottlieb watched the workings of her face he knew she was wondering whom among her acquaintances she could possibly ask.

'Tomorrow you will stay in the house all day,' Gottlieb said.

'Yes, Manfred, I will.'

Gottlieb watched her closely.

'You will tell no one?'

'No, Manfred.'

Gottlieb issued one more warning. 'You will remember that you are an accomplice, and just as guilty as me if anything goes wrong.'

'Yes, Manfred, I will remember.'

'And that will make you behave with responsibility?'

'Yes, Manfred. I feel very responsible already,' Riva said, with a glance over her shoulder at an unexpected footfall outside the door.

The sound happened to be the approach of Sylvia, who had come to ask Riva for some advice about a dress which Riva had grown tired of and which, as she did with most of her dresses, she had handed on to Sylvia. Sylvia was now adapting the dress for her own use, and had come to ask Riva about the length of the hemline. For in her room in the backyard of the house of her master and mistress, by the light of a single bare electric bulb, Sylvia read with great care the fashion magazines that Riva handed on to her along with the dresses, and Sylvia lengthened and shortened her skirts as the magazines directed. Sylvia and Riva began retreating to the kitchen, where Sylvia had set up Riva's sewing machine, but Gottlieb called them back. 'I hear there was some trouble this afternoon,' Gottlieb said; and heard again the story that Riva had told him, this time from Sylvia. Sylvia's voice was loud, indignant, sorrowful:

Gottlieb cut the recital off by asking her why she had called the offending boy a lazy kraal kaffir.

'But that's what he is,' Sylvia replied. Her brown face laboured under the little serving-maid's cap as she said, 'I am nearly white, master, the master knows what I am. And the missus too. But these kaffirs don't have respect for us.'

'I am sorry,' Gottlieb said, and signified that Sylvia could go.

A little later Gottlieb heard more cheerful voices from the kitchen, where the two women were busy over the dress. Had the dress been designed and made in Paris expressly for Sylvia, in Lyndhurst she could still not have sat in it on a park bench, gone to a cinema, ridden in the front seat of a bus; but she would clearly, gladly lock upon others the doors that had been locked upon her. 'So it goes,' Gottlieb said aloud, touching the box in his pocket through the cloth of his trousers.

While the two women were in the kitchen, Gottlieb sat by himself for a few minutes, wondering whether it would be possible for him to find here in the house a hiding place for the diamonds which would escape the vigilance even of that imaginary observer who had plagued him in the office. The simplest and most effective way of hiding the little box, Gottlieb decided, would be to dig a hole somewhere in the garden and drop the box into it; but Gottlieb was a little worried about the chance of a passer-by in the street looking over the fence and seeing him dig a little hole and then drop something into it. Even the most unvigilant and unimaginative of passers-by might think that rather odd – so, Gottlieb decided, he would have to dig like a gardener, in a bed of flowers, and only then would he be safe. For who could suspect anything in the sight of a householder digging like a gardener in the evening after a day in the office?

Gottlieb went outside: it was already darker than he had expected it to be, but there was still light enough for a good dig.

Despite the care of the houseboy, the garden had a dusty, light-brown look, but that was only to be expected at that time of year, and the lawns were coming on green quite well, low down. Gottlieb got hold of a spade and chose one among several flowerbeds near the fence that would benefit from a little digging up. And he set to work; but before he could throw the little box into the special little hole that he had prepared for it among the rest of the sandy, turned-up earth, Benjamin, the houseboy, came running from the back of the house to see if he could help his master.

'I want to dig,' Gottlieb told him brusquely.

But Benjamin lingered nearby, his hands reaching forward involuntarily when Gottlieb struggled with a particularly heavy spadeful of earth, or when he struck a rock and jarred his hands and shoulders. Solemnly, Gottlieb dug; wonderingly, Benjamin – whom Gottlieb felt he could not send abruptly away without arousing suspicion – watched Gottlieb at this unaccustomed exercise.

'Please, baas, I will dig for the baas.'

Gottlieb straightened himself over the spade, and felt the evening breeze touch with a sharp chill the sweat down his back. 'I'm digging because I like it,' Gottlieb said, struggling for breath. 'You can go.'

Benjamin did not go. He sank on his haunches, his black knees projecting from his khaki shorts. '*Au*, baas,' he said admiringly, 'the baas is working too hard.'

'Yes,' Gottlieb said, acutely aware of his age, of his inefficiency with the implement, of the alternating warmth and chill of the sweat that was collecting in the small of his back. The garden was losing what little colour it had had when he had come out: a light blue shadow was beginning to fill the spaces under every shrub and between the branches of the small trees.

When Benjamin at last got to his feet, Gottlieb stood up and rested; no sooner did Benjamin go than Gottlieb began digging furiously at a brand-new hole, for the other had been filled long before by a carelessly dropped spadeful of earth. There was sand in Gottlieb's shoes, sand in his trouser turn-ups, sand in his eyes from where he had wiped his brow with a sandy hand; he dug like a demon for a moment, but Benjamin was back too soon, with a pitchfork in his hand.

'I will help the baas,' Benjamin said.

He began working behind Gottlieb, breaking up the clods in the dry earth that Gottlieb's spade had turned up. So they worked together, the master and the servant, the white man and the black, until the lights from the house were yellow and square, filling each window, and the light blue shadow under the shrubs had become a near-black shade everywhere, and Gottlieb could work no longer, and went tottering inside, the box still in his pocket.

Riva looked at him with pity, as he made his way to the bathroom.

'You shouldn't do such things, Manfred, at your age. If you want things fixed up in the garden you must tell Benjamin. That's why I sent him to help you – it's what you pay him for, isn't it?'

3

For fifteen years an enamel sign hanging down from the concrete portico over the pavement had said, '*Fink & Gottlieb Ltd., Manufacturers' Representatives*', and the same words were emblazoned in gold on the green windows to either side of a door that was usually ajar. Through this door passers-by could get a glimpse of the long wooden-floored room behind the windows, but on most days the sunlight outside was so bright, and the office was so dim inside, that even when anyone entered the office it took him some time before he was able to read the sign that hung above a counter that ran the full length of the room. '*Sample Department*' the sign said, but the shelves behind the counter and those along the wall on the other side were quite bare of samples or anything else. At the end of this office there were smaller offices made of whitewashed beaverboard, on both sides of a narrow passage. The windows on the doors of the first two offices were frosted white, and in gold lettering similar to that outside there appeared on the left-hand door the words, '*T. H. Fink, Managing Director: Knock Before Entering*'; and on the right-hand door, '*Manfred Gottlieb, Managing Director: Please Knock Before Entering*'. The passage between the offices ran on, to a door right at the back of the building; on this back doorstep a native frequently squatted with his hands on his hips and his attention directed to a kettle that stood on the floor of the passage and that was usually about to come to the boil. Both Fink and Gottlieb drank innumerable cups of tea, even on the hottest day. The other offices, between the back wall and those of Fink and Gottlieb respectively, were small affairs, in one of which there sat Miss Scholtz, the white girl typist; the others were almost empty but for the signs that Fink had had erected and that declared them to be *'Dispatch Department'*, *'Packing Department'*, *'Special Department'*, and *'General Department'*. ('We will be a big firm,' Fink had said. 'Like the Legemco.') When he was not making tea Amos, the native, could be found in a brown drill jacket at the high desk in the General Department, casually sorting files of the firm's old correspondence, and reading silently but with much movement of his lips letters chosen at random to help him pass away the time.

But it was an unusual visitor who managed to get as far as the typist's office without his shadow falling on the frosted windows of either of the first doors between which he had to pass. And if they had not already been roused by the sound of the visitor's footsteps on the uncarpeted boards, the sight of his shadow invariably produced an instantaneous reaction in the rooms of both partners. Their doors would open, their heads would appear, and peremptorily they would greet the visitor with such remarks as: 'You knocked? – you knocked, hey?' 'What is your business?' 'Why don't you come in?' The partners would glare at one another, and when the surprised visitor announced his business, 'That's Gottlieb's,' Fink would say angrily, pointing at his partner's head, not more than two feet away from his own; or 'That's Fink's,' Gottlieb would say – and as the visitor followed Fink's retreating head into Fink's office Gottlieb would shout after him, 'What do I know about the soft goods? It's all Fink's.' Or if the business were Gottlieb's, Fink might say, 'Novelties? (or "Stationery?" or "Mealie meal?") Speak to Gottlieb, not to me. I've got no time for novelties, I'm a busy man with the soft goods.'

By custom each left it in this way for the other to direct the stranger; but when either of the doors closed behind the visitor the remaining partner stood in the passage and listened intently to every word that passed behind the beaverboard partition, and occasionally shouted from outside his opinions on the discussion within. 'We don't want it, we got enough,' or 'Don't argue with the man, tell him yes, it's all business, grist to the mill.' And back the reply invariably came through the partition, 'I remind you that novelties is my affair.' 'Who knows the soft goods, you or me?' Then the two partners would conduct a loud and animated exchange about the merits or demerits of the visitor's proposal, until the matter was settled one way or the other. Business then put behind them, Gottlieb or Fink would offer the visitor a cup of tea, which the other partner was always formally invited to join. 'Fink, why don't you come in and drink a cup of tea with Mr Smith?' 'I don't mind, Gottlieb, I'm coming in a minute.' When the visitor declared that it was time for him to go, back each of the partners went to his own office, where he worked and shouted at the other until it was time for lunch.

Fink, poor fellow, was a widower, and each of his daughters had said that she would rather be dead than live in a dump like Lyndhurst, so he had to live all by himself in the Diamond Hotel, near the office, on the other side of the Market Square. The food at the Diamond, Fink said, was giving him an ulcer in the stomach, so he ate his lunch with Gottlieb, at the Gottliebs' house. Carefully they drove to Gottlieb's house for lunch – one day in Gottlieb's car and the next day in Fink's – and ate the lunch that Sylvia and Mrs Gottlieb served them both. Then Gottlieb retired to his bedroom with the newspaper and had a little sleep until two o'clock, and Fink did the same in the lounge, with his shoes off and his stockinged feet pointing to the ceiling from the end of the sofa.

'It's no life for a man without a wife,' Mrs Gottlieb reported to her husband. 'He had holes in his socks today.'

'Holes in his socks! A fine advertisement for his soft goods!'

Mrs Gottlieb was not amused. 'It's a shame. I'd offer to darn them, but he'd be offended. You know what he's like.'

'Very well,' Gottlieb nodded. 'Poor fellow.'

'He'd be hurt that I saw the holes in his socks. He has such terrible pride.'

'Fink's pride is a terrible thing. It is eating him away.'

Sometimes Riva cast about in her mind for a suitable widow for Fink. 'It's what he needs,' she said. 'Then he'll be happy again.'

Gottlieb was more cautious. 'Perhaps he would be a little happier, and not so proud.'

At other times Gottlieb reminded her that the man had *three* daughters, not one of whom had made it her business to stay in Lyndhurst and look after her father. Instead each one of them, as she had reached maturity of a sort, and eligibility without doubt for marriage, had deliberately gone off to Johannesburg in search of the professional man that each had succeeded in marrying. 'A girl has to get married,' Gottlieb admitted to his wife, 'but is it impossible to manage it in Lyndhurst?'

And when he wanted to goad Fink, Gottlieb always inquired after Fink's daughters. 'What has happened to Althea?' he would ask. 'She married the lawyer?'

Fink would know what was coming. 'Yes.'

'He's doing well?'

'He's making a living.'

Gottlieb would think this over for a moment or two.

'And Lynda? She married the doctor?'

'Yes.'

'And how is his practice?'

'Very good. An excellent practice in a good suburb.'

'And Claire, her husband is also making a living?'

'A first-class living.'

'That's a good thing to hear. Three daughters, all married to good men, all making a living.' Gottlieb would nod, Gottlieb would suck at his tea, absently Gottlieb would deliver his blow.

'I haven't seen them for a long time. I'd like to see them again. Are they coming down to Lyndhurst soon?'

'Yes.'

'Oh – so?'

'Yes.'

Gottlieb would smile, Gottlieb would know he was on top. 'When?'

'I don't know,' Fink would shout. 'I don't know their plans.'

But if Fink had been really angered by Gottlieb's inquiries, he would tell Gottlieb, 'They're coming down when your Irvine comes down. On exactly the same train, that's when they're coming down.'

'My Irvine?' Gottlieb could see no connection between his Irvine and the questions he had been asking. Haughtily he asked, 'My Irvine? He's very well. He's learning hard to be a specialist.'

'And when he's finished he's coming to practice in Lyndhurst?'

'Perhaps,' Gottlieb would lie uneasily; and Fink would reply with a pitying shrug of his shoulders: 'Perhaps is as good as a feast.'

Often when he regarded his partner, especially after Fink had just said such a thing, Gottlieb wondered how he could ever have become the partner of a man like that. Fink was a small, sharp-featured man with thin white hair hanging in a wispy way over his curved reddish forehead, and hard bristling eyebrows starting upwards, above his eyes, as if in fierce reproof of the softness, thinness, and vagueness of the hair of his head. Then his face dwindled away, down the cheeks, past the small slightly open mouth to the receding chin, leaving behind it with any assertiveness only the pointed nose which Fink was in the habit of lifting in the direction of the ceiling whenever his partner talked to him. How, Gottlieb asked himself, could he have gone into partnership with a man who looked like that? A man who was clearly, from his face alone, unreliable, impetuous, given to sulking and private thoughts, a man with no strength of character, only the curses of obstinacy and pride. A man who would, without warning, have the words, '*T. H. Fink, Managing Director*' painted on his door.

What an argument they had had, that Monday morning, when Gottlieb had come into the office and had found that over the weekend Fink had got hold of a coloured sign-painter and had paid him to paint that sign on his door.

'Who appointed you managing director?' Gottlieb screamed. 'I did.'

'And who are you to appoint yourself managing director?'

'The managing director,' Fink replied, with a finger to the words on the door.

What could Gottlieb do with a man like that but get the same coloured to come and paint the same words under Gottlieb's name on the other door – only adding '*Please*' to the '*Knock Before Entering*' in the hope that visitors would notice how much better were the manners of the right-hand managing director than those of the one on the left?

But there were other matters that were less easily settled. 'Sometimes,' Gottlieb confessed to his wife, 'I feel ashamed when I walk in the street with Fink. I ask myself: What must people think when they see a man who looks like that? And what,' Gottlieb asked, with greater concern, 'must they think of a man who walks with a man who looks like that?'

Mrs Gottlieb pointed out that in her opinion Fink did not look any more strange than her husband. 'He is thin and you are fat, and that is all the difference.'

'I wear glasses, and Fink doesn't.'

'So? Does that make you more beautiful?'

'No – but it – it sets me off,' Gottlieb said, having chosen his phrase. 'And how can you say that I look no better than Fink? Fink is no figure of a man. Fink has no proportions.'

'And you have proportions?'

'Certainly I have. I am a man of generous proportions.'

'You mean you are fat.'

'I mean nothing of the kind. I am taller too,'

'You look shorter because you are fatter.'

'What nonsense! Fink looks shorter because he's thinner. If it wasn't for me,' Gottlieb exclaimed, silencing himself and his wife with the angry inconsequence of what he was saying, 'no one would so much as notice Fink when we walk together.'

But when the two of them walked in the street together, Gottlieb looked censoriously at his partner, and pulled his shoulders back and thrust his chin into the air; when they met acquaintances Gottlieb talked effusively in an effort to divert the attention of the stranger from his partner's appearance and manner – both of which, Gottlieb was sure, were so much less pleasant and urbane than his own. Despite Gottlieb's efforts, often enough Fink did manage to put in his word, and then Gottlieb listened to what Fink was saying with an embarrassed smirk on his dark countenance and a conciliatory tilt of the head towards the stranger. Then they would resume their stroll, Gottlieb occasionally pressing his chin deeper into the flesh that supported it to have another sideways, disapproving look at his partner. Down the street outside their office they would walk, and at the corner they would stop and consider which way to go farther. And here Gottlieb would be faced with the least easily settled matter of all: here Gottlieb would be faced with his partner's ideas.

The bottom half of the street was a little grander than the top half in which their own offices were situated, for across the intersection were the offices of the Lyndhurst General Mining and Exploration Company, the company which owned all the diamond mines around Lyndhurst, and a considerable part of Lyndhurst too. Great as was the Legemco in Lyndhurst, in itself it was only one of the companies of an even larger company with its headquarters elsewhere, so its offices in Lyndhurst were modest enough, or would have been thought modest enough in any other town. But in Lyndhurst, with their three-storey blocks of white concrete on either side of the street and their noticeable lack of corrugated iron anywhere, even on their roofs, these offices were sufficiently imposing to make grand the lower reach of Old Mine Street, and with their solid wooden doors and their glinting brass nameplates and their shadows falling across the street, were enough too to discourage the partners from continuing their stroll in that direction. To the left the street petered out into corrugated iron garages and shops with windows that displayed nothing and that were kept together only by strips of gummed brown paper; and then, with no gesture at all, and only a barbed-wire fence to indicate that it was about to do so, the road fell into a hole, the biggest open mine in Lyndhurst – a hole so deep that its bottom could be seen from one point only, where the pigeons that dared to fly into its depths looked no bigger than midges, a hole so wide that from where Fink and Gottlieb stood, only a few minutes' walk from the Market Square, and across the road from the offices of the Legemco, the houses and trees on the far side of the hole were at the very rim of their sight. Between themselves and that horizon there lay only the savage great hole that men had dug in their search for diamonds, and had then abandoned.

And it was here that Gottlieb was faced with Fink's ideas. Gottlieb may have been discouraged from going down Old Mine Street, but Fink refused to do so, because of the hatred he bore for the Legemco. 'We are surrounded,' he told Gottlieb.

'They are all around us. They starve us, they deprive us of opportunity. Isn't it enough that they have those offices, and that mine there, and everything else that you can see? Must I walk between their buildings like a slave? Never, Gottlieb, never.'

Sometimes Gottlieb argued with Fink. 'Fink, you exaggerate. Of what opportunities do they deprive you? They don't own every building, nor every mine. You are no one's slave, you are a free man in a free country.'

'A free country!' Fink shook his head. 'Gottlieb, you talk like a child. How can it be a free country when this Legemco across the road has all the diamonds in the world and keeps them all for itself, and puts them on the markets one by one, when it pleases itself? Is that freedom to you, Gottlieb? To me it is slavery. And you know what is happening down the river. Seventy-five years ago they had to dig a big hole like that to get the diamonds. Now,' Fink said, repeating one of the rumours most persistently current in Lyndhurst, 'the diamonds have been found lying along the river, anyone can pick them up. And what does the Legemco do about it? It owns them all – and does it let people come and take the diamonds and sell them for the best price they can get? No, Gottlieb, it does not. It puts barbed wire around the diamonds, and it brings its own policemen and the policemen of the government too, and they come with their cars and their aeroplanes and their guns and their dogs and they go up and down the wire. And when they catch a poor devil taking one of these diamonds that they don't use themselves, but just leave lying there – when they catch one of these fellows, they put him in prison for ten years under the I.D.B. laws. Just a trickle of diamonds the Legemco lets out of its hands, just enough to keep the prices high, and that's all. Is that freedom to you? No, it is slavery! And you want me to walk between their buildings? Never, Gottlieb. Do you hear what I say? Never!'

'Fink, you are a kind of a socialist.'

'Gottlieb, you are a slave. With a slave's mind.'

These abstract ideas and speculations always impressed Gottlieb more than he cared to admit. As Gottlieb saw them they were the expression of an ambition which goaded Fink to see himself in direct, immediate, and competitive relationship with forces that Gottlieb could not believe had anything to do with himself; and Gottlieb was more impressed than he wished to show by the sort of thing that Fink so often did in the service of that ambition.

There was, for example, the occasion when Fink phoned up the offices of the hated Legemco, and instructed the person who answered the phone to tell the managing director of the company that he, Fink, was about to leave for Europe on a business trip – an urgent trip, on some very big business – and that all inquiries from the Legemco during his absence should be referred to his partner, Mr Manfred Gottlieb, who would give them his best attention. Now there were two aspects of this call that were inexplicable to Gottlieb: the first being that Fink was not going to Europe and had no business there; and the second being that the Legemco had never done any business at all with Fink & Gottlieb Ltd. For the next two or three months whenever Gottlieb saw anyone whom he knew to be employed by the Legemco he hurried past with face averted, lest the man should ask him the same question that he had asked of Fink: 'What the hell is all that about?'

Gottlieb would have been unable to reply to the Legemco employee in the way that Fink had replied to him: 'Don't get excited. It does no harm.'

'No harm? Are you mad? You make a laughing stock of me.'

'They won't laugh, they'll have more respect for you the next time they see you. They'll think you have a partner who does big business in Europe. They're so big that if you tell them they've done business with you they don't even know that you're wrong. Gottlieb,' Fink said firmly and pityingly, 'the trouble with you is that you have no visions.' And later Fink explained: 'It does no harm if it confuses them. Then it is sabotage, then it is like striking a blow for freedom almost as good as working in the I.D.B.'

Once Fink pointed at the great hole near the office and told Gottlieb that with one-thousandth millionth of the diamonds that the Legemco let lie on the ground down the river and put people in jail for taking, the company could afford to fill up the hole and build where it had been a most beautiful garden suburb.

'Fill it all up?' Gottlieb asked incredulously, staring at the tiny houses at the far rim of the hole.

'Of course fill it up, and build houses.'

'But who would live in the houses?'

'People.'

'What people? Are there so many people living in Lyndhurst who are looking for houses?'

'If they built the houses in a beautiful garden suburb, then the people would come to them, and then Lyndhurst would flourish, and our firm' – Fink said, with a glare across the road at the impervious offices of the Legemco – 'would also flourish and everything would be fine and free.'

'It's not so bad now.'

'What?'

'Our firm.'

'You have no ambition,' Fink said. 'You are content to be a little manufacturers' representative for the rest of your life.'

'And for the rest of your life what do you plan to be, Fink? Disraeli?' Disraeli, in Gottlieb's opinion, had reached the very highest position that any Jew could aspire to; and Gottlieb tried to show his scorn for what Fink had said by calling him 'Disraeli' for the next few days. But Fink drew the teeth of the joke by answering to the name with a straight face, as if it were no more than his due.

'He is proud,' Gottlieb said to his wife.

And all Mrs Gottlieb's efforts to find a suitable widow for Fink were unsuccessful. There was Mrs Berman from Leeudorp: there was Mrs Bethel from Johannesburg who was visiting her sister in Lyndhurst: there was Mrs Yankelowitz, poor woman, living right in Lyndhurst with no one to look at her. But Riva Gottlieb always shrank from suggesting to Fink by hint or casual remark that it might be good for him if he were to remarry. 'He would snap my head off,' she said, 'and what good would that do?' She organized card-parties and saw to it that at Fink's table there was a suitable widow, but none of these card-evening acquaintances that Fink was forced into making ever went further than that one evening. 'He is obstinate,' Mrs Gottlieb said, and her husband added more portentously: 'He has ideas.'

'His ideas I don't know. But his obstinacy I know very well. There was Mrs Weintraub, there was Mr Fink – but would he offer to drive her home? No, no, no. He drove home by himself in his big car. What can you do with such a man?'

'My partner,' Gottlieb groaned.

She too sometimes blamed Fink's daughters for the way their father lived, but for a different reason than that of her husband. 'They're frightened that if the man marries again he'll leave all his money to his new wife. They've terrorized the poor man.'

But Gottlieb pointed out bitterly that Fink was not so easy to terrorize. 'There is nothing that Fink is afraid of. A man who is not frightened of the Legemco – would such a man be frightened of his daughters? Never. That Fink is fearless.'

Bitterness had become admiration when Gottlieb went on to say boastfully and without conviction: 'Sometimes I wonder if I'll be able to go on keeping him in control.' And Gottlieb told his wife how Fink had that day asked him what chance in a general election he thought there would be for an anti-monopolist political party dedicated to a full exploitation of the diamond fields and a general amnesty for all those convicted of I.D.B.

And whenever Fink opened the door of Gottlieb's office, and looked in to say with a crooked smile and his head tilted to one side, 'Gottlieb, why are you working so hard? There is more money in the diamond fields that the Legemco won't let you touch than you can make if you stay here for a hundred years. And to take it would be a service to humanity, not a crime' – when Fink said this sort of thing, then Gottlieb would be touched with fear, and in a low voice warn his partner: 'Fink, don't get an obsession.'

But Fink was unafraid. 'If people like you, Gottlieb, would help the heroes, the martyrs, the fighters for freedom in the I.D.B. then in a year we would throw off the shackles of the Legemco, and the diamond fields would be worked, and we would all be rich and freer.'

'Fink, it sounds to me like an obsession.'

'I am not frightened of such an obsession, Gottlieb.'

'Would you like a cup of tea?'

'Yes.'

'Good.' And Gottlieb called for a cup of tea for them both and endeavoured to engage Fink in the details of the particular item of business with which he was engaged. For Fink's ideas alarmed his partner; and it was this alarm, with the difficulties and incomprehensions that accompanied it, that Gottlieb and his wife tried to indicate and isolate in a general, pitying way by their talk between themselves of Fink's 'pride' and Fink's 'obstinacy'. Usually their talk helped them – though occasionally when Fink offered some new provocation they broke down and confessed to each other that Fink was a strange fellow, that they did not understand him, that

41

sometimes he was so cheeky it seemed almost dangerous to be in his company.

So though to the outsider the relationship between the partners might have seemed an equal one, and the one partner as responsible as the other for the vagaries of them both, within, on Gottlieb's side at least, there was a certain disarray and puzzlement. Not that this affected the business adversely. They were busy, and they did well. They were manufacturers' representatives, and the manufacturers they represented made a great variety of things. They represented clothing firms, they represented milling firms, they represented stationery firms, toy firms, manufacturers of vegetable oils and soap and cattle feeds: they represented firms that made patent-medicines, and bicycles, ashtrays, bricks, beaverboards, glass, timber, sugar and sugar by-products: they handled paints and tents and jute bags and tinned goods. 'If you want it, we can get it for you,' Gottlieb said to customers, and Fink in the passage shouted through the beaverboard, 'And if you don't want it, why don't you say so?' 'We carry no stocks,' Gottlieb said, 'but when we make an order from the manufacturer it's put down just where you want it as fast as the train can bring it.' 'Or the boat,' Fink shouted through the beaverboard. 'We indent from abroad. We do big business.' 'You hear my partner,' Gottlieb said gravely.

They were as good as their word. The partners were hardworking, even, in their own way, efficient. They dictated letters to the girl in their barbarous, old-fashioned business English ('Yours of 2nd inst. re ours of 24th ult. to hand ...' either of the partners might drone at the girl in beginning a letter, and continue in that style), and each of them had a copious memory for the facts of business, for such things as prices, discounts, due dates on bills of exchange, names of shops and shopkeepers and the purchasing habits of each; they were liberal in the use of the telephone to call customers across their territory; once a month Amos the tea-maker donned a white travelling jacket and a cap with shiny black peak, and the partner whose turn it was took a three- or four-day trip into the country. Across the dry, flat veld, southwards into the Karroo, or north, east, west of the town, into the pale grassveld, Gottlieb's or Fink's car would tear, raising dust, scaring sheep, overtaking and being overtaken by other dust-shrouded metal monsters that appeared and disappeared on the otherwise deserted sand roads in the twenty, forty, and seventy miles between the forlorn little dorps in which Gottlieb and Fink stopped to do their business. The country shops were crammed with at least one item each of all the lines that Gottlieb and Fink represented, and many more, and leaning over the wooden counters, sitting on open sacks of meal and drinking tea, counting the bicycles that hung from the ceilings, the partners would urge the lean, shirtsleeved, unshaven country shopkeepers to buy more of this and less of that, advise them on what would be going up and what would be going down, what would soon be in short supply and of what there would soon be a glut. On business trips there could not possibly be a distinction between Gottlieb's side of the business and Fink's; and when the one who had been away returned the partner who had remained in Lyndhurst took the sheaf of orders brought to him, went through them in the privacy of his office, perhaps grumbling softly to himself, and then called in the girl and began dictating letters.

The girl, in Fink's phrase, was a pudding. Miss Scholtz was a girl with a large family that was a continual strain upon her: her brothers were numerous and young, her father was very old, her mother was dead, she had no sisters to help her. To her stories about her family the partners listened with pity and discomfort, and when they were alone they agreed that it was a shame that such a hardworking girl should be burdened with such a difficult family. At Christmas time they gave her a bonus and a raise in salary for the coming year; and then Miss Scholtz wept and said that there was nothing in the world better than a good Jewish gentleman. 'A good Scotchman is also a fine man,' Gottlieb said, distressed; and Fink moved his eyebrows up and down like darts. They had taken on Miss Scholtz when she had just left school: in their office she had reached the bloom of adulthood, and in their office she was beginning to lose it. Sometimes – with an irony that Gottlieb shared with his wife – Fink worried about the fact that Miss Scholtz had no suitors. He knew, he said, that if she got married she would probably leave the office, and that would be a pity; but all the same, for her sake, he thought it a shame that there was no young man who seemed to be interested in her, and he speculated about this or that *shaigitz* who called at the office as a possible mate for Miss Scholtz. 'The girl is a pudding, but a pudding is a comfortable thing,' he said. This concern about Miss Scholtz infuriated Riva Gottlieb when she heard of it from her husband.

'He has holes in his socks, but he worries about Miss Scholtz! What can you do with a man like that?'

'Nothing,' her husband replied. 'I know him too well. There is nothing that can be done with Fink.'

So Fink's partner built up in his own mind and in the mind of his wife the character of Fink: his loneliness, his pride, his unreliability, his rebelliousness against the social order which Gottlieb believed that he accepted without question. Gottlieb could not help seeing himself as a timid, weak, conservative, conforming fellow compared to Fink; and the more he admired and was alarmed by the wild things Fink did and the wild things Fink said, the more Gottlieb had to denounce them, for the sake of his own self-respect.

They had had a particularly severe quarrel about Fink's 'obsession' just before the last trip Fink had made into the country, before he left for his three-week holiday with his daughters in Johannesburg. Gottlieb had gone into Fink's office and to him Fink had announced that he was drafting for the local newspaper a notice to the effect that Fink & Gottlieb Ltd. had no connection in any respect whatsoever with the Lyndhurst General Mining and Exploration Company. When he heard this Gottlieb did not laugh or smile or shake his head, or ask his partner who on earth had ever flattered the partners by assuming that there was a connection between the two firms. For the moment Gottlieb was startled; then, the angrier for that momentary shock, and the angrier for his wonder at a man who could think of such a thing, he told Fink that he was just a big talker, a boaster, a fellow with ideas out of all proportion to his natural size. To drive this last point home Gottlieb leaned over the desk and braced his arms in a kind of circle, to make himself as large as he possibly could. 'Fink, I would be happy to leave you alone with your mad ideas and your obsessions. But I am human, I am not a calculating machine without flesh and blood and natural feelings, and when a man comes talking wild talk, and always about the same nonsense, then I am not an Englishman to pretend I don't hear him. Then I must tell you what I think, and I must tell you, Fink, that you are a man whose words are just noises in the wind, not even dust. Your head is swinging, Fink, and as it goes round and round you think you are going somewhere. But you are not, you are staying in the very same place. Your talk is worth nothing, until you come with proof that it is not just talk. Do you hear me, Fink? Proof I want, or I despise your boasting.'

Gottlieb would have been pleased if Fink had shrunk himself from the unusual ferocity of the attack; but Fink sat with his head drooping, and seemed merely to be regarding the edge of his desk as if to make sure that it was quite straight.

'So? What have you got to say to that?' Gottlieb made a clutch of the hand for each word. He shouted the name at the end as if it were the worst insult that he had grabbed from the air: 'Fink!'

Fink said nothing. After a pause Fink said that he said nothing.

'What do you mean?'

'You tell me that I am just a big talker, so from now on I say nothing. You will see who is the big talker in this establishment.'

'I know already, Fink.'

Fink lifted his nose so that it pointed at the ceiling, and Gottlieb turned his back on him and went out of the office. Alone in his office Gottlieb said loudly, hoping that the words would carry through the partitions, 'Boasting … big-talking … a mouth, a mouth, and that is all.'

The next day, before there had been any reconciliation between the partners, Fink had left for his trip to the country customers, and had returned from it to Lyndhurst only to take the train to Johannesburg, to spend his holiday with his daughters.

And when Gottlieb remembered that scene with Fink – as he did, late the night the diamonds had come into his possession – with a start that jerked him out of the doze in which he had been lying, Gottlieb suddenly wondered how he could for a moment have imagined it had been by mischance that the diamonds had come to Eleven, Old Mine Street. By mischance the diamonds had come into Gottlieb's hands; but clearly, obviously, unmistakably, they were diamonds that Fink had bought on his trip to the country, when he had, in fact, visited the villages down the river. Clearly, after the challenge Gottlieb had issued Fink had been determined to show Gottlieb that he was not merely a boaster and a big talker, but a man of action, and these diamonds were the proof of Fink's words that Gottlieb had demanded: Fink must have arranged for the parcel to be made up, and for the runner to bring them to town;

but he had not arranged for the diamonds to fall into Gottlieb's hands.

Wide awake in his bed, Gottlieb couldn't help feeling grateful to Peter, the runner, for being unable to tell Fink from Gottlieb, one old Jew from another, when he had seen neither, and both lived at the same address. For Gottlieb knew how amazed and impressed he would have been if Fink one day had produced from a drawer of his desk a little packet of diamonds, and casually tossed it across to him; Gottlieb knew he would have stammered, shown fear, pleaded with Fink to put the terrible things away; Gottlieb knew – in short – that he would have acted no better than Riva had earlier that evening – and what a victory for Fink that would have been! Whereas now, Fink was the one who would be surprised, and not merely at the miscarriage of his plans, but at the way his partner had managed to deal with the situation. And of Gottlieb's fear, of amazement, of the wonder that Fink had intended to arouse and which Gottlieb did indeed feel as he lay in bed – of these Fink would know nothing.

Gottlieb had a whole night in which to prepare what he was going to say to Fink. 'Fink,' Gottlieb imagined himself saying, 'I have a small surprise for you.' Or, 'Ideas is one thing, that I don't mind, but action is another that I must watch, Fink, when it carries you away.' Or, 'Trouble may well be upon us, Fink, but you will be surprised to see how ready I am for it, how very cool.' And Gottlieb rehearsed in his mind how he would tell Fink of the visit from the stranger ('To me he looked a little fanatical, Fink,' was one phrase he particularly favoured); Gottlieb pictured to himself how he would smile to see Fink's discomfiture at the miscarriage of his plans; Gottlieb even permitted himself to imagine Fink congratulating him on his coolness in the encounter with the stranger, and in keeping the stones with him overnight. 'A man does what he has to do,' Gottlieb replied to these congratulations. 'But I meant to test you by showing you these diamonds,' Gottlieb then permitted Fink to say, 'and here I find you have been even more severely tested than I planned, and, Gottlieb, you are unruffled. How did you manage it?' 'I have my reserves, Fink.' 'I can see that you have reserves of iron, Gottlieb,' Fink was then encouraged to say. 'Thank you, Fink – but please – don't embarrass me with such praises.' And with these last imagined words of his own in his ears, Gottlieb fell asleep.

4

The main platform of the Lyndhurst railway station offered few facilities to the small group of people waiting for the early morning train from Johannesburg. They could buy a newspaper or a magazine from the bookstall, fruit from the fruitstall, sweets from a ramshackle set of automatic machines, and ice cream from a native vendor with a wooden tray slung in front of his chest; they could also pass the time by weighing themselves, or by having their fortunes told by a female gipsy-figure painted on a sheet of glass, who for a penny made several revolutions and then came to a halt with her forefinger pointing at one of the fortunes conveniently stencilled around her. Gottlieb weighed himself and bought a newspaper, but he did not have his fortune told. Eventually, like the others, he simply stared at the rails that stretched flat northwards, from which direction, out of the sunlight, the train would come.

The train came down upon the station, the black engine passing with a clank and a hiss and a gust of heat. Then there were the coaches with their brown-painted wooden walls – the first in the heat and grit from the engine being crammed with natives, and the rest inhabited more sparsely by whites lolling on green leather, to whom the station was merely one other on the thousand-mile drag to the sea. Faces were vacant after the night on the train, in anticipation of the day to come, but there was a certain amount of getting off the train and getting on it

49

again; the native ice cream vendor walked up and down along the platform with a little more animation than he had shown before the arrival of the train. Fink was nowhere to be seen.

Then Gottlieb saw him, in a brown suit, one shoulder advanced farther forward than the other – a small, white-haired, red-faced old man, with a bag in his hand. 'Fink,' Gottlieb called, but Fink did not hear, and went on. Gottlieb trotted heavily behind, and caught up with him in the wooden-floored booking office.

'Fink, wait for me.'

When he heard Gottlieb calling, Fink stopped and turned, warily, lugging the case around with him. Then he saw Gottlieb approaching.

'Gottlieb, what are you doing here?'

'I came to see you, Fink.'

'But that's very nice of you.'

'No –' Gottlieb said.

'But it is nice. How are you, Gottlieb? How are things?' Fink stretched out his small red hand, which Gottlieb met with his own.

Gottlieb was smiling; he did not know why he was smiling, but he could not help it now that he saw his partner again. 'All right,' Gottlieb said, as their hands moved up and down. 'How are the girls? What kind of time did you have?' Still Gottlieb smiled; and Fink too let his lower lip droop, showing an edge of his teeth, in an expression that Gottlieb recognized as the nearest Fink ever came to a smile.

'The girls are fine. Why shouldn't they be fine?'

'And the husbands?'

Fink lifted the shoulder that he carried slightly forward. 'If the girls are fine then the husbands are fine too. You know how it is with the girls.'

'And the children?'

50

'Beautiful children, all of them.' Fink gestured as if to continue walking down the booking office, and Gottlieb made a grab at Fink's case. Fink refused to yield it. 'Gottlieb, what's the matter with you? Do you think I can't carry my own case?'

'But you are the visitor.'

'A visitor in Lyndhurst!' Fink looked around the booking office. 'Gottlieb, this is where I live.'

'And me too.'

'We both live in Lyndhurst, and, Gottlieb, I'll tell you one thing.' To tell Gottlieb this one thing, Fink put the case down between them, and leaned over it towards Gottlieb. 'I'm glad to be back. It was very nice in Johannesburg, I'm saying nothing against the girls, and they've all married good men, and they have beautiful children – but no, it isn't my place, and I don't belong there. There's no one to blame: they have their own lives, Gottlieb, and there isn't too much room in those lives for me. And I have my own life here, and that's why I'm glad to be back.'

'And I'm glad to have you back.'

'You are?'

'Fink, what do you think? Do you think I wouldn't be glad to have you back?'

'Well, that's fine. Because this is my place,' Fink said, with another glance around the booking office at the timetables and the railway maps on the walls, the sign that said: '*Europeans Only / Blankes Alleen*'. 'I don't like Johannesburg,' Fink told Gottlieb, 'I don't want Johannesburg. There's a rushing and a jumping and a shouting and a hooting. What for? What for, when you can live peacefully in a town like Lyndhurst, and there's no one to jump on you?'

'How I feel!' Gottlieb said with an emphatic shake of his head. 'How I've spoken to my Irvine many times!'

'I phoned your Irvine,' Fink said.

'You did? How is he? But that was very kind of you, Fink.'

Fink denied the kindness with a shrug of his shoulders. 'I was in Johannesburg, he's in Johannesburg, why shouldn't I phone him?'

'And how is he?'

'He's all right. He's learning very hard to be a specialist. He tells me that he has to work hard.'

'He does, yes.'

Fink stared at a timetable on the wall across from him. 'I told him it doesn't matter how hard he has to work, a weekend in Lyndhurst wouldn't make him fail his exams. And it would make his mother very happy. Yes,' Fink said, with a shake of his head, 'I told him.'

'What did he say?'

'I think he's coming. He was very impressed with what I told him.' Fink shook his head again, several times, in demonstration of how much Irvine had been impressed.

'Thank you, Fink, his mother will be very happy when I tell her. He didn't say when he was coming?'

'No,' Fink admitted reluctantly. 'He didn't say *that*. But he did say that he would be coming, and I spoke to him very forcefully.'

'Then perhaps he will come.'

'For sure he'll come, Gottlieb.'

The two men smiled at each other.

'Tell me, Gottlieb, how has business been?'

Now was the chance for Gottlieb to deliver one of the speeches that he had prepared in such detail the previous night. But he let the chance pass; he said merely, 'Not too bad. Keeping up.'

'That's good.'

'You weren't worried, were you, Fink?' Gottlieb asked with a smile; and Fink almost smiled in response.

'No, I knew you could look after my affairs.'

Again Gottlieb could have delivered one of his speeches. Or not even a speech: he could have said just something brief and shocking which would have brought Fink's lower lip abruptly against his upper lip, which would have made Fink stare wildly at him before fear and surprise could be overtaken by admiration. But Gottlieb remained silent – there was no need to rush like a schoolboy he told himself. He remained silent long enough to make Fink lift his eyebrows and give Gottlieb a stare from his small, bright blue eyes; then Fink picked up the suitcase and began walking down the booking office, towards the sunny pavement outside.

Gottlieb followed, and as he did so he silently addressed Fink's back: 'Fink, if you knew what I know! I could make you jump!'

On the pavement Fink hesitated, not knowing where Gottlieb had parked the car. Gottlieb pointed it out to him, and the two men set off across the road. They crossed the sandy traffic island in the middle of the road, and came to Gottlieb's car without exchanging a word. They did not speak until Fink stretched himself in the car and told Gottlieb, 'I slept like a log on the train.'

Gottlieb thought that if Fink had known what Gottlieb knew he perhaps wouldn't have slept at all.

Aloud Gottlieb said: 'That's lucky. I can't sleep in the trains.'

'Nor can I, usually,' Fink said, in defence of his sensibility. 'But last night – I don't know – I had a drink in the saloon before I went to the compartment, and perhaps that helped. But they come so early with their coffee in the morning! Rat-tat, bang-bang! I woke with a start, I could feel my own heart beating. And what for? – a cup of railway coffee. The noise they make you'd think it was something terrible – a fire on the train, the police at least.'

'The police!' Gottlieb's foot jerked on the accelerator pedal; and the car jerked too, towards an approaching stop sign. So

DAN JACOBSON

Gottlieb had to press the brake hard, and the car came to a halt
that threw both their heads back.

'Your driving –' Fink said cheerfully. 'One day, Gottlieb, if
you're not careful the police really will come after you for your
driving. Bang-bang! – in the middle of the night.'

'Please, Fink,' Gottlieb said, turning fiercely to face his
partner. 'Don't say such things. I don't like to hear them.'

'All right, Gottlieb, there's no need to snap my head off. I
made a joke, so it wasn't such a good joke, but why be so cross?'

'Because you are in no position to make such jokes.'

Almost, Gottlieb would have gone on. But in the street,
hitherto empty, a car had pulled up behind theirs: this car
began hooting and with a jerk Gottlieb's car crossed the
intersection – to the dismay of its only other user, a native
cyclist coming across the path of Gottlieb's car, who had to
swerve and brake and come to a halt in the gutter. But when the
white men drove past him he could do nothing but smile
propitiatingly at them from the gutter.

'Poor fellow,' Fink said to the glass of his window. Then he
turned to Gottlieb. 'Why am I not a one to make such a joke?
Have you got a word to say against my driving? Do I chase
poor kaffirs into the gutter?'

'Your driving!' Gottlieb exclaimed. He was about to go on;
then he said quietly, 'Your driving's not so bad.' He drove,
looking straight ahead; and Fink did the same.

Eventually, with a sideways look at Gottlieb, Fink said, 'It
strikes me that you are in a funny mood, Gottlieb. First you
come and meet me at the station, for which there was no call,
though I appreciated it very much, and you were so friendly;
but now you are cross. Is everything all right, Gottlieb?'

'Everything's fine.'

'Well, if you say so.'

They drove towards Gottlieb's house. Silently, Gottlieb was telling Fink that Fink would have a heart attack when Gottlieb had told him a thing or two.

But by the end of the day Gottlieb had still not told Fink what he had planned to tell him.

Gottlieb was too much enjoying not telling Fink. For the first time in his acquaintance with Fink, Gottlieb had the feeling that Fink was at his mercy. When he saw Fink eating his bowl of cornflakes and drinking his coffee at breakfast, Gottlieb thought how the spoon or the cup would rattle in Fink's mouth when Gottlieb told him what he had to tell him. When they drove to the office together, Gottlieb wondered if the buildings they were passing would shiver for a moment in Fink's sight as the office had done in his own when he had found what was in the box that the stranger had left with him. When Fink greeted Miss Scholtz warmly in response to her greeting, Gottlieb thought how false and abstracted Fink's response would have been if he, Gottlieb, had let drop so much as a word of what had happened to him. When Fink sat down in his office and took off his jacket, Gottlieb thought that Fink would feel cold and small when Gottlieb told him what he was going to tell him. And when Fink started shouting for this and that, and grumbling about this letter that Gottlieb had written during his absence and that cut in their commission that Gottlieb had accepted during his absence, then the initial anger that Gottlieb felt was followed by the silent warning: 'You wait, Fink – you will learn soon to whom you are shouting in this way.' And Gottlieb patiently went to fetch the letter in question, and explained patiently why he had written the letter in such terms, and why he had accepted the cut in their commission and what benefit he hoped would eventually accrue to the firm from it. For in Gottlieb's heart every sentence that he uttered in reply to Fink's irascible demands was followed by the still-silent warning:

'Soon you will learn, Fink, what kind of a man I am, that you speak to with such disrespect.' In the meantime, Gottlieb felt, he could afford to let Fink shout; there was no need yet for him to break his silence on the one particular matter which seemed to him now to put the audacious, irresponsible, cocky little Fink at his mercy. His silence gave him – the timid, simple, easily cowed Gottlieb – the upper hand over Fink the man with ideas, Fink the man who was not frightened of the Legemco, or anyone else, Fink the thinker, the planner, the man of action.

Gottlieb was not a hard-hearted man, but he kept his silence. He would tell Fink, he would tell him soon, but – in the meantime, meekly, enjoyably – soon having no need to utter even silently his warning, it was so much part of all he did – Gottlieb brought Fink the files on this shaky little shopkeeper and meekly explained to Fink why he had extended the man's credit, or why he had refused to have anything more to do with another, whose file too he brought for Fink to see. When Fink shouted and cursed and asked Gottlieb if he kept his eyes in his pocket, then Gottlieb meekly replied no, in his head, like everyone else.

Gottlieb was not a hard-hearted man; he found that he pitied Fink.

He was going to tell Fink soon, Gottlieb told himself; as, at Fink's behest, he went backwards and forwards.

But he had not told Fink by the end of the next day, nor by the end of the day after that, nor the day after that. He still had not told Fink by the end of the week; and during that week, Fink had behaved in a way that Gottlieb, who thought he knew what Fink could be at his worst, found surprising. The man was impossible, Gottlieb told himself; and added: 'Poor fellow.' Often he had said 'Poor fellow' about Fink in the past, but now he knew that he had always said it more as a way of comforting himself than as a genuine expression of pity for Fink. Now he was able to say it with a patronage and a pity that was quite wholehearted. 'Poor fellow, poor Fink.'

And Fink swore, complained, shouted at customers, turned away business, and reserved for Gottlieb all his most insulting phrases, some from the past, as if he had culled them for use on just such an occasion, and others that Gottlieb had never heard from him before. 'A hawker,' he called Gottlieb. 'A peddler, a man with no ideas.' 'Gottlieb,' Fink told his partner, 'you can't handle a business like this one. What you can do, Gottlieb, is to get a little pushcart, and in the little pushcart there must be bones and bags and empty bottles. In your pocket, pennies to give your customers change. In your boots, holes.' 'Why don't you take a little holiday?' he asked Gottlieb. 'You need a rest, your powers are failing and it's a pitiful sight.' He told Gottlieb at different times that he was a drunkard, a real *Dvinsker*, a mouse, a cat, and a fat fellow. He asked Gottlieb, 'Why do you speak like you've got a potato in your mouth? It's something I've noticed for many years, and it makes me a little uncomfortable.' 'Not a gentleman at all,' he called Gottlieb, and a *beigel*, a traitor, a bottle. 'Why a bottle?' Gottlieb asked mildly, taking Fink by surprise. 'Why not a bottle?' was the only reply that Fink could think of at the moment, but later he told Gottlieb that a bottle was fat and round and had no brains. 'Not your best,' Gottlieb said, wrinkling his broad nose judiciously.

'Poor fellow,' Gottlieb said to himself when he drove alone in his car; when he dressed, when he was alone in his office. 'Poor Fink.' In the past any one of the phrases flung at him, any one of the questions Fink asked of him, would have caused Gottlieb to rage, slam doors, rack his brain for insults in reply, even to take a week's unscheduled business trip into the country in an effort to assuage his feelings. But now the insults came daily, came sometimes hourly, and Gottlieb merely smiled; or dropped his head to show how they passed over him; or warned Miss Scholtz that Mr Fink was in a terrible temper but that there wasn't anything to be worried about, because she knew how he could be, poor fellow. To speak in this way to Miss Scholtz was unprecedented; but even that Gottlieb permitted himself, though hitherto the partners had been careful not to drag Miss Scholtz into the quarrels between them, and Miss Scholtz for her part had remained sturdily neutral, saying only to them both, on occasions, 'The things you say!' or 'The noise you make!' Either of these exclamations was enough to make the partners drop their voices and come together defensively, each wearing an expression of innocence, surprise and disbelief – though later the one might accuse the other of making a shame and disgrace of himself in front of the girl. At this particular time, however, Fink was never at all impolite or abrupt with Miss Scholtz, so that when Gottlieb broke the unwritten code, she was able to reply in bland but unmistakable reproof: 'He isn't cross with me, Mr Gottlieb.'

'No,' Gottlieb said with pleasure, 'he's cross with me.' But Miss Scholtz so obviously disapproved of these disloyal confidences that Gottlieb had to retire to his own office, where he could mutter safely to himself: 'Still, poor fellow.'

Once or twice Gottlieb remonstrated with Fink, not in a tone of anger, not as if he could so much as imagine that the things that Fink was saying had any reference to himself, but entirely in a tone of pity and patience. 'Fink, you should be careful. You're not a young man any more, and I'm a little worried about you that you get worked up over such small things. That is the place where ulcers come from, Fink.'

But Fink would not be curbed; and just as, in the past, the less attention Fink in making his wild plans had paid to Gottlieb so the more Gottlieb had had to nag at him, now the more Fink talked the less Gottlieb cared what the man said. 'He thinks he is a wild fellow,' Gottlieb said to himself or his wife, 'but he is nothing of the kind. He is just a poor fellow.'

When Fink called Gottlieb a criminal – as he did once over a letter that Gottlieb had neglected to write – Gottlieb was able to reply coolly, 'You can call me what you like, Fink, because we are in a free country for the white people; but I am no criminal. My conscience is clear in every respect. I hope yours is the same.'

'Why shouldn't mine be clear?'

Gottlieb smiled. 'Do I know the secrets of your heart? No, Fink, I do not, no more than you know mine.'

'Ha!' Fink said scornfully. 'You think you are a man of mysteries. I see through you, Gottlieb, all the way.'

This alarmed Gottlieb. 'So what do you see?'

'Nothing. I see nothing because there is nothing,' Fink said, and Gottlieb's relief at this reply was greater than his resentment of it. He listened attentively, smiling again, as Fink went on, 'All there is is that same fat Manfred Gottlieb who has been my partner for fifteen years.'

'A man can change, even after fifteen years.'

'A man can think he is changed, Gottlieb. But all the time you are settled in your foolish ways.'

'That's what you think!' Gottlieb crowed in triumph. 'And that shows how little you know. If you had understanding and respect, you would know better than to talk with such certainty about any human being. We are all men of surprises, Fink, not you alone. So perhaps you will choose your words more carefully in the future.'

And Fink continued to choose his words. And Gottlieb was able to shrug and remark pleasantly, 'A huffing and a puffing means nothing to me, Fink. I judge by actions, not words. My actions, and the words of another.' Gottlieb also told Fink that it must be sad to be living entirely through the mouth, like Fink, and not through the hands and the heart and the brains, like Manfred Gottlieb. 'And the eyes, too,' Gottlieb added, remembering the little box which every morning and every night he took out of the place where he kept it, in the drawer of his wardrobe, behind the handkerchiefs and the socks and the rolled-up parcel containing old letters of Irvine's that the boy had written in his first year at the university. Every evening and morning Gottlieb took out the box and opened it, and looked again at the sharp little stones, and touched them, feeling their edges and their hard little surfaces with the tips of his fingers, sometimes rattling them in delight close to his ear. They were the source of his power, which poor little Fink could never guess at. Fink talked; but simple, cautious, meek little Gottlieb looked every evening and every morning at the diamonds he kept so casually at the back of a drawer in his wardrobe.

And what Gottlieb had said to Fink about his conscience being clear was true. Occasionally he would have a pang of contrition for the trick he was playing on his partner; but these pangs were never severe, nor did they ever last long. For Gottlieb would remind himself that Fink had wanted the diamonds only to use as a weapon over Gottlieb; and Gottlieb would thus feel justified in using them as a weapon over Fink. And it wasn't as though he actually told any lies to Fink, Gottlieb told himself; he merely kept silent, and he – like any other man – was entitled to his silences.

And the fact was that Gottlieb did intend sooner or later telling Fink that he had the diamonds. That intention hadn't altered at all, Gottlieb believed, ever since the first morning when he had rushed to the railway station to meet Fink, so that he could break his news early; all that had altered was the timing and the manner of his announcement. For if Gottlieb knew anything at all about Fink – and after fifteen years who in the whole world knew Fink better? – then the man wasn't spending his time in speculation about what had happened to the diamonds that should have been coming for him. Having gone as far as he had, having arranged for the diamonds to come, having spent money on the diamonds, Fink wasn't the sort of man who would shrug, smile, and feel secretly relieved that the diamonds hadn't after all come to him. No, Fink was a man who would go at his first opportunity to the person from whom he had bought the diamonds and ask what had happened to them; Fink was a man who would trace the runner and have him sent back to Lyndhurst, so that he could find out exactly where the diamonds had been delivered, and to whom.

The confrontation that would follow was what Gottlieb was now waiting for. When Fink met the runner, and the runner identified the building and the man to whom he had delivered the diamonds, then Fink would have to tackle Gottlieb on the subject; and Gottlieb spent much of his time imagining the ways that Fink might do this. Fink might be carefully casual; he might ask Gottlieb if he had any memory of a funny kind of a poor white fellow coming into the office one day and perhaps talking about a message he had to deliver – some crazy stuff like that, from a poor white. 'There are poor whites here every week,' Gottlieb imagined himself saying innocently. 'A shilling is what I give them, and that's all I have to do with them. Out! Out! is my motto for the poor whites.' No, Fink might then say, this one wasn't an ordinary fellow; and perhaps Fink would describe the man, mentioning his eyes, his hair, his clothing. Then Gottlieb would think deeply, trying to remember such a man; and eventually would obligingly come to remember him. 'Ah yes, there was such a one. What do you want to do with him, Fink?' Did he perhaps leave a message – or a little paper box, Fink might ask desperately. 'A box? A box from a poor white? Let me think if he did … Ah yes, there was such a box … I remember, Fink.' Then Fink would be unable to contain himself; he would ask Gottlieb if he still had the box, please, because it was important. 'Yes,' Gottlieb would say calmly, 'I still have the box.' Then Fink would sweat, grow red, tremble as he asked, 'Gottlieb, do you know what is in that box?' And Gottlieb would smile, relenting. 'Of course, Fink. There are diamonds in the box.' At this point in the dream the amazed, anxious and humiliated Fink always cried out so loudly that Miss Scholtz came running in to see what was the matter. 'It is nothing, Miss Scholtz. Mr Fink is just a little excited about what I have told him, but he will get over it.'

In the dream Fink cried out sooner or later, and Miss Scholtz came running in – whether the dream was of a casually inquiring Fink, or of an indignant Fink demanding point-blank if Gottlieb had his diamonds. And when Miss Scholtz had left, in all the dreams Gottlieb gave Fink a little lecture about how Fink had shown himself unfitted to handle such dangerous things as diamonds, how Gottlieb had acted only to protect Fink from the consequences of his own folly, and how cool and calm Gottlieb had been throughout in the whole matter.

Sooner or later, Gottlieb was sure, what was now a dream would become a scene which would be enacted between himself and Fink (and Miss Scholtz), and while he waited for this to happen, and because he was waiting for this to happen, Gottlieb's conscience was clear. So why should he go running now to tell Fink of what had happened? Why should *he* – who had the diamonds, as Gottlieb put it to himself, in his upper hand – be the one to talk? Why should he take trouble to save Fink from inconvenience, discomfort, and embarrassment, when through these things Fink would be taught a lesson about Manfred Gottlieb that he would never forget?

And in the meantime, Gottlieb felt that he had Fink as his slave, and the wilder Fink's words were the more were they like nothing but the clanking of the chains that bound him to his place. And the more humbly Gottlieb walked, the more he heard without protest Fink's insults, the more intensely he was aware of his own power. Until, in time, secure in his power, Gottlieb was able to mock Fink, urging forward the day of confrontation with such words as, 'Fink, why don't I hear you talking so much about the diamonds? Why have you grown so quiet about that, when you used to be so cross?'

And inwardly Gottlieb smiled to hear Fink's chastened reply. 'How can I worry about the diamonds when I have a partner who does not care if the partnership goes bankrupt?'

'But think what you have always told me about the diamonds, Fink! Think that if the Legemco didn't lock them up behind the barbed wire how rich and how free you have always said we would be! Then what does it matter, a rubbishy little business like ours? Who cares in such a case for Fink & Gottlieb, Ltd.?'

'I do.'

Gottlieb was not a hard-hearted man, but he watched with pleasure Fink struggling to confine his answer to these two words.

'You have a small imagination, Fink,' Gottlieb said.

And even Riva asked Gottlieb fewer questions and spoke to him much less about the diamonds than he at first could have hoped she would. She spoke less than he had expected even in the course of the very first day of Fink's arrival, when the possibilities of not telling Fink had suddenly and invitingly opened before Gottlieb. At the end of that day she had eagerly asked him: 'What did Fink say about the diamonds?'

Gottlieb replied: 'The diamonds are well under control.'

'With Mr Fink?'

'Very much with Mr Fink. Fink and I are both busy with the diamonds.'

'That's good,' Riva said. 'I am glad to hear that. I trust Fink with such things more than I trust you.'

'Why?'

'Because he is so fierce.'

'There is nothing fierce about him, ' Gottlieb said, irritated by her words.

'But he is always talking of such things, and so has more experience of thinking about them,' Riva suggested.

Within him Gottlieb felt the unfamiliar surge of power and silence, and his irritation was lost. He was able to say calmly,

'He does talk a lot about it. So between him and me the diamonds are in good hands.'

Since then Riva had asked him a few times what they were going to do with the diamonds, whether or not they had been to the police with them, what Mr Fink was saying about them now. And each time Gottlieb repeated that everything was under control with the diamonds and that there was nothing to worry about. It was all under *his* control, he said, and that was just fine.

'And Mr Fink's.'

'Oh yes,' Gottlieb agreed. 'And Mr Fink's. Poor fellow.'

'A widower,' Riva said obediently.

Gottlieb had to cast his mind far back into the past to remember a time when it had been with such things that he had had to console himself about Fink. Gottlieb smiled. 'A widower, yes.'

But he did not forget to ask her: 'And you have told no one?'

'Oh no, Manfred. Anyone who knows, you have told.'

Gottlieb looked in surprise at his wife, working this out. Then he smiled. 'That means no one at all. Except Mr Fink,' he remembered to add reassuringly.

'Yes, Manfred,' Riva said. 'You told me that I must tell no one.'

'That's what I did.' Gottlieb glowered at his wife, and then let his expression modulate into one of quiet power. 'And I am a man whose words mean something.'

'Yes, Manfred.'

'I am a man that people must listen to.'

'Yes, Manfred.'

'I am not an ordinary fellow.'

'Oh no, Manfred.'

'I have my powers, and my ambitions too.'

'I suppose so, Manfred.'

5

In any other country Lyndhurst would have been considered a small town, a market town – not a 'city'. Yet in a more thickly populated country Lyndhurst could never have been spread over as wide an area as it was. There were about twenty thousand whites in Lyndhurst, about the same number of coloureds, and the same number again of natives; and these sixty thousand people had spread themselves over miles and miles of what had once all been veld, and was now veld in stretches only, between this suburb and that, or merely between just one little group of houses and another. These waste stretches of veld could comfortably have carried as many houses as the number that were built around them, though houses, gardens, backyards were all spread over the widest possible space for each. The mines too – all those great gaping holes in the earth – had forced the town to spread itself, the town having been built after the holes had been dug. Under the arch of the sky the town lay wide, and so flat that from any rooftop one could see for miles – miles of corrugated iron roofs, veld, mine dumps, corrugated iron roofs, sand.

The first people to live in Lyndhurst had not bothered themselves with such niceties as town planning, or even individual street planning. Nothing had attracted them to that particular stretch of veld but the diamonds which could be found under its soil, and they had simply thrown down their belongings and immediately set about looking for diamonds. Later, this heap of belongings had been joined to that heap of belongings by a street; and if by that time there happened to be an enormous hole in the ground in between, then the street ran around the rim of the hole; and if this heap of belongings happened to be set back from two others, then the street obligingly crooked itself like an elbow to take in all three. And to these streets were given such descriptively ornamental names as Muck Street, Dump Street, Old Mine Street, New Mine Street, and Billy's Street.

The first people to come to Lyndhurst had none of them considered staying in Lyndhurst. But when the various diggings were combined together in a single company, and when it became clear that many people would have to spend the rest of their lives in Lyndhurst, the citizenry of the town began to organize their town for permanent settlement. By that time it was too late to do anything about, say, the Market Square, into which there ran at least fifteen side streets, only one of which managed to make a right angle with the square. But there was time to lay out the more expensive parts of the town in a rather more orderly way, and to name the streets in these areas after Governors or Lieutenant-Governors of the Colony rather than purely local celebrities; time to build a few elaborate double-storeyed houses that threw out wings and turrets and gables without a thought for the day when because of these wings and turrets and gables they would be perpetually, forlornly 'To Let'; time even to lay out on a rather grand imperial scale a few public gardens, and to place in these gardens of dry sand and dry trees such unlikely things as a massive wrought-iron gate, a band stand with a cupola roof, and a stone statue of Queen Victoria. Seventy years later Queen Victoria stared in the heat down a sandy lane of trees along which very few people ever came, and small boys climbed up the statue and broke the sceptre in one hand and prised the orb out of the other; they put cigarette ends between the stone lips, and these were left for the infrequent rains to wash away, streaking the lower lip with yellow. To one side of the statue could be seen the harsh brown and white of the veld; to the other one went between the small trees and over the hot sand deeper into the Lyndhurst Botanical Gardens, as this particular park was called. There were three or four of such deserted parks in the town, each with its own neglected statue of queen or empire builder; for it was noticeable that the present-day townsfolk were inclined to leave these alone when in search of their amenities, and to build their own more modest and directly useful playing-grounds for cricket and rugby away from what seemed on the barren sand of Lyndhurst as strange as the relics of a centuries-forgotten civilization. Some six miles out of town there was a building that had once been a country hotel, and that had once actually had a ballroom, a billiard room, a glassed-in promenade, lawns, trees, and an artificial lake on which swans had sailed; now the glass was shattered, and the lake was dry, the swans were dead, the lawns were so many sunken sandpits, and the place was looked after by a solitary native watchman in the employ of the Legemco. And in the heart of the town, in Old Mine Street, on the other side of the Legemco buildings, there was a be-steepled building of brick and iron that still declared itself to be 'The Lyndhurst Stock Exchange' though its windows were filled with nailed-in grain bags and its doors with sheets of corrugated iron. The town was littered with such things, as silent as the abandoned mines, and they all took up their spaces too.

So it was quite possible, Gottlieb found, to live in Lyndhurst and to go about it in a motorcar every day, and never so much as to see parts of the town which lay beyond some man-made abandoned hole, or which hung on to the centre of the town from miles away by a single road that went between the artificial mountains of green wrinkled sand taken from the mines. And this was true of the white and coloured areas alone, for the natives lived in their locations, towns of their own, at the end of their own roads.

Gottlieb had gone first to the King's Hotel, the Ritz Hotel (but not the Diamond Hotel) – they were the largest hotels in Lyndhurst, and kept up standards in the way of white jackets on the waiters, carpets in the foyers, potted ferns in the lounges. From these he had gone along devious roads to the inferior single-storeyed hotels, whose pretensions were confined to their names: the Crown and Anchor, the Comet, the Universal. Thence to the boarding-houses that had no names at all, but did have indoors a plentiful supply of overstuffed furniture and framed hanging texts that called for the protection of the Lord on those who dwelt in the house and forbade those who dwelt in the house to spit, swear, or bath between the hours of ten and four. And in these places Gottlieb spoke to this, that, or the other person, and won from the best of them practically no response at all.

Yet so open, so flat was the town to the sky that arched above it, and so few were the people on its lengthy, twisting, sandy or tarred roads, that it seemed impossible to Gottlieb that he shouldn't be able to find within it the sort of person he was seeking. Gottlieb followed up hints, jokes, threats, remarks half-remembered, even a particular inclination of the head and the roll of the eyes at the mention of a name. He threw out his own hints: he said, 'You weren't born yesterday,' and 'There are some crimes that are no crimes as far as I'm concerned.' But the eyes that met his stared in suspicion or amusement, the heads shook in negation, or nodded disconcertingly in an agreement so placid that it could clearly lead to no action at all. His manner, Gottlieb told himself, put them off; but for the life of him, in these strange surroundings, he could not alter his manner. In the lounges of hotels, the stoeps of bars, in the drive-in yard, where, in the middle of the yard, a little grey structure described as *Lavatory* carried another sign saying: *Flick Lights for Service, Stay in Cars, Mixed Grills and All Kinds Sandwiches, Coca Cola* – in such surroundings, Gottlieb could not feel at ease, could not be hearty, alert, and in the know. He could only feel himself – in these unfamiliar and distant parts of the town, so far from his solid house – a stranger, a curiosity to the others there, most of whom he suspected of regarding him as an object of scorn, kindness, anti-Semitism, or help which he did not need.

There were humiliations for Gottlieb. There was the time, for instance, when he was accosted by Thomas, the coloured signwriter who had once done some work for Fink and then for Gottlieb, and who on seeing Gottlieb outside the Pathways Bar came running to him from the coloured entrance, crying, 'Your worship, Mr Gottlieb, what the hell do you do here?' The Pathways Bar was in the middle of a rundown block of tin shanties, among which its brick walls and single neon sign stood out nobly; and in no time a small crowd of white and coloured children, women, and drunks had gathered to before the bar to watch Thomas repeatedly bowing low to Gottlieb as he shouted, 'I'm glad to see your worship again. Such a surprise, but welcome, welcome, welcome · your worship.' Thomas swayed and yelled; he crouched low and came forward, weaving from side to side, snapping his fingers, driving Gottlieb towards the entrance for whites. Now he was offering his services to Gottlieb. 'Reliable, your worship, always sober, much too ambitious.' He lunged again at Gottlieb, but always with a snake-like, dangerous servility of movement. 'Overtime,' he yelled, 'summertime, wintertime, what do I care? We only live once.' Gottlieb went into the 'European' bar, and there Thomas could not follow him; and when Gottlieb went out again he was accompanied by a self-appointed bodyguard of two young men in shirtsleeves, whose sensibilities had been offended by this raucous non-white voice entering the only way it could into their sanctuary. Gottlieb told them for God's sake to leave the drunken fellow alone, which they did only after Thomas had convincingly shown them that drunk though he was he could run faster than any of them. A block away Thomas stood on the corner and shouted, 'To hell with you your worship.'

When he reached home on that particular evening Gottlieb swore that that would be the last time he went out to such a place and among such people. A day passed, a second; by the third day Gottlieb was persuading himself that the incident with Thomas the drunken signwriter had been dangerous, dramatic, something that a man like Fink, for instance, would never have been able to deal with.

In truth, Fink was a great disappointment to Gottlieb, for Fink was still going about his business in a very matter-of-fact fashion; he was no longer even cursing Gottlieb as much as he had been; and – most disappointing of all – he had not raised the subject of a mysterious visit from a poor white, and seemed to have no intention of ever doing so.

For Gottlieb to hold his own silence on the subject was all very well; but Gottlieb had found that the enjoyment it gave him was not one that increased as the weeks passed and Fink held his silence too. To himself Gottlieb accused Fink of cowardice, obstinacy, bad faith and deliberate perversity; but every day more and more of Gottlieb's exhilaration and excitement in keeping the diamonds was turned stale by Fink's silence, Fink's slowness to act and expose himself, Fink's busy-ness with the day-to-day affairs of Fink & Gottlieb Ltd. Intensity of feeling prolonged breeds fatigue and indifference and a sense of defeat; it was from these that Gottlieb fled into a fantasy that promised what he had so far tasted of danger and power and surprise in keeping the diamonds, and mastering Fink would be as nothing to what he might yet know.

There was no point to which Gottlieb could look back and say: there I first thought of this; here I first acted on it. There was indeed no point from which Gottlieb could look back, for when he gave himself over to the fantasy then it would remind him of how much he had already done – how much had been real, spoken, seen, held, heard, and not merely imagined; and when Gottlieb acted he found that his action only encouraged the fantasy to assume another and more dangerous shape. If a long-cherished dream of silencing Fink had already become an. unsatisfactory reality, then a speculation as to what sort of people they really were who dealt in Illicit Diamonds could become a reminder that he, Gottlieb, merely by being in possession of the stones, was one himself. It was a never-to-be-committed stroke that would release him from the thrall of his own silence and put him in a position to crow over Fink for the rest of his life; but it was also true that that stroke would be, after all, not so very much more than he had already done. And then the problem of his relations to Fink would hardly matter at all. Then he would be independent of Fink, indifferent to Fink, a man alone, a hero.

But wasn't he that already? Did Fink do any of the things that Gottlieb did? Did Fink stand under the lamplight outside a bar and see strange coloured and white faces moving in front of him, with a drunk man shouting and dangerous white hooligans coming up behind? What a question! Gottlieb was the man who did these things. Gottlieb was the man who had already – just for curiosity, not committing himself one little bit, but just for the sake of finding out and seeing and hearing a thing or two, very coolly and calmly, knowing just where he was going to draw the line, no matter what thoughts he sometimes had by himself – Gottlieb was the man who in this way had said to that big Dutchman, 'Lyndhurst means one thing in the world.' 'What's that?' the Dutchman had asked. And Gottlieb was the one who had come right out and replied,

'Diamonds. Diamonds. Diamonds.' And hadn't the Dutchman looked over his shoulder when he had heard these words, hadn't he leaned to Gottlieb and said, 'I knew a bloke once, he said he had some but he was puffing my leg.'

That had been very early; now Gottlieb was bolder. Still, Gottlieb told himself, he knew exactly where he was going to draw the line; still he was taking great care not to put himself in any danger. But it was a matter of fact now that a man like Carlisle knew from Gottlieb's winks and nods and stammered words that Gottlieb was in possession, illegally, of diamonds. For surely if he didn't know this Carlisle wouldn't talk so strangely and at such length to Gottlieb about his friend Jimmy Stuart? For that matter, Carlisle actually seemed under the impression that Gottlieb wanted to *sell* the stones. That was where Carlisle was wrong of course, Gottlieb knew, because Gottlieb was not the kind of man who would step over a line that he himself had just drawn. He was listening just out of curiosity, and he listened carefully to Carlisle, for Carlisle was the first to speak in quite such an open way.

Carlisle had a great trunk of a chest, broad shoulders that seemed to curve over his neck, almost in a hunch, a big pale face, and short thin legs that were bent at the knees by the weight they had to bear. And though Carlisle was the first to speak openly, and though Carlisle's body was powerful and misshapen, there was no need, it soon became clear, for Gottlieb to be in any fear of him. If anything Carlisle was afraid of Gottlieb, because of the plot that Carlisle suspected. Gottlieb tried to find out from Carlisle the details of this imagined plot, but soon fell behind, for Carlisle spoke with a Scots accent so broad that Gottlieb had difficulty in translating the rolling r's and the glottal stops into the r's and t's that he himself had had to learn; and in any case Carlisle kept what he suspected to himself. 'Forty years I've been in Lyndhurst, Mr Gottlieb, and I've learned a thing or two in my time.' Carlisle shook his head and told Gottlieb, 'Jimmy Stuart fell for something like this in the old days, and they put him away for a long, long time. I'm too old to let that happen to me. Not that I'm afraid, Mr Gottlieb, I won't have you thinking that. But age brings caution and the ability to learn from the experience of others. Like Jimmy Stuart. He never recovered from what they did to him.' Gottlieb was not prepared to admit that he knew neither Jimmy Stuart nor what 'they' did to him. 'You may be right, Mr Carlisle,' he said, and nodded knowingly. Carlisle's large, loose-skinned pale forehead moved still closer to Gottlieb, as if he were about to speak fully and confidentially at last, but all he would utter were fragments – 'The same as you – a respectable man of business, and that was the end of Jimmy Stuart ... It was a fellow who'd never touched them before that finished him off ... They know what they're doing, and it's people like you they use ...' 'Is that a fact?' Gottlieb said, though he remembered to add, 'I did think as much, but it's very interesting to hear you actually say so.' Casually, putting his head to one side, Gottlieb asked, 'And who exactly now – but exactly – are these people? I mean, I know in a general kind of a way of course, but ...' 'In general and in particular they're exactly the same people,' Carlisle cried excitedly. 'I wouldn't have a thing to do with them. Nor with you. I've got nothing against you, but take your goods elsewhere, Mr Gottlieb.' 'Goods? Goods? What goods? I have no goods to sell you, Mr Carlisle, you misunderstand me.' Gottlieb winked and fluttered one plump hand above the table. 'But say now, Mr Carlisle – just say, for the sake of argument and interest, I did have certain goods – not that I have, at all, don't misunderstand me – but say I did, now where exactly would I take them? I'm curious to know. I'm a curious fellow, my wife has often said so. She's said to me, "Why do you always want to know about things that don't really concern you?" And I've replied, "Intellectual curiosity." That's a thing you respect, not so, Mr Carlisle? Now you tell me that because of certain things that happened to your friend Jimmy Stuart you wouldn't be interested at all in what I have ...' Gottlieb broke off suddenly; for a moment he could only stare at Carlisle, but he recovered with another flutter of his hand. 'Out of the same curiosity that brings me here, I ask, where would a man in my position go next, Mr Carlisle? How about that, for an intellectual inquiry?' Gottlieb sat back, exhausted and fearful; and Carlisle pondered the matter. 'If I knew, Mr Gottlieb,' he said, eventually, 'I wouldn't tell you.' 'Quite right! Quite right!' Gottlieb cried in relief and disappointment.

'It's a broadening experience to meet such people,' Gottlieb told himself. And there were many more of them that he still could meet; and, after all, if Carlisle knew that Gottlieb had some goods – and obviously Carlisle had known – then why shouldn't a man like Aporto know too? Aporto's name was a big one in the town, much bigger than Carlisle's, who was just a finished old man. Probably if Gottlieb mentioned the subject to Aporto, Aporto wouldn't be shy or frightened to tell him where to go next, as Carlisle had been. Very possibly Aporto would tell Gottlieb to go no farther, because he was there already, with Aporto, whose name in the town was so big, and who could do for Gottlieb whatever Gottlieb wanted. Then, Gottlieb swore, Aporto would find out what a big mistake he had made, for this was just a matter of intellectual curiosity, really. A man could talk, ask, look, hear without committing himself; a man could do these things, and perhaps commit himself a little later; a man was free to act as he thought best in such a business that someone like Fink, for example, poor simple fellow, had never dreamed about. Fink might be able to make some inefficient arrangement somewhere far away and safe down the river, where the stones lay to be picked up by any kaffir in the employ of any reckless white man, but Gottlieb went out whenever he felt like it, among all sorts of dangerous people and crooks and smugglers and gangsters and drunkards and men who probably carried on with other people's wives – men who it seemed to Gottlieb were beginning to know him already, and who greeted him and smiled and waved a hand when they saw him. He would be a fool not to go to Aporto; and then there might be fireworks; but only if he wanted them, and of that Gottlieb wasn't so sure. 'Better be safe than sorry, yes,' Gottlieb told himself, and then: 'But also, and at the same time, better be strong than weak, like people who know nothing, who live their whole lives without having the strength to finish once what they secretly want to do.'

Gottlieb's call on Aporto was to all appearances accidental, Gottlieb happening to walk slowly past Aporto's garden at a time when he knew Mr Aporto walked in his garden. To Mr Aporto – after having been invited in, after drinking a cool drink – Gottlieb dared to say, uncomfortably, that he had heard that there was a lot of – you know – things going on these days – more than before – Mr Aporto would know what he meant. Mr Aporto did know what he meant. 'Na,' Mr Aporto said, 'Na, na, Mr Gottlieb.' Mr Aporto put his head to one side, as if to listen through the uppermost ear, out of which dark hairs grew thickly. But that was apparently the position in which Mr Aporto found it most comfortable to speak, and speak he did, with a flashing of his teeth and a screwing of his features and a rubbing with one hand of his scraped but nevertheless blue and bristling chin. 'You're a respectable man, Mr Gottlieb, and to you it's a damned good joke. I tell you straight, when such a respectable man comes to see me with such damned good jokes, I grow sad for Aporto. Why sad? Because if every Tom, Dick, Harry, and other respectable people make such jokes, who can Aporto see over garden fence and say, come in, have a drink, accept some hospitality? Then house, car, garden, swimming-bath, all other fine things that he has built in a fine suburb help not at all – no, no help, Aporto must sit alone in middle of fine things, and think people will make jokes if he gives them orange squash. A good joke, to make Aporto sad? No, a damned bad joke. And why bad jokes when you are a businessman, and can tell interesting things of business, sport, politics, weather, like other people I see sitting talking nicely in other gardens?' 'But –' 'Nothing but, Mr Gottlieb. So sorry. Good afternoon.' 'I didn't mean to hurt your feelings.' 'I have feelings like dog, cat, human being – Aporto is the same thing exactly.' 'Of course.' 'Now you say and so I thought when I see you passing by.' 'I'm sorry, Mr Aporto.' 'If so, please debate weather and climates.' So they discussed the weather until it was time for Gottlieb to go. Then Mr Aporto saw him to the front gate, and shook his hand, and invited Mr Gottlieb to come over again some time and break up some more loneliness; and Mrs Gottlieb too, he assured Gottlieb, would be very welcome too.

Gottlieb walked home cursing himself for a fool and a coward. What was Aporto to him that he should have been so tender to him? Why should he have let Aporto curl like a well-bred girl at a dirty word when Gottlieb mentioned – barely mentioned – what he had to him? In the dusk, through the empty, be-hedged, respectable streets, Gottlieb walked home, and every house he passed, some with a light in a front room, others still in darkness with the families at leisure in the darkening gardens, gave him a kind of answer. As his own house did, when he reached it and opened its clean white gate and walked up its trim garden path.

'Where are you always running, running?' Riva challenged him that evening.

'No one is running.'

'I don't know what's come over you. You used to be quite happy to sit at home in the evenings. But now – now it's a walk you must take, then it's a drive, and then you must go and see a fellow, and every evening it's the same thing. What is this?'

'I can't explain.'

'You must explain.'

But Riva hadn't chosen her time well, for Gottlieb was in a thoroughly bad mood. To have had both his intellectual curiosity and his surreptitious hopes balked by Aporto had not been for him a pleasant experience; and to Riva he could express his anger, as he had not been able to with Aporto. And in berating Riva, to his surprise and pleasure Gottlieb found that the hope with which he had gone to see Aporto was confirmed; he was able to forget how meekly he had fallen in with what Aporto had wanted of him, and was able instead to see himself again as a dangerous man, with a secret life among secret people, that Riva knew nothing about – certainly not the kind of man who would put up with questions from a foolish and anxious wife. Hadn't he just spent an hour with one of the biggest I.D.B. names in Lyndhurst? 'What do you think?' he asked her. 'Do you think I run around with other women? Is that what you're so frightened of, after all these years? Because if you are, then you can stop right now, because I have more important interests than other women. You know nothing about these interests,' Gottlieb boasted loudly to Riva. 'You never will know, because they are not things that a woman must know about. They are too dangerous altogether.'

'Manfred!'

Gottlieb was afraid for a moment that he had gone too far – for surely she remembered, even if she did not talk of it, that he had come home one night with a packet of Illicit Diamonds. But Riva had picked up one thing and one thing only from what he had said. 'Manfred, what's this about other women? I have never thought about other women!'

'Then don't begin now.'

'But why do you talk about them?'

'To tell you what I'm *not* doing,' Gottlieb shouted. 'I have no other women, believe me.'

'Manfred, I hope not. At your age, to be thinking of other women!'

'My age is not so old. If I wanted to I have enough life to think of other women. I am young enough to do all sorts of things that I have never done before, you wait and see. I am doing them already, but until it is done and finished I am saying nothing, I am keeping quiet. And it will be done, then you will know and see what a young man in heart I am, how little I am frightened, what recklessness and pride there is still inside me.'

'Inside you?'

'Who else? Do you think I'm talking about Mr Fink with his cold feet? So please, please, know the man you are dealing with, and leave him alone.'

'Who? Mr Fink?'

'No! For God's sake! Me!'

'Yes, Manfred.'

'That's much better,' Gottlieb said kindly. 'That's how you must talk to me.' He suddenly shouted again, 'Because I will not be talked to in any other way.'

'Yes, Manfred.'

Timidly Riva added, 'Such a thing has never happened to me before, Manfred, that I have to think about other women. But as long as with you it's just thoughts, Manfred, I will not mind. I suppose it's in the nature of a man to have thoughts like that.'

'Like that and like others, that a woman can't understand. She can only leave alone, and admire from a distance, and that is what you must do.'

Reassured and strengthened by this exchange, Gottlieb was able to reflect that Aporto was not the only fish in the sea. There were others, and with those he would be able to do all that he had threatened Riva he would do – if, of course, he should want to, when the time came.

He was even surer that he would want to after his conversation with Cloete – and he felt like this precisely because in its way his meeting with Cloete was hardly any more satisfactory than his conversations with Aporto and Carlisle had been, though at the time Gottlieb had felt proud enough merely to be sitting with Cloete on the stoep of the Cartwheel Hotel, drinking beer with him, leaning back as Cloete did to watch the cars pass on the road below. Across the way from the Cartwheel Hotel there was a wide and shabby stretch of ground divided into smallholdings, and the setting sun turned black every hencoop and house and gilded every rock and stick of grass. And Gottlieb glanced at Cloete's large and furrowed face, with the flat brow set back and the nose and mouth set forward, and Gottlieb dropped what he thought would be a meaningful name. 'Don't talk to me about Carlisle,' Cloete replied with scorn. 'I don't like that bloke, and just thinking about him upsets me here.' Cloete patted his capacious stomach, and then belched a little, to prove the truth of what he was saying. Cloete's body was altogether capacious, but his clothing was skimpy: he was wearing a pair of khaki shorts, a khaki shirt, and a pair of slippers: perched right on top of his hair *en brosse* was a very small green felt hat. Yet when he saw friends of his he greeted them with condescension, and his friends all seemed glad to receive his greeting and came over and thumped him on the back and only left when he waved them imperiously away. 'They all know me,' Cloete explained to Gottlieb. 'Everybody knows me.' It was not for nothing that he had stood for so long behind the Town Hall, in a sky-blue uniform with a peaked cap as the symbol of his authority to chase away the piccanins who made a nuisance of themselves among the crates of fruit, vegetables, fowls, cool drinks and other evidences of commerce that piled up in the open market, and whose supervision on the spot had been his task. Since then Cloete had come mysteriously into money, and retired. Retired apparently to the stoep of the Cartwheel Hotel, where he sat in state among his friends and Gottlieb tried to engage him in conversation. 'They're my friends,' he told Gottlieb. 'You stick to your friends, and I'll stick to mine. I don't want to hear about Carlisle, he's no friend of mine.' 'Well there are other people we can talk about,' Gottlieb suggested, and smiled in what he hoped was the way he had often imagined himself smiling: knowingly, coolly, daringly. But Cloete – instead of dropping the lid of his eye and jerking his head to the interior of the hotel, for Gottlieb to follow him – merely smiled back. And when the smile faded the look of concern that replaced it had nothing to do with Gottlieb. For a moment Cloete moved his large body from left to right – 'It gives me hell sometimes,' he said, in explanation – and then belched loudly. 'Shall we talk about Aporto?' Gottlieb asked. Cloete reached for his glass of beer, tilted it to his mouth, drank deeply, wiped his mouth with the back of his hand, and expressed the opinion that that was the stuff to give to the troops. 'Mr Aporto,' Gottlieb persisted, with a kind of small desperation, feeling that any talk of Mr Aporto must lead to the topic that had brought him to sit at the same table as Cloete on the stoep of this hotel. 'That Portuguese kind of a bloke?' Cloete asked. 'That one,' Gottlieb said. 'He's always in trouble,' Cloete said cautiously. 'That's right,' Gottlieb said. 'I don't know him,' Cloete said, with an air of absolute finality. But he weakened: 'I just read about him in the newspapers sometimes, and then I think: poor old Portuguese.' Gently, as if to show his sympathy, Cloete belched. He swished the dregs of his glass about, brought the glass halfway to his mouth, put it down suddenly, as if on a suddenly remembered thought, and said that he was hell of a sorry but it was getting late and he had to be going now. He added that as a matter of fact he was leaving town, so he didn't think he'd ever see

Gottlieb again. Then he got up, sauntered down the stoep of the hotel, and sat down by himself at an empty table, where one of his friends soon claimed him; and Gottlieb left.

Gottlieb had dreamt for himself many difficulties, dangers, and uncertainties: it was in hope of these, indeed, that he found himself doing what he was, and not just dreaming about it. But he had not imagined that he would find it so difficult to reach a position where the difficulties and dangers might begin to operate. 'What is this?' Gottlieb asked himself. 'Do they think I am to be brushed off so easily?' He was puzzled and disappointed, until he decided to blame himself for the treatment he had received. It was his own fault – Gottlieb decided – because his shoulders were bent, his brow was furrowed, his head was bald, his voice was uneasy, his gestures were cramped as he made them, his smiles were strained, his very waddling walk betrayed his fear. 'I will teach them who they are dealing with,' Gottlieb vowed. 'I'll make them shake in their boots before I'm finished with them. Then there will be respect and admiration for Manfred Gottlieb from the whole town-full of I.D.B. rascals. They will shake their heads, they will say, "What a man he is!" And Gottlieb brandished his fists in the air. 'I am what I want to be,' Gottlieb swore – 'independent, making my own way in everything.'

And so the very reluctance and shyness of those to whom he spoke served to make Gottlieb more determined still – and, as he had promised himself, already he was acting for his own sake now, not Fink's.

It was not of Fink that Gottlieb thought when like a miser he gloated over the packet of diamonds that he still kept in his wardrobe. The fact that the raw little stones seemed no more remarkable or beautiful in themselves than they had the first evening he had seen them, did not lessen his pride in having them, his delight in handling them. Sharp they were, and hard, and when he touched them he felt his own fingers to be large and clumsy and padded; he held them individually to the light and rattled them collectively in the palm of his hand, for it was the very arbitrariness of the value attached to them and the stringent laws applied to them that appealed to him, in his mood of recklessness and defiance. And once, when he was handling the stones in this way, it came to him with a pang that if he should sell them he would no longer have them to play with and gloat over; but then with a sense of lightness and pride he remembered that if he should sell these there would be others. There was a world of diamonds around him, under the ground, behind barbed-wire fences; and the next that came into his hands would not come accidentally as these had, and so the handling of them would be all the more satisfying. The selling of the diamonds was not the conclusion that he had thought it to be, but merely a beginning; and Gottlieb marvelled at the boldness that had brought him this far, by such simple steps, and would still carry him so much farther, as far as he would ever want to go.

It was just by chance that shortly after his meeting with Cloete, Gottlieb happened to see Susskind, for Susskind was not often in town, in any town. Most of Susskind's time was spent in travelling in his car about the hottest, farthest, least inhabited areas of the country – and both Susskind and his car showed the marks of these journeys. The car was pale, dusty, and battered; Susskind was equally dusty and battered, but red-faced; both the car and its owner were noisy. Any rare metal that one could think of, any stone ending in 'ium' or 'ite' was Susskind's enthusiasm: and many were the farmers in those northerly deserts whose farms Susskind had bounced across in his car; many were the farmers who had been approached by Susskind to sell the mineral rights on their properties, or options on mineral rights, prospecting rights, digging rights, exploring rights, rights the farmers did not know they owned and were only too happy to sign away to the passionate Jew who assured them that the metal, stone or chemical he was sure would be found on their lands was invaluable in the manufacture of the most secret and internal parts of aeroplanes, radar screens, television sets and a hundred other such modern devices. Cadmanium, lebenite, hallite, bromium: these were the things of which Susskind spoke, and found too – hundreds of miles from the nearest railhead, or in such small quantities as to make their exploitation commercially impractical. But back Susskind would go to Johannesburg, and he would sell options here and options there to other Johannesburgers; sometimes he even succeeded in dragging unhappy, perspiring Johannesburgers to Lyndhurst, and then two hundred, three hundred, four hundred miles westwards, to inspect the lebenite concession they had just bought, and over which they stumbled, watched by the patient Boer and his wife who hoped but did not believe that these alien urbanites would make them as rich as a second cousin of the wife had become in the Free State, once. Susskind invariably disappointed them; invariably he disappointed himself; a hundred times he said, 'If I'd had some capital I would have been a millionaire today.' 'Capital!' was Susskind's cry, 'Capital!' But no one gave it to him, and a man who is so short of capital, who roams around the country and is so interested in the stones in the ground, must necessarily become involved in diamonds, and Susskind had suffered after diamond ventures which he had been sure would bring him in some capital. And when Gottlieb seized upon him and tried to interest him in the diamonds, Susskind would talk only of dagenite, and pulled out samples of the soft, crumbling, pale pink rock and forced them into Gottlieb's hands as if they were sweets for Gottlieb to eat. 'Ten Jews like you from Lyndhurst,' Susskind cried. 'Just ten solid men to put in a thousand pounds each, that's all I want! Why should I run to Johannesburg to get capital when there's rich men like you in Lyndhurst? And on the spot,' Susskind added, overlooking the three hundred miles of atrocious dirt road he had traversed the previous day. 'It's under your nose, Gottlieb, can't you smell a fortune?' Susskind thrust the rock under Gottlieb's nose and kept it there. 'Speak to your friends, Gottlieb. They know you're not a hothead – they know you for a cool head, a shrewd businessman, a credit to the community!' Susskind leaned against his car, the stones in each hand, his shirt open at the neck, his trouser pockets bulging with more lumps of stone. 'In America they'll go mad when they're told about it. Mad! There's people in Johannesburg who'll want to kill me when they hear I've given you the first chance –' 'Susskind, there's more valuable things than your dagenite in this world.' 'What? Just tell me what's more valuable than dagenite, and I'll listen.' 'There's – there's – look down there,' Gottlieb said, and pointed down the road towards the offices of the Legemco, for it was outside his own premises, opposite the Ritz Hotel, that Susskind had parked his car. Susskind looked in the direction of Gottlieb's pointing finger, and then his red, soft face twisted with distaste. 'They'll be chicken feed before we're finished with the dagenite.' 'You didn't used to think so.' 'Aha! Is that it? Is that why you're so stand-offish when I present you with a first-class, cast-iron proposition with the dagenite? A man makes one slip,' Susskind mourned, 'and it's thrown into his face for the rest of his life. Give a dog a bad name, hey, Gottlieb, even when he comes with a proposition that an ignorant kraal kaffir would jump at. Then he's told that he's just an I.D.B. crook and a loafer. A fine state of affairs! Well,' Susskind said, with a shrug of his broad, jacketless shoulders, 'it's your loss. You'll be sorry one day. I won't.' Susskind stuffed the samples of dagenite into his overweighted pockets and walked bumpily into the hotel.

Mr Bannerjee conducted his business at the junction of three entirely unimportant streets. Opposite his general dealer's store was a small and unsuccessful garage, and on either side were small houses, pavements of sand, and one long brick wall behind which there lived an old lady rumoured to be enormously wealthy 'from the old days'. None of this rumoured wealth had ever entered Mr Bannerjee's pocket, but whenever the old lady appeared in the street and Mr Bannerjee happened to be standing in the door of his shop, he unfolded his arms and smiled and bowed, and construed as a response to his greeting a particular nod of the many the old lady gave as she nodded and staggered down the street. None of his customers were ever greeted by Mr Bannerjee, for they were – coloured, native, and white – extremely unsatisfactory to a man of his temperament, as was the view at which he had to stare. Indeed, when Gottlieb came in Mr Bannerjee apologized for the view, and remarked that the world they lived in was a world for men who worshipped only pecuniary gain, and in such a world, Mr Bannerjee said, a man like himself did not stand a chance of success, because he cared so much for ideas and idealism. Gottlieb hardly knew Bannerjee, and, unlike Mrs Bannerjee, he did not know that any reference by Mr Bannerjee to ideas and idealism would be followed by an attack on Mr Bannerjee's wealthy brother-in-law, his own wife's brother, who had not, as Mr Bannerjee explained to Gottlieb, helped Mr Bannerjee financially but had condemned him to this little shop in such a sad street as this one. Mr Bannerjee's fine dark countenance, with its plump cheeks and high-bridged nose was fully expressive of what he felt about his hard and grasping brother-in-law; but later he smiled: he was telling Gottlieb these things, he said, because he knew that Mr Gottlieb was a man who shared his own interest in beautiful thoughts, and the many problems of the world, and the nature of life, which was a most interesting topic in itself. Gottlieb did have a small business matter to raise with Bannerjee, and when he had done so he went on with a large, false heartiness to inquire whether Mr Bannerjee was still interested in another line of goods, highly portable, risky to handle, but available, as one might say, to anyone who wanted them. For an instant Mr Bannerjee frowned; then he said that he knew perfectly well who was going around spreading such stories about a man who had never had his general dealer's licence revoked for any cause whatsoever. Well, if it came to that, Mr Bannerjee said, his brother-in-law himself was the man who would be interested in such a proposition. Only if his brother-in-law were ever to go in for the nefarious trade (and that seemed to Mr Bannerjee just the sort of thing his brother-in-law would do) then he had no doubt at all that the stones he passed on to others would be made of glass. And with this merry joke – as he described it – Mr Bannerjee rapidly ushered Gottlieb out of the shop.

In his desperation Gottlieb even approached Amos, the office-cum-driver-boy, who came from somewhere down the river, and asked him if he knew of the people who bought and sold the *steentjies* – the little stones – but Amos laughed and said in Afrikaans that the *steentjies* were dangerous stuff and he did not like them. Amos was clean, quiet, smooth-skinned, an indefatigable reader of the firm's old correspondence and the father of a son who he hoped would grow up to be a schoolteacher: Amos was incorrigibly respectable and knew nothing about diamonds.

After such treatment to have that Fink come snooping and inquiring and trying to find out what he could was something that Gottlieb was simply not prepared to put up with; and Gottlieb told him so too, 'I have my own life,' he shouted, 'and you have yours. That's good, that's excellent, that's the way it always has been. So since when must I account to you for what I do with my time? Who are you to come and ask me such questions? Who are you to talk to me like I don't talk to my own Irvine any more? It is ridiculous.'

Fink was quiet, stretching out one hand to pacify Gottlieb. 'Please, Gottlieb, there is no need to use such words, or to speak in such a loud voice. I mean no harm with my questions. It's natural that I should be curious, when I go for my walk in the evening, and I see you pass in a motorcar by yourself, so late at night, and I don't know where you've been or where you're going to. And when I drive in my motorcar after I have been playing cards, I see you sitting like a drunken *goy* on the stoep of the hotel, then I must wonder. And when Riva says to me that she doesn't understand why you are going out so much these days in the evenings, and that she is left alone so much that sometimes in the evening she gets frightened, and has to ask the girl, that Sylvia of yours, to come in and keep her company. When I hear such a thing about my own partner, of course I must ask him if he is all right, or in some kind of trouble, and if there is anything I can do. I am accusing you of nothing, Gottlieb, so why do you shout at me?'

Gottlieb sat behind his desk and glared at Fink, as if he had not seen the outstretched hand, or heard the friendliness of Fink's voice. 'So now you are coming between a man and his wife.'

'Gottlieb!'

'No, Fink, nothing, there is no need to look at me in such a shocked way – there are more ways than one of coming between a man and his wife, and one way is for a man to listen to the wife's complaints about the husband. It is a little thing, but it is not a harmless thing, especially when it is typical.'

'Typical of what, Gottlieb?'

'Of blindness, of not understanding, of talking too much when there is no knowledge behind the talk.'

'Excuse me, Gottlieb, you are jumping from point to point in a way that I don't understand at all.'

'Am I not entitled to jump from point to point, if that is what I feel like doing? Why do you come to reprove me for this or for that or for the other thing? I am a man who does what he likes whenever he likes, Fink, or haven't you noticed that yet? Then notice it now, once and for all times. I do what I like, and when I jump then I jump, I don't look to see if Fink is following me. I am independent of Fink, I am indifferent to Fink, Fink. If you choose to follow me as far as you can, well and good, I have no complaints, because you are free to do what you like; and if the best that your little imagination can reach to, Mr Fink, is following your partner like a puppy-dog, then well and good, do it with pleasure. And it's only because I am a man of a generous disposition that I take the trouble to warn you, Mr Fink, that if you follow me all the way you might find yourself in places that you don't like and in scenes that you won't understand and among people who will frighten you. They don't do such a thing to me because I am not a follower, a little partner, a salesman; but a man altogether.' Fiercely Gottlieb shook his head at Fink. 'And now perhaps you will tell me that I was jumping again. I meant to jump, Fink, and if you don't like it, then you know what you can do.'

'And what is that, Gottlieb?'

'Lump it, jump it, do what you like, but please don't have the impudence to come and complain to me.'

'Gottlieb, you go too far!'

'Fink, I haven't begun yet.' It was the truth of this statement that infuriated Gottlieb again; for even as he shouted at Fink he knew that as yet he had actually done nothing to warrant the threats and dark words that he used to Fink. But he told Fink nevertheless, 'I have matters in my life that you can know nothing about until they are concluded, so please, Fink, for your sake don't try to find out. Because that makes me angry, and you know my temper by now.'

Fink did not reply; he sat on the other side of Gottlieb's desk and examined in silence his own small hands, as if ashamed. And when Gottlieb saw the man's hesitation he felt the malicious impulse to counter-attack. 'And while we are on the subject of each other's private life,' Gottlieb said, and when Fink looked up Gottlieb met his gaze severely, and a little scornfully, 'may I ask you, Mr Fink, if there is anything that is troubling you?'

'Why do you ask?'

'I have some concern for you, Mr Fink, after all. Sometimes you annoy me when you go out of your depth, but I try my hardest to forgive you a little, as I am doing now. And then I think that this poor Fink has been my partner for many years, and so when I see him so humble and quiet as you are now, then I would try to help him.' Gottlieb could not stop a smile appearing on his lips, at the thought of his own magnanimity, and of the discomfort it must be causing Fink. 'A man's nature is his nature, and I can see that yours is quiet, cautious, very worried about little affairs of business and such things, so I try not to blame you, nor do I worry about it. Only when I see you are especially quiet as if there is something on your mind, then I do want to help you, Fink.'

'That's very kind of you, Gottlieb.'

'I am glad you appreciate me, Fink.'

'Oh yes, I do.'

Gottlieb nodded, and leaned back in his chair, pushing it away a little from his desk. And the strain of the days and the evenings he had spent so unsuccessfully made him soften towards Fink, towards the idea of being appreciated, at last, even by Fink. He did not relax his masterful grip with both hands on the desk shoved away from himself, but he did say, 'That is what a man has friends for, people who appreciate him at his true worth. Or –' Gottlieb added with an inclination of the head, so that he stared at Fink over his spectacles – 'not at his true worth, for the fire and courage of some men is not known until they choose to reveal it themselves. But their friends have a little idea of it, and that is a comfort to him, in his loneliness and his ambition, in the efforts that he is making.'

'I have felt that way too, sometimes, Gottlieb.'

Gottlieb was suspicious. 'What do you know of loneliness and ambition, Fink? You are happy with Fink & Gottlieb Ltd., you can't understand what I am talking about.' But Gottlieb waved this away. 'Let us not quarrel any more, we are talking from different planes. You tell me what is worrying you, Fink, and then I will see if there is any way that I can help you.'

Fink said slowly, 'There is one problem that I've thought I should perhaps speak to you about, Gottlieb.'

'What is that, Fink?'

Then, before Fink spoke, Gottlieb knew with fear what it was – that Fink was going to tell him about his diamonds that had gone astray. And Gottlieb feared it because then he would have to admit that the diamonds had come into his hands, and that he had been keeping them. Fear quickened to disgust as Gottlieb looked back to the days when precisely that admission on Fink's part had been the summit of his ambition. How puny, how limited, his thoughts had been! And yet that – if Fink spoke of his diamonds – would be all that in the end he had accomplished.

And like a fate, as though with an intended deliberate malice, Fink did go on to say slowly, 'It's a difficult thing for me to admit, but – you know, Gottlieb –' Fink paused and examined his hands, and spoke even more slowly – 'You know how busy I always was with the diamonds, always talking and always saying I wanted to do something to show what I thought of the laws and the Legemco and the government and all that. And that's what my problem is connected with now, that I was wondering if you knew – or could help me –'

'Fink, that is a problem that I want to know nothing about! Nothing, do you hear me? It is your madness and your obsession, not mine. I know nothing about diamonds, I hear nothing about diamonds, I talk nothing about diamonds, because I have absolutely nothing to do with diamonds!' Gottlieb was shouting, but still he sat back in his chair, as if trapped in it, unable to move; and the blood crept up and darkened his features and made them swollen even while he spoke. 'Don't talk to me about it. Talk to the walls and the ceiling, because they know more about diamonds than I do, and because they are more interested than I am. The subject is closed, Fink, finished: you hear?' And when Fink did not answer, Gottlieb screamed again, 'You hear?'

When Fink said quietly that he had heard, Gottlieb was able to move, to slide himself deeper into his chair. And with this movement came horror at what he had done. But it was done; it was too late now to retract; and though for the moment Gottlieb could not speak, and sat with his eyes staring forward as if at what they had just seen of himself, already in his mind there were words, sentences, gestures, forming. 'What poor white? Who poor white?' Gottlieb did not say them, but the words waited, ready to answer Fink if he should persist with his questioning. 'If such a man left such a box in the office it was swept out immediately by Amos. This is a place of business, and I have no time to worry my head about nonsense from crazy poor whites.' Gottlieb's lips moved; he pressed them firmly together. Then, lifting his head, he opened his mouth again. 'Well, Fink, is that all you had to say to me? I thought you had a serious problem for me, but I see you are just as mixed-up and childish as ever.'

By the bristle of Fink's eyebrows, by the pointing finger that Fink brought up, Gottlieb knew with relief that he had succeeded in angering Fink, and that an angry Fink would not seek help from anyone. Gottlieb knew he would have to lie no more, for his lies had served their purpose: the diamonds were safe.

Fink stood up and warned Gottlieb, 'I am watching you. I don't need your help for anything, Gottlieb, and when I spoke it was because I thought that might make you sensible again –'

'A likely story!' Gottlieb interrupted.

'But you are too far gone!' Fink raised his voice above Gottlieb's. 'You need the help of a doctor. When your son comes to Lyndhurst again perhaps in the next twenty years, you must ask him what is the matter with you. A non-medical opinion is that you are a fool, a boastful fellow, a windbag, and a hopeless partner. And that is why I warn you: I am watching you, Gottlieb, think of that, I am watching you. You have had your last chance from me, from now on I watch you like a spy.'

'And what good will that do you?'

'That is none of your business. You will see when you have done with your folly.'

'What folly?'

'Running around the town like a loafer, neglecting the business, neglecting your wife, shouting at your patient partner, and follies like that.'

Gottlieb forced himself to laugh. 'They are nothing to what you will see if you really watch me, Fink. Fleas and flies you worry about, when there is an eagle flying alone over your head.'

6

In his stay in Lyndhurst Detective-Sergeant Groenewald had as yet had no occasion to forgive the staffing-officer in the C.I.D. Provincial Headquarters in Cape Town who had posted him to the town. 'You look simple enough,' the staffing-officer had said; and when he had heard this Groenewald had known that the job which he would be sent to fill would not be a pleasant one. Words like these had followed Groenewald throughout his life, and their consequences had never been pleasant for him. As a boy, when he had gone with other boys to steal fruit somehow or other he had always been the one who had been hoisted over the fence to do the actual stealing – for, his companions said, if anyone should see him they would believe him when he said that he was merely looking for a ball or a kite or a runaway cat. At school experienced teachers had blamed him instinctively for misdeeds committed by others, and when he had managed to prove his innocence, the teachers had wanted to know why, if he wasn't guilty, he made a point of looking so suspiciously and provocatively innocent. At twenty-five Groenewald's age was still occasionally questioned in bars; and girls whom he knew to welcome the advances of others often laughed at his. 'Who'd have thought you'd try such a thing?' they said, as if from his face they had thought him less than male, or more than human.

But the staffing-officer in Cape Town seemed to have been right, at least as far as Groenewald's superior in Lyndhurst, Detective-Inspector Conroy, was concerned. Conroy – Groenewald had soon learned – was not a man who ever looked either pleased or displeased about anything; but if he had not been pleased with Groenewald's appearance he would not have said, after staring at the young man in silence for a full two or three minutes, 'Good. You'll do. We want people who look like you, not people who look like crooks, or policemen.' Was that a joke, Groenewald had wondered anxiously, but he had not dared to meet Conroy's stare with a smile, let alone break the silence with a laugh. Conroy's silences and Conroy's stares were in themselves a sufficient reason for Groenewald's unforgiving attitude to the staffing-officer in Cape Town.

There were other reasons for this attitude, among them being the town of Lyndhurst, which to Groenewald seemed drab, spiritless, and ugly, made up of altogether too much sand and too much corrugated iron and too few people. And yet there were times when he was positively glad to be able to walk about the town's tortuous and wide-flung streets, for the effect that the town as a whole had upon him was stimulating compared to the moods that the New Temperance Hotel could induce when he had spent a long enough time in it. Groenewald did not know when the hotel had been 'New', and did not try to find out. There was no question at all but that it remained 'Temperance'; and in a town where there were still in use so many things rickety, rusty, clanking, unpainted, unfashionable and overdecorated, the New Temperance Hotel managed to look as though it had been built and furnished entirely by stuff pilfered or donated from other people's attics. Groenewald's bedstead was made of cast iron cunningly spun at the head and the foot to look like a spider-web, each axial ray of the web being held to the ovoid rings by a clasp of solid and tarnished brass. It had obviously been an expensive bed, once upon a time; the washstand too had been an expensive one of its sort, for it was made of red marble, though the basin which it supported was of sensible, yellowed enamel. Such, with a chair or two, and a black overwhelming wardrobe, were the furnishings of his room; and the only other facilities which the hotel offered him were the bathroom at the end of one long corridor, and the parlour, at the end of another. The most noticeable object in the parlour was a glassed-in sideboard that stood on four ball-and-claw feet – the balls of these feet were the largest Groenewald had ever seen, and the claws were correspondingly ferocious; but what they supported was all of a rather delicate nature. There were three or four dolls' tea sets, all laid out, and three Coronation mugs, and several plates and ashtrays bearing the crests of the cities in which they had been purchased, and a snowstorm in a glass ball. In the room there were also several armchairs and sofas equipped with velvet cushions that looked high enough when they were unoccupied but surprised Groenewald each time by sinking so disconcertingly low when he sat on them. The proprietor and his wife never came into the parlour, for they had their own; they left the other to the three drowsy widows, who, with Groenewald, seemed to be the hotel's only permanent guests. Other people Groenewald sometimes saw in the shadows of the corridors, or emerging from the bathroom; he sometimes heard male and female voices from other bedrooms at night; but none of these others, transients, ever put in an appearance in the hotel parlour, and nor, after a while, did Groenewald, though he was all too permanently settled there.

They would have to see, Conroy had said, how long he could stay in Lyndhurst. It might be as long as a year, it might be six months, he might have bad luck or do something foolish and have to leave within a week. Often in the few weeks he had been in the town Groenewald had wondered what 'something foolish' might be. If he had known, he felt, he would have done it, for the sake of cutting his term short. But at other times he would remember that if he left with a black mark against him it would hinder his career in the future; and Groenewald was a reasonably ambitious young man. And yet again at other times Groenewald would reflect what folly it had been for a reasonably ambitious young man like himself to enter the police force in the first place, where opportunities for promotion were so severely limited by seniority, and where the pay scales were so wretched, and where there was no opportunity at all for a man to strike out for himself.

Such were the reflections to which a few weeks of loneliness in Lyndhurst had led Detective-Sergeant Groenewald. His loneliness was complete, for it was professional. He had been forbidden to join any of the church or social bodies through which a young man in a strange town might hope to meet people; he had been cautioned against letting himself be seen too often in bars or at dances or in the town's one roller-skating rink. The New Temperance Hotel had been chosen as his place of residence precisely because so few people either knew of it or lived in it and the latter were known to be of no importance or interest whatsoever. If the occasion should arise when Groenewald would be forced to say who he was and what he did, he had been instructed to give his name, which was innocent enough, but to say that he was an official of the Provincial Rural Roads Board – a body of whose existence very few people were aware, as it had no office in Lyndhurst – and that his work took him too much into the country. Even among the police there were few who knew Groenewald was a member of their force.

'We want you to remain unknown in Lyndhurst,' Conroy had said. 'Someone no one here will be able to trace or pin down, or, so far as it's possible, even know, socially. When you come in to see anyone, you must come in as an absolute stranger. We have thought of having your job held by a man who lives out of town altogether; but that isn't possible, because sometimes we do need you immediately, in a day, and we need you for days on end, and it would be hopeless if you had to keep coming and going. So you'll just have to put up with the other times, when there's nothing very much for you to do. Go to the bioscope, read books, go and watch rugby, do what you like; but do it by yourself. It's not a very pleasant assignment this one that you've been given; the only comfort that I can offer is that it's a temporary one – it has to be – and that the rewards are great.'

Conroy's face was big, with a broad brow and a narrow chin – it was like a shield, and not only in shape but in the smoothness and impassiveness of its surfaces. His eyes were hidden behind faintly green lenses of glass, and when he spoke Conroy opened his mouth as little as possible, hardly moving his lips and jaws. He sat upright behind his desk; he held his arms close to his sides; his clothes fitted him perfectly, and his collar was always very white. 'The rewards are great,' he repeated, and fell into silence, unmoving, the discs of green glass over his eyes directed blankly towards Groenewald. Then he said: 'I'll show you what I mean. Go to the window.'

The command came so unexpectedly and with so little change of tone that for a moment Groenewald did not move. Conroy did not repeat the order; but then hastily Groenewald got to his feet and went to the window. Then he looked back at Conroy, fearing that he was still doing the wrong thing. Conroy did not turn his head to see him go. 'Now look out of the window.'

Groenewald leaned forward. He saw from the height of the second storey of the building across the courtyard of the police station, and then up a street outside – the sort of Lyndhurst street he was beginning to recognize, with its tar and pavements of sand, and its tall old-fashioned lamppost, a curve in the neck of each and a large bulb dangling naked at the end,

97

as if caught in a beak. The street lamps led towards the Town Hall and the Market Square – the Town Hall a ramshackle, grey-cemented building with Doric pillars in front and a roof of corrugated iron on top; and the Market Square simply an expanse of tar marked out with white lines for the few cars that were exposed on its flat surface. And all around the square were low, tin-roofed, white-plastered buildings, in which were sold cool drinks, hardware, watches, ties, hot dogs, and a hundred other commodities necessary for civilized life – name succeeding name and advertisement succeeding advertisement in a chain that was broken only by the roads that ran at oblique and acute angles into the square. The tallest structure to be seen was the elaborate, crenellated clock tower of the magistrate's court, the hands of the clock stuck fast together at noon or midnight. The sun shone on it all from a sky whose paleness was a warning of the heat to come, and in the shadows under the shopfronts and in the sunlight across the square, a few cars and buses and a donkey cart – all the wheeled traffic of a small town – and the silent little figures of the black and white pedestrians went about their business.

'Not a thing that you can see would be there,' Conroy said from behind Groenewald's back, 'If it weren't for the diamonds. There would not be a building, there would not be a road, there would not be a person walking in the street. There would be the veld there – the same veld that you crossed to come here: just grass, and sand, and rock. But because of the diamonds we have people and a city, that you can stand here and look at. Think about that, for from it you will realize the importance of the work we are doing.'

When Conroy fell silent Groenewald did not know whether he was expected still to stare out of the window, or simply to return to his chair. He glanced quickly at Conroy, but Conroy did not nod, or jerk his head, or smile and say, 'Sit down again, now.' He did not even look in Groenewald's direction, but spoke as before, looking down at his desk, leaving Groenewald hanging irresolutely at the window. 'You can see,' Conroy said, 'that a thing as important, as essential as that can't be left for people to come and do what they like with. There have to be laws, there have to be regulations, it has to be controlled and managed from above, otherwise there would be only chaos. There was chaos here, in the early days, before all the diggings were organized together, and before there was a system of I.D.B. laws. Now things are better.' Conroy paused, and Groenewald took the opportunity to step away from the window, hoping to reach his chair before Conroy started speaking again. Each step was anxious, but in the end Conroy held his silence not only until Groenewald had reached his seat, but for so long after that Groenewald began to fear that by returning to his seat without permission he had offended his superior. So, as a placatory contribution to the discussion, Groenewald threw in, 'Ja, that's something to think about.'

It was not in reply to this remark that Conroy spoke again. 'My job – and your job while you're here, and that of everyone else who works under me here – is to see that the law relating to the discovery, mining, sale and purchase of diamonds is strictly carried out. The only people who are permitted to handle uncut diamonds are licensed miners, traders, cutters, and companies thereof – that is the law that has been passed by Parliament and confirmed by subsequent statute. Anyone who hasn't been licensed by the government, and who handles uncut diamonds in any way, or for any purpose, is committing a serious crime.'

'I.D.B.,' Groenewald said, to show Conroy that he knew exactly what was going on.

Again Conroy ignored his words. 'This town owes everything that it is to the diamonds. So you can see how serious is the crime that we have to stop; you can see what kind of laws they are that we have to carry out.'

Groenewald was not sure that he knew or could see, but he nodded and frowned, enacting both.

'You could call them the laws of life for Lyndhurst,' Conroy said, and this time Groenewald neither nodded nor frowned, but stared deeply at his hat in his lap.

Conroy, who had been watching him, looked at his watch, and told Groenewald, 'Come again at the same time tomorrow morning. And here in the meantime,' he said, giving Groenewald a large, taped folder, 'is some homework for you. Read those cases – you will see the sort of work that we do, every day.'

'You're not here to deal with the regular buyers of Illicit Diamonds,' Conroy told Groenewald at a later interview. 'Your task will be with another kind – people who, if it weren't for the special circumstances in this town, would never become criminals. There are twenty thousand white people living in Lyndhurst, and of those twenty thousand perhaps only three or four thousand have anything to do with the mines and the mining companies. But though the other thousands have nothing to do with the mines, and though most of them have never in their lives seen an uncut diamond, they all know, as you do, that they would not be here, and that there would be nothing here, if it weren't for the diamonds. They know what has made this town to be built out of the veld, they know what it is that has brought them to live here, under this sky, on this ground, in these buildings. That is why you will not deal with the regular buyers in Illicit Diamonds, whom we handle quite separately, nor will you be dealing with the natives and the coloureds and the Indians and the poor whites; but only with the respectable citizens of Lyndhurst. They can be clerks and artisans, businessmen and professional men, city councillors, government officials, even people who hold high and responsible positions in the Lyndhurst General Mining and Exploration Company – sometimes the richest and most powerful men in Lyndhurst. People always want to do what they should not – they always want to touch, to feel, to bargain with the thing that is vital, that gives them their life here, even though the law has forbidden them to do it. We have to hold them back – these people who are unable to live their lives on ground that carries diamonds without trying to get at least one diamond, one uncut stone into their hands. Sooner or later they try: they want to hold a diamond between their fingers, to feel it, to see it, and then to sell it, to pass it on to someone who is in the same bad way as themselves. They start looking and asking; and soon we are looking at them, and asking about them. There isn't a man in Lyndhurst who hasn't at one time or another at least wanted to do what the law has forbidden; and there are hundreds who have wanted it so badly that we have had to watch them, to see how far they will actually go. Some I've brought in here and warned, when I thought they could be saved; others simply become afraid and abandon the idea without any pressure from us; but others again – well, you will be busy with the others.'

Often when Groenewald came into Conroy's office at the time he had been given, Conroy would not yet be there, and then the young man had to wait alone; he had to pass the time by staring at the closed doors of the bureaus and cupboards, at the blank walls of the office, at the covers of the taped-up files on Conroy's desk. Groenewald listened at those times to the cheerful whistling and door-slamming and boot-stamping of his fellow officers in other rooms, and to their muffled and indistinguishable conversations as they passed briskly down the corridor outside the office, and Groenewald yearned to go out among them, to greet them, to give them his name and tell them what he was doing. In return they would tell him their names, they would tell him about their jobs, and he would be able to argue with them about which job was worse, and to laugh, shrug, tell them he had to go now but would see them again, hey. If only he could have done that Groenewald was sure that Conroy would not have seemed as formidable to him as he did now; but Groenewald could not go to his fellows, and could not find out from them what they thought of Conroy, of Conroy's wife, or if Conroy had a wife, of what they thought of Conroy's future prospects, of Conroy's moods, of Conroy's silences, of the way Conroy sat at his desk; he could not say to them, 'That Conroy is really keen, isn't he?' or, 'That Conroy's a bugger,' or, 'Old Conroy gets me down sometimes, but he's hell of a good at his job'; he could not hear their agreement or disagreement of his own judgment; no one said to him, 'No, man, don't let old Conroy get you down,' or, 'He's big stuff here, but at home his wife gives him a time, I can tell you.' These conversations Groenewald had to have with himself, and from them he got no satisfaction; for whatever he said or thought was a guess, and he had no confidence in his own unsupported guesses. He had very little confidence in his own unsupported self.

As a matriculant with a good scholastic record, and as a nephew of an uncle who was high up in the C.I.D. in Johannesburg, Groenewald had entered the Police College at an early age; and neither the cheerful gregariousness of his schooling nor the formal organization of his profession had prepared him to withstand the loneliness he suffered under such mean and shabby circumstances in Lyndhurst. There is no self-confidence that loneliness cannot undermine; no will that loneliness cannot enervate. Groenewald's conviction of his own worth could hardly survive when there was no one around him who shared that conviction – in this strange town, where he was to pursue people who were admitted to be as respectable as himself for a crime whose nature he did not fully understand. And from the confusions and bewilderments that his loneliness bred Groenewald could not even obtain the relief of confession. He did not dare to breathe a word of them to

Conroy, who seemed to Groenewald so forbiddingly impersonal and impassive, and who apparently had no doubts at all on any subject.

The effect on Groenewald was therefore all the greater when Conroy revealed that the only doubts he did feel were doubts about Groenewald; Conroy wondered aloud once whether Groenewald was responsible, active, intelligent, honest and serious-minded enough for the work that he had to do. 'You look all right,' Conroy said; and Groenewald heard this with as much equanimity as he ever felt on hearing anything from Conroy, for he had heard this before from others. 'But why haven't you asked me more questions?'

'I didn't know I was supposed to, Mr Conroy.'

'But I suppose you've been asking yourself questions?'

'Sir?' Groenewald said.

'It would be much better for you if you asked me the questions. Because I know the answers, you see, and you don't.'

'Of course, sir.'

'So you say now.' Conroy was silent; and Groenewald tried to meet with due deference but without shiftiness his superior's gaze. 'You haven't been getting any ideas, have you, Groenewald, that you've been keeping to yourself?'

'Ideas?'

'Yes. There's no need to look at me like that, Groenewald. I'm not one of the people you're supposed to fool.'

'Mr Conroy – ?'

'Do you suppose it hasn't happened before? Do you suppose the people who work for me haven't the same ideas come into their heads as the people they're supposed to be chasing? And do you think that I couldn't guess that the same thing might be happening to you, Groenewald? You've been keeping too quiet.'

'I think I'm just quiet by nature,' Groenewald suggested hopefully.

Conroy had not smiled once since Groenewald had met him. Nor had he shown any signs of anger or displeasure. He did neither now as he went on. 'I warn you, Groenewald, put those ideas out of your head. Listen to me when I tell you never – never – to question what I tell you. Do what you're told: that is all you have to do. Then – but only then – you will be carrying out the law, and that's what you're here to do.'

'I'll try,' Groenewald said. And then, as if there were some kind of admission of guilt implicit in this: 'I am trying.'

'I'll be able to see if you are or you aren't,' Conroy answered calmly. Conroy's lips hardly opened, as if speech were a trick that he hoped to perfect one day, when he would not have to open his mouth at all and the words would still come out; but at what Conroy said Groenewald opened his eyes wide. 'And if you aren't, Groenewald, and if it's for the reason that any questioning of my orders and of the law will lead you to – must lead you to, if it goes on for long enough – then there is nothing that will help you. You will be caught, trapped, held, put in jail, Groenewald. It has happened before, it will happen to you if you invite it.'

'No sir,' Groenewald said. 'Yes sir, I mean.'

But as he walked up the garden path to the house of the first man whom he was to investigate, Groenewald could not help regarding himself with almost as much suspicion as Conroy apparently did the owner of the house. That was all his reward, so far, for a loneliness so acute that he had got into the habit of extending for as long as possible his conversations with people from whom he bought cigarettes, or from whom he sought directions that he did not really need.

When Riva opened the door Groenewald was delighted to see her. 'Mrs Gottlieb?' he said. 'How do you do? May I come in? I have something to discuss with you.' It was the ingenuousness of his face, coupled with the urgency of his appeal for simple human communication that persuaded Riva to smile in reply and open the door wider. Besides, she too was always eager for a chat, and especially in these days, when Manfred – who was no longer going out at all – now sat so mysteriously glum, sullen, and silent, evening after evening in the house, never saying a word to her and letting her say none to him.

7

Middle-aged, well-to-do Jewish women were not really in Groenewald's line; but by the end of the first fifteen minutes of his talk with Riva, Groenewald couldn't help feeling that he wasn't doing too badly. He also couldn't help liking Riva. She was a real lady, he told himself; and though Groenewald did not consciously compare the furnishings of the Gottliebs' living room with those of either the New Temperance Hotel or Conroy's bare and uncarpeted office, he nevertheless enjoyed to the utmost the firmness of the cushion beneath him, the smoothness and the high polish of the wood on which his arms rested, the elegance of the curtains that were drawn aside to let the sun fall in vague yellow squares on the patterned carpet. And there was a bookcase, a vase or two of flowers, and the large portraits of Riva's mother and father – her father heavily bearded and her mother daintily be-capped in what looked to Groenewald like a kind of d'oyley. 'They look like grand people,' Groenewald said politely, and Riva said modestly that she didn't think they had been so grand, but they'd been very nice all the same.

Riva was embarrassed at this praise, especially when Groenewald went on to say that you could always tell what kind of a person a person was if you knew what kind of a family he came from. Fine people had fine children, always, he said; and he, asked Riva if she had children.

'Only one, but a doctor,' Riva said.

'There you are,' Groenewald said. 'You must be very proud of him.'

'Oh yes, I am. We both are.'

'Mr Gottlieb is proud of his son?'

Riva smiled and leaned forward. Her hands were working a little nervously together, but she said, 'He shouldn't be proud of a son who is a doctor?'

'No – he should be.'

'Well, that's my point. He is.' Riva paused. 'He always has been. Even now he still is, when he thinks about it.'

'I'm sure.'

'But I don't know how often thinks about it these days,' Riva was forced to admit.

'Is Mr Gottlieb very busy in his work?'

'In his work I don't know so much, but –' Riva considered what she had said, and what she was about to say. She sat back in her armchair. 'He's a busy man in all ways.' She crossed her stockinged, plump legs; and Groenewald couldn't help glancing down and thinking them rather handsome for a woman who to him seemed so much advanced in years. Riva said, 'But his interests are very interesting to him, so that's all right. You can't expect that a man should have the same feelings as a woman, isn't that so?'

'That's very true, Mrs Gottlieb. It's the woman who thinks more about her children, and things like that, and it's the man who has outside interests.'

When Riva uncrossed her legs Groenewald admired them again; but the obtrusive irrelevance of his own thoughts prompted him to remember both the ostensible and the real purposes of his visit. 'If Mr Gottlieb is so busy then that's all the better reason for you to think about this proposition that I'd like to put to you,' he said briskly.

107

'I can't talk without my husband. I'm sorry, I know I'm taking up your time while we're talking, but when it comes to propositions then I must find out what my husband thinks. Then I know what to do.'

'That's a spirit we don't get much among modem wives, Mrs Gottlieb,' Groenewald said gallantly; and then he thought that this had perhaps not really been so gallant. 'I mean –' he began.

But Riva had not been offended. 'If Mr Gottlieb could see it in that way – a spirit you said? – I would be happier. He doesn't believe that I have any spirit at all, except to make mistakes.'

Groenewald sniggered politely.

'Don't laugh!' Riva commanded him. 'It is true. But perhaps you are a married man, Mr Groenewald, and you will know what I mean.'

Groenewald denied that he was a married man. 'I haven't yet met the lady, much as I would like to,' he said; and he meant what he said. If he had been a married man he would never have been given an assignment like this one, for one thing, where the only chance he had to sit in a pleasant room and talk like a human being to another human being was through lies and deceits, and then only for a very short time. Groenewald couldn't help feeling a little sorry for Mrs Gottlieb, whom he was deceiving so completely. For she had brought him in; she had listened to his preposterous talk about how the All-Watchful Mutual Assurance Society had decided to approach the wives of potential clients as well as the clients themselves – 'for insurance is a family affair, or it is nothing at all, and the All-Watchful Mutual Assurance Society is anxious to know how the women of South Africa feel about insurance,' Groenewald had said persuasively. 'We value your opinion so much – please –'

Now they chatted about marriage, for Riva was distressed to learn that Groenewald was not a married man, and told him to exchange his single state for a better one as soon as he had the chance. And Groenewald said that he was anxious to; he told her that he wasn't one of those blokes who tried to pretend that they preferred being single. 'A foolish pretence,' Riva said in dismissal; but she also told Groenewald that married life was not all joy and good times. 'Especially if you get a worrying wife,' Riva said, and shook her head, in reproof of herself. 'That's what my husband says.' To this accusation Riva returned subsequently. 'If it's the nature of a man to have outside interests, perhaps it's the nature of a woman to worry about them,' she suggested to Groenewald. 'Perhaps all women do it, so there will be no escape for you from that, when you are married too. And then you must be patient,' Riva appealed to Groenewald on behalf of his bride-to-be. 'You mustn't snap and shout first and then sit silent afterwards, like a dumb man. Of course,' Riva admitted, in an effort to be fair, 'it's better if you get a wife who doesn't worry at all, but it's my belief really that there is no such wife in the whole world. And it's also my belief that if a man did get such a wife he wouldn't like it in the end, but would worry because she didn't worry.'

Riva talked; Riva ordered the girl, Sylvia, to bring a cup of tea for the gentleman and herself; Riva poured the tea and passed Groenewald a plate of biscuits; Riva ate several biscuits herself.

And over the emptied teacups, Groenewald listened to Riva telling him earnestly: 'I plead with him: why should he first go running out so much, and now sit in his own house evening after evening without saying a word, like a man who has forgotten how to speak? But he just tells me to mind my own business. And why all of a sudden should I mind my own business when for all these years his business has been my business? Except, I don't mean his business – Fink & Gottlieb Ltd., that's a different kind of business from the one I mean. What I mean is the business of what a man does in the evenings or in weekends, which is a wife's business too. And the latest of all,' Riva said, 'is why do I go running to strangers with my problems? Can you imagine, that's what he accuses me of doing! Is Mr Fink a stranger?' Riva demanded. 'Are you – ?' Riva stared at Groenewald, and her mouth closed slowly, before opening again even more slowly.

'Tell me,' Riva asked, 'have you been long in Lyndhurst?'

Groenewald hesitated. 'No,' he said. 'Not too long. And I'll be leaving again – it all depends where the company posts me.'

Riva was satisfied. 'Then what harm does it do if I talk to you?'

'No harm,' Groenewald assured her. 'And besides, the representative of the All-Watchful Mutual Assurance Company is never a stranger, Mrs Gottlieb.'

'That's good,' Riva said, and went back to her preoccupations. 'And Mr Fink is even less of a stranger than you are, even though Manfred talks about him so strangely these days. Would you believe it, Mr Groenewald, that after being my husband's partner for fifteen years, my husband could be so suspicious of him these days, and worried about him? And I've told Manfred not to worry, I've told him that he knows what Mr Fink is like, so why should he sit here night after night worrying?'

'It's hard to believe, Mrs Gottlieb,' Groenewald said sympathetically, to keep her going.

'Partnerships and marriages are both things that have their ups and downs, Mr Groenewald, as you'll learn when you get married, and should you ever go into partnership,' Riva told her listener. 'And it seems to me that there's a down at the moment in the partnership. Manfred denies it, and won't let me talk of it, and I wouldn't dare talk of it to Mr Fink, because he would snap my head off. But I see what I see, and I hear what I hear: it's always Manfred so cross and worried and arguing with himself against that Fink, under his breath, when he thinks I can't hear him.'

Groenewald hesitated, but a glance at Riva's absorbed and worried face, as she bit at her fingernails, was an encouragement to ask, 'And what does he say?'

'Under his breath he says, "Fink, it is all your fault." And, "Fink, you are the guilty partner." And, "Fink, you force me to betray you, and that is not what I meant to do." And, "I'm sorry, Fink, believe me, but give me an alternative now." And things like that. And when I tell him that he shouldn't worry so much, then – after all his muttering – he snaps at me that Fink means nothing to him, that he doesn't care what happens to Fink! And then he falls silent again. And later still, I see him and I hear him, muttering the same things. And sometimes he swears against Fink, terrible words he uses, that I don't even know the meaning of, except that they mean that he is swearing. And so it goes on, and I worry.'

'I'm very sorry to hear it,' Groenewald said.

'It's a shame,' Riva said. 'That there should be such bad feelings between them now, that Mr Fink hardly ever comes here for lunch any more! But there has always been a problem with Mr Fink, he is so proud. The things Mr Fink used to say! The things he used to talk about, without a care or a fear in the world! He would make Manfred's eyes grow big, when he talked about wild and strange things, like even breaking the law.' Riva laughed uncertainly. 'Don't get the wrong ideas, please, Mr Groenewald, about my husband's partner. There isn't a nicer man in Lyndhurst, and I'm not the only one who says so. I don't know why I'm saying such terrible things about him – except,' Riva said helplessly, as she sat exposed in her chair, with only the hand at her mouth to shield her, 'that when I hear my Manfred talking about him in such a worried and suspicious way, then it's a comfort to me that he has always had problems with Fink. Mr Fink was afraid of no one. Even diamonds he used to talk about.'

'Diamonds!'

Riva's hand fell of its own weight from her mouth. 'I know nothing about such things.'

'I'm sure you don't, Mrs Gottlieb. But – but – Mr Fink, you say, does?'

Having gone so far, Riva made the best of a bad job by being proud of it. 'Certainly.'

'That's Mr Fink – your husband's partner?'

'Of course he's my husband's partner. That's the man I've been talking about.'

Expressing the deepest interest in the possibility of issuing an insurance policy to cover the life of Mr Fink, Groenewald had soon found out from Riva where Mr Fink lived ('By himself, poor fellow, in the Diamond'); how old he was ('No one knows exactly, but he's older than Manfred, who is older than he thinks he is'); how large his family was ('Three daughters in Johannesburg, and Mr Fink by himself in an hotel'); and the sort of thing he used to talk about ('It was always heroes and liberty, and defy the Legemco, and wild talk like that. And when we would tell him that it was none of his business he would reply in his fiercest voice, "Ha! You say that, when you live in Lyndhurst?" ')

'This is very interesting,' Groenewald said. He also said: 'The company will get in touch with Mr Fink, he sounds a likely prospect,' and, 'You are being most helpful, Mrs Gottlieb, more helpful than I could ever have imagined.'

'Don't mention it, why shouldn't I help you? You're just a young fellow trying to make a living. And if Mr Fink doesn't want to have anything to do with you, then he won't be shy to tell you so, that's for sure.'

'Perhaps Mr Fink will have no choice,' Groenewald said absently; but Riva laughed at the idea.

'He always makes a choice for himself. You don't know Mr Fink, or you wouldn't say such a thing about him.'

'Well, I'm going to try to get to know him very well indeed.'

'I wish you luck. He is an interesting man to know.'

'It sounds like it, yes.'

A pause followed; and though Groenewald had gathered more information than he had hoped for, he was reluctant to go out into the bare street that would lead either to his room in the New Temperance Hotel or to Conroy's office. But eventually he got up to go, thanking Mrs Gottlieb again for her help, and assuring her how pleased he had been to hear what she had told him. 'You see, Mrs Gottlieb, when someone has been as kind to me as you have been,' Groenewald said, making a little speech, his hat clasped firmly in front of his buttoned-up little waistcoat and his shoulders moving within the cloth of his jacket, 'then I don't want to be a nuisance or worry to them. So it's been nice for me to hear all this about Mr Fink, you understand?'

And with further expressions of thanks and esteem, Groenewald took his departure, Riva's last words to him being, 'For such a young gentleman like you there should be something better than going from door to door. You must try to think of another way of making a living.'

'Find out as much as you can about this Gottlieb,' Conroy had said to Groenewald. 'And in any way you can. Speak to his wife, speak to his servants, the people who work for him in the office. Find out where he goes, what he says, where he keeps things that are especially important to him – anything. It will all come in useful.'

At the time Groenewald had asked, 'But how did you find out about him?' but Conroy had refused to answer. 'That isn't your department. Do your job; find out how we can best get at him, and when we know enough, then get him to commit himself. That's all you have to do.'

'But perhaps it would be easier if I knew –'

'It would be easier? To find out how we work – yes, it would be easier for you, in all sorts of ways, wouldn't it, Groenewald?' The silence that followed had been even more unpleasant to

Groenewald than such silences usually were. 'Your job,' Conroy resumed, 'is not to find out how we work, but to find out how Gottlieb works, We know enough to send you after Gottlieb: he hasn't committed himself yet – you are to make him. And when we are finished with him, there will be others. There'll be lots of work for you – you'll know quite enough if you do it properly.' And Conroy had followed this with further, detailed instructions, which – Groenewald felt after his interview with Riva – he should act on without further delay – if only to prove Conroy wrong.

The thought that Conroy might be wrong in anything he said was one that had not occurred to Groenewald before he had heard what Riva had to say about Mr Fink. But once the thought came, it filled Groenewald with pleasure – for if Conroy could be wrong about Mr Gottlieb, then very possibly he could be wrong too about Groenewald.

As he waited for his bus, and when, after a long wait, he eventually rode in the rattletrap bus along one of Lyndhurst's main residential streets that led with many a change of direction to the town's business area, Groenewald was able to think with a simple sense of relief that perhaps he wasn't such a crook after all. Already, in doubting Conroy's word Groenewald had struck a blow for himself; all he had to do now was to prove Conroy wrong and wrong again, and he would know himself once more.

Groenewald did not reflect that such a determination might well lead to his proving the zealous Conroy right and right again. Already, though he did not dare to disobey Conroy directly, Groenewald did dare to obey him with such speed that it amounted practically to disobedience. Groenewald got off the bus; he entered the offices of Fink & Gottlieb Ltd., and surprised himself by the casualness and firmness of his own greeting to Gottlieb. Gottlieb looked to Groenewald like a suitable husband for Mrs Gottlieb – and she had helped so much already that he was confident Gottlieb would do the same.

8

So casual a greeting or so direct an approach, Gottlieb felt, was not really to be expected from such a young fellow, who looked so much like a little clerk, in his grey suit, white shirt and tie with a knot no bigger than a thumbnail. And it was Gottlieb who hesitated, temporized, pretended he could not understand what the man was talking about. It was Gottlieb who said, 'Article, Mr Groenewald, what article? I have a thousand articles. I am not a manufacturers' representative for nothing.'

'No, I don't mean that –'

'What else can you mean? In this office, Mr Groenewald, when people talk of articles they mean soap, bicycles, ashtrays, patent medicines, and innumerable other things which we can get delivered to your doorstep in no time at all and at factory prices. That is,' Gottlieb said, with a doubtful glance towards Groenewald, as if assessing his youth, his inexperienced manner, 'if you are in business. We do not deal direct with the public at all, only with the trade, who find us useful in one way and another, very often.'

'I'm sure,' Groenewald said politely.

'So you may be.' Narrowly, Gottlieb watched him, where he sat in the chair on the other side of the desk, one straying hand buttoning and unbuttoning his jacket. Groenewald's eyes were small, set closely together on either side of his small upturned nose; his voice seemed to pass through his nose when he spoke, coming out with a reedy and youthful note. And like a boy, Groenewald seemed unable to leave alone anything that he said; but was always shoving it into place with his hand, or swinging it about with an elbow, or pushing it up with both hands extended, or stretching it with an upward movement of his head that exposed his neck. 'Oh yes,' Gottlieb said to the man, 'many articles, but only from the manufacturers, and only for the trade.'

But the young man persisted, despite Gottlieb's hedging. 'I wasn't thinking of that sort of article at all.' He moved his shoulders to bring his jacket higher up on his neck, in a friendly but conspiratorial gesture. 'It's another kind of thing altogether.'

'And what would that be, please?'

Groenewald did not speak. He looked around the office as if to make sure that they were alone in it; he looked up to the beaverboard partition which did not meet the ceiling but left a gap through which their words might escape. Then he shook his head.

'Speak, speak,' Gottlieb said – the more impatient for the pang that came again within him, as it had done a few minutes after the young man's arrival. 'My partner is out, and there is only the typist here, and she cannot hear a word that you say. So what are you? What do you want?'

'I've heard, Mr Gottlieb, that you are interested in a rather special kind of article –' Groenewald said. He broke off and looked again at the gap near the ceiling. He edged his chair closer to Gottlieb's desk. 'It's not easy for me to speak, Mr Gottlieb. You understand from this how special the article is. But it's a well-known one here in Lyndhurst.'

'From whom exactly have you heard such a story about me?'

'People, Mr Gottlieb.'

'I never for one moment imagined, Mr Groenewald – is that what you said your name was? – that you had heard anything at all from dogs or walls or lampposts.' Gottlieb smiled at his own joke, but Groenewald merely looked puzzled.

But he got to his feet hastily when Miss Scholtz came into the office, carrying some papers for Gottlieb. 'Oh, excuse me,' she said when she saw that Gottlieb had someone with him. 'Can I come in?' She came forward and laid the papers on Gottlieb's desk, peeping over her shoulder at the visitor as she did so. 'They're all in order,' she told Gottlieb sincerely, to make up for her peeping.

'Yes, yes, Miss Scholtz.'

'Is there anything you still want?'

'No, I don't think so, Miss Scholtz. You can go back to your office.'

'Oh yes, Mr Gottlieb. I will, right away.' But she did not. She looked about the office, happening again to look at the visitor. 'I'm sure there was something else you wanted me to do,' she said blankly. She laughed and said directly to Groenewald, 'I'm so forgetful, you see.'

'So'm I,' Groenewald said in immediate response.

'It's terrible,' Miss Scholtz said. 'But Mr Gottlieb doesn't mind too much, does he?' She looked back at Gottlieb, who was pushing the papers back and forth on the side of the desk. But Gottlieb did not disagree, so Miss Scholtz was able to say: 'There, you see.'

Groenewald nodded solemnly.

'Well, I've interfered enough, haven't I?' Miss Scholtz asked. 'Interrupting the business. It's wrong of me, isn't it, Mr Gottlieb?'

'No, Miss Scholtz,' Gottlieb said.

Miss Scholtz laughed and left the office. Groenewald turned and watched her go; when the door closed behind her he stared at it for a few minutes longer, as if he did not trust her not to reappear through it. Then he turned to face Gottlieb again, and seeing that Gottlieb had been watching him he apologetically dropped his eyes to his hat, and took his seat.

'Perhaps,' Gottlieb said cautiously, 'people have given you the wrong information.'

'I don't think so.'

'And what exactly did they say to you?'

The young man ducked his head and told Gottlieb that he had heard that it wasn't a manufacture, no it was – well – something – well – out of the ground that Gottlieb was interested in.

'And who the hell are you to come and say such a thing to me?'

The young man was not offended. He merely said that Gottlieb had a right to ask.

'I should hope so. And who are you?'

'Groenewald.'

'Your name you've told me already. What I want to know is, who is Groenewald?'

Groenewald did not seem surprised that Gottlieb did not know who he was. He was, he said, just a bloke; and when Gottlieb said that he could see that for himself, Groenewald said, 'Yes,' in an entirely reasonable manner.

'You are a simple fellow,' Gottlieb said. 'Do you think – even if I had anything to say – I would say it to a stranger, a bloke who is no more than a bloke in his own words. A man who has never before been seen, and comes to me with strange words from people of whom I know nothing.'

'And if you did know about me?'

Gottlieb thought this over before he spoke, leaning forward across the desk, 'Then you would no longer be just a bloke. I don't talk to blokes, I talk to people, grown-up men, serious business people. That is the right thing to do, you agree?'

Groenewald agreed for all he was worth, to judge from the way his head jerked up and down. So it was a kind of reference Gottlieb wanted, Groenewald said.

'Like a man looking for a job,' Gottlieb jeered.

Groenewald said that he supposed in a way he was a man looking for a job. Because, he added frankly, he was pretty new to all this sort of thing.

'A man is never too old to learn,' Gottlieb said proudly.

'No, I suppose a man never is, Mr Gottlieb. And I do want to learn.'

'Have you got a lot to learn?' Slowly Gottlieb wagged his head from side to side. 'Mr Groenewald, you are in the wrong line of business altogether. I tell you this not because I know about your business so well, and not because I have anything to say to you even if you should come back with your references – but because I am a man who knows a thing or two, about all kinds of business.' Gottlieb's caution suddenly threatened to become as much a joke to him as his recklessness now was. They were both unreal: because they were unreal Gottlieb closed one eye, squinted at the man in front of him and listened carefully to the man saying that he was sorry to hear that Gottlieb thought he was in the wrong line of business, because it was one that he was very interested in. And Groenewald ventured to suggest that Gottlieb might be mistaken, for he hoped to be able to prove the strength of his interest in a way that Gottlieb would recognize. This morning he had merely been making the most preliminary inquiries, he told Gottlieb, but he would be back, if Gottlieb didn't mind; he would be back soon.

Gottlieb was tempted to close both eyes; he felt that if he did, and kept them closed for a little while, when he opened them again the young man would no longer be there. But Gottlieb kept one eye open, and told Groenewald, 'You are a strange young bloke. You talk in certain respects just like a child.'

119

'I'm trying to learn, Mr Gottlieb.'

There was no real harm in the young man, Gottlieb decided, even if he didn't know his own business, and even if his business was such a wretched little one. So Gottlieb restrained himself no longer, but spoke on the understanding he had had a moment before – the understanding that had forced him to half-close his eyes, squinting against its very glare. He gave Groenewald a word of advice. 'Look, Mr Groenewald,' Gottlieb said, 'go back to the person who sent you and tell him that Gottlieb isn't a damn fool, to be caught in such a simple way by such a simple fellow as you. Do you think I know nothing? Do you expect me to swallow such an openness, a coming-in – and a saying hullo – and – and after a mock hesitation an asking of your kind of question, about an article that comes from a hole in the ground? To such a question, Mr Groenewald, believe me, the answer is always no. Have I seen nothing in my time, that I should think that that is how such people manage their affairs?' Gottlieb's head shook several times, in reply to his own question. 'I know a thousand times better,' he said, thinking for once without anger of his own numerous and unsuccessful forays into a world that he had imagined would be peopled with just such reckless, casual and happy-go-lucky people as this young fellow in his ignorance had pretended to be. He had pretended to be just what Gottlieb himself had tried to be, in equal ignorance; and Gottlieb said now, 'The way I feel about you at the moment, my boy, is so strange that I feel like laughing in your face.'

Groenewald regarded Gottlieb with an expression of interest, as if he was thinking of obligingly presenting his face to Gottlieb for Gottlieb to laugh into.

'Why, you ask?' The young man had not asked, but Gottlieb told him nevertheless. 'Because that is what I plan to do to Fink. Go back to Fink –'

'Fink!'

'You jump now, when you hear the name.' And when he saw the smile on Groenewald's face, Gottlieb smiled too, momentarily. 'You see, I know a thing or two. He's the man, he's the man,' Gottlieb said in triumph. 'Let him not try such tricks on me, probing and thinking to catch me this way. If he wants to know my position, let him ask like a man, not send such spies to me, so that he will have me as his victim, caught in his trap, making a fool of myself. I have been watching that Fink too long; I know with what jealousy and hopelessness he is being eaten. But that he should now in this way try to trap his partner!' Gottlieb was smiling no longer. 'I have no message for him. Just go back to Fink, Mr Groenewald.'

Groenewald stood up. 'Mr Gottlieb, I will.'

'I will have the last laugh on him,' Gottlieb said, though still there was no smile on his face. 'He is a desperate man, to try such a thing on me. But it will help him not at all.'

'Nothing will help him now, Mr Gottlieb. I'll see to it.'

Gottlieb frowned at the higher tone of Groenewald's voice. 'He is a foolish man to admit strangers into such affairs, and to try and trap his partner.'

'A very foolish man, Mr Gottlieb.'

Gottlieb's frown deepened, but before he could say any more, Groenewald had put his hat on his head and gone to the door of the office. Only when he was at the door did Groenewald say, 'Oh – the lady –'

'What lady?'

'The lady who brought you the papers.' Groenewald rubbed the back of his neck for a moment. 'I think I've – No, nothing,' he said. 'Thank you for your help,' he added. 'You won't regret it, even if Mr Fink does.'

Gottlieb's chin sank into his neck. Over black-rimmed spectacles he watched the young man go; but a few moments later Gottlieb had rallied sufficiently to call in Miss Scholtz. 'It looks to me as though you've made a conquest of that young fellow. I wish I could give him a better recommendation, but he doesn't seem to me to be a very reliable young man.'

'Mr Gottlieb! Why do you say such things?'

'Running around on messages like that –'

'No, conquests! Honestly, Mr Gottlieb.'

Gottlieb bore with her reproofs. But when she left his office Gottlieb heard her go to the front door, to see if the conquered Groenewald were still in sight. Alas, he was not – if Gottlieb could judge from the slowness and heaviness of her tread as she went back to her office.

But when Gottlieb got up to go home, some hours after Groenewald had left, his tread was slow and heavy too. Fink had come back to the office in the meantime, and had left again: Gottlieb had waited for Fink to say something about the caller he had sent; but the silence in the office had been as deep on this afternoon as it had every other afternoon and morning since Gottlieb had told the outright lie to Fink about the diamonds.

Gottlieb did not feel remorse for the lie he had told – or so he assured himself. All he felt now was suspicion and resentment of Fink. For days Gottlieb had sat in his office, listening to Fink in his office across the little corridor, wondering what Fink was thinking and planning, suspecting Fink's every entrance and departure. When he was with Fink, Gottlieb confined his exchanges to the necessary details of business; and when Gottlieb left Fink each time he searched Fink's words for double meanings, threats, hints, reproaches, and then was the more suspicious for his failure to find them. Suspicion grew from silence, and silence from suspicion, so that there could be no end to either.

And suspicion was manifold and destructive; and Gottlieb was as much the object of his own suspicion as Fink was. In search of certainty Gottlieb might flail around him, without discretion and without judgment; but suspicion was subtle, and made all that he struck seem doubtful and uncertain no sooner than he touched it. Already, as he drove home, Gottlieb was wondering if he hadn't been too hasty in his treatment of Groenewald. Perhaps, Gottlieb was wondering already, the man had been a real I.D.B. man, a crook, a gangster, whom he had failed to recognize, but had sent on to Fink.

Gottlieb had told his lie to Fink so that he would be able to go on – on his own – to achieve the success of selling the diamonds. As a result of the lie Gottlieb had indeed found himself on his own: so very much on his own that there no longer seemed to be any point in going on. For Gottlieb knew that even if he should achieve the success of which he had dreamed, Fink could now never learn of it, because of the lie he had been told; Riva could never learn of it, because of the lies she had been told; there was no one who could know, except the stranger to whom Gottlieb might sell the diamonds. And when Gottlieb had realized this, the bottom had simply dropped out of the whole thing, without warning, without a possibility of recovery.

Gottlieb no longer went out in the evenings. He stayed at home, silent, muttering occasionally in reproach and apology and accusation to Fink, shouting at Riva when she told him that she was as worried about him now as she had been when he had gone running out of the house every day like a wild man. 'Why don't you go out any more?' Riva asked him often. 'If it cheers you up, please do go, Manfred.' But there was nothing that Gottlieb could think of doing now that would have cheered him up.

'I wish I had never seen those stones,' Gottlieb told a Lyndhurst road, lying flat in the sunlight before his car, as he drove home. 'Why did that Fink ever send them to me? They make me sick. Sick! Sick!' There was some satisfaction for the moment in shouting the word, but another voice was treacherous and promptly interrupted him, as it had done a

123

hundred times before. 'You've still got those stones, all the same.' 'I know, I know,' Gottlieb said angrily. 'You don't have to tell me things that I know already.'

One voice spoke aloud, the other silently; their unhappy debate took Gottlieb home, through his supper, and so through yet another evening.

9

Early on the next morning Gottlieb was phoned from the Lyndhurst General Hospital, and was told that Fink had been brought into the hospital the previous night. He had been in an accident, the voice said, and his condition was serious.

'What kind of an accident?' Gottlieb screamed.

'It seems that he was attacked. The police are investigating.'

'Who attacked him, for God's sake?'

'The police don't know.'

'And how is he?'

'I have told you already. His condition is serious.'

'How serious, please, tell me! Is he in danger?'

'Yes.' Then the voice said, 'Thank you, Mr Gottlieb,' and Gottlieb heard the receiver being put down at the other end of the line. No sooner had the voice gone than Gottlieb could not believe that it had spoken the truth – he could not believe it, so early, on such a quiet, sunny morning, into which the ringing of the telephone had wakened him. But his next thought was for Fink's daughters, to the eldest of whom he sent a telegram saying that her father had been injured in an accident, and that his condition was serious.

Then he had to go and see Fink at the hospital'. 'You can go in,' they told him there, for though it was not the visiting hour, Fink was in a private ward with a single bed in it; and Gottlieb was able to go in on tiptoe.

125

From the expression on Fink's face it seemed to Gottlieb that he could have clumped into the room in a pair of metal-shod boots and Fink would not have heard him. Fink lay with his eyes closed, his cheeks drawn in, as if listening to sounds other than those that could come to him from outside. To these Gottlieb listened: he heard the sound of trolley wheels from the passage outside the room, of dishes rattling, of pails clanking, of nurses passing in the corridors, their rubber-soled shoes seeming to kiss the material on which they trod. Fink heard none of these sounds; he did not move. His chin had disappeared into the sheets, and against the whiteness of the pillow his forehead looked very red, his hair, which Gottlieb had always seen as white, looked almost golden.

'Fink,' Gottlieb whispered, but Fink did not stir.

Gottlieb shifted his weight from one foot to the other: he was carrying his hat in his hand and he wanted to put it down, but did not know where; he could not put it on the bed, lest it should disturb the white sweep upwards of the bedclothes over Fink's reclining body. He put his hat insecurely on the arm of the ward's one armchair, and scratched his bald head, and again whispered, 'Fink?' A moment later he did not know whether he had said the name aloud or merely thought of saying it aloud, for the expression of withdrawn, inward concentration on Fink's face did not change at all. Gottlieb had steeled himself against seeing Fink bruised and battered, seeing bits of Fink's face peeping without expression between forbidding, impersonal swathes of bandages. But there was nothing of the kind: Fink looked as though he were fast asleep, and Gottlieb knew less than ever what to feel.

'But how serious is it?' Gottlieb asked the matron in her clean, gleaming, flower-bedecked little office.

The matron turned her nun-like headgear towards him and replied: 'He is in danger.'

Gottlieb turned his hat in his hands. 'Ah, is that what you say?' He saw the matron's fingers on the desk: they were clean, almost colourless, only the fingernails showing the faintest of colours. Her brows were black but the rest of her face seemed to Gottlieb as colourless as her hand, where it lay on the desk.

'You have informed his family?' she asked.

'Of course.' In the office where everything was pale and gleamed subtly, Gottlieb stood in his dark suit. 'There are no marks,' he said.

'None that you can see,' the matron replied.

Gottlieb could see that she wanted to get on with her work. 'Well, thank you.' He turned to go.

'Good morning.'

'You are sure?' Gottlieb asked, turning back in appeal at the door.

'No one is ever sure. We must hope for the best.'

'Yes,' Gottlieb said. Hopefully, he told the matron: 'His son-in-law is a doctor, and he will probably be coming down. He will know how it seems to him.'

The matron's black eyebrows drew together. 'Yes, Mr Gottlieb.' She stood up, and turned her back to him, letting him see only the back of her headgear hanging down.

'Well – good morning, miss.'

With her back to him the matron said: 'We are doing our best for Mr Fink. We do the best that we can for anyone who comes into the hospital.'

'For sure,' Gottlieb said in surprise. 'How – ? What – ?'

'Mr Fink's son-in-law will have nothing to complain of.'

'Oh,' Gottlieb said. 'Oh, miss. I meant nothing different. It was something I said –'

But the woman would not turn around to face him, and Gottlieb left her.

At first anxiety came in pangs, but as the day passed it was as though each pang was extending itself, was going forward to meet the next, so that they came without intermission, and Gottlieb was enchained in anxiety. And heavier even than his anxiety there was within him his guilt, which lay unstirring and voiceless.

Guilt did stir when, in the evening, the front door bell rang, and Benjamin appeared agitatedly at the door of the living room.

'Baas, you must come.'

'What is it?'

Benjamin made no answer; he could only shake his head and roll his eyes towards the front of the house. When Gottlieb went to the front door Benjamin stayed back, hiding himself behind the folds of the hall curtain, out of sight but for his bare black feet.

There was a policeman at the door. He was big in his dark-blue encasing uniform; his boots were black on the red cement stoep; his badges glinted gold; only his face was naked under the rounded shell of the helmet. He blocked the doorway; and Gottlieb could see over one heavy shoulder just a corner of the sky, where there was a single green glow – the open and aloof light of an early summer evening.

'What is it?' Gottlieb asked, when he was still within the hall. 'Why don't you come in?'

The policeman did not move. 'Mr Gottlieb?'

'Yes.'

'Mr Gottlieb, I've come in connection with the attack last night on Mr Fink.'

'Yes. Why don't you come in?'

The man did not move. 'I don't want to take up your time, Mr Gottlieb. There's just one question I have to ask. Do you know of any reason why Mr Fink should have been attacked? Is there anyone you know or can think of who might have done it?'

Gottlieb wiped his chin with one hand, and then with one finger rubbed the place that he had wiped, like a man thinking something over – though there was no thought in his head.

'No,' he said. 'I know nothing.'

'You have no ideas? Even just guesses, anything that might help us.'

'I know nothing.'

The policeman had begun to take a notebook out of his tunic; now he shoved it back into the pocket. 'Mr Fink never talked to you about anything that might have led to this?'

'I know nothing.'

'Well, thank you, we're sorry to have troubled you. And if you should think of something, Mr Gottlieb, you know where you will be able to find us.'

'I know noth–' Gottlieb began to say. 'Yes,' he said. 'I will remember what you have said.'

'Good.' The policeman had taken a step or two back while Gottlieb had been talking, and he cut off less of the garden from Gottlieb's view than before. The trees and bushes were all black; in the quiet street there was diffuse, weak light of a streetlamp; farther back the sky was still green, and wider now.

'What do you know?' Gottlieb called out. 'Tell me, please.'

The policeman turned, and for the first time Gottlieb saw the young, unlined features of the face, the straight sunburned nose and the blond moustache beneath it. He saw the paler lips moving and heard the voice saying, 'Very little. He was found at about twelve o'clock last night, in Straight Street, just off the Market Square. We don't know who did it to him, or why. Perhaps it was just kaffirs, or hooligans – but they didn't seem to rob him or anything. We're working on the case, and we'll get hold of the people who did it, don't you worry, Mr Gottlieb.' The lips ceased moving, and Gottlieb no longer heard the sound of the voice; yet time seemed to pass before he found that he was standing in his own doorway, with the policeman a few paces away from him.

'Thank you,' Gottlieb said.

'Good evening,' the policeman said, nodding. His boots clinked as he went down the path, and then Gottlieb saw him carefully closing the gate behind him.

'They said – ?' Riva asked eagerly, coming into the hall. 'I couldn't hear everything, but I didn't want to come and worry you –'

Gottlieb was not listening to her. 'I'm going to the hospital,' he said, 'I must find out how he is.'

'Manfred, you were there coming back from work, there'll be no change. Sit down and have some supper, and perhaps afterwards you can phone. Please, Manfred, give yourself a chance.'

'What have I done to deserve a chance? Oh, Riva,' Gottlieb groaned, 'what have I done?'

'Nothing, please, Manfred.'

But Gottlieb went to the hospital, and came back to the house a little later. There had been no change, he told Riva. 'But he'll be all right. It's a nasty business, but I don't want to hear you say that it won't be all right.'

Riva had not made any prophecies; but hearing her husband's words she warned him now, 'I don't know, Manfred. We must be prepared for the worst. He is not a young man any more, and the head is a delicate thing.'

Gottlieb put his elbows on the table, and sat with his hands over his ears, and Riva did not finish her story about how strange it had been that just the day before a man should have called about selling insurance. When Riva went to bed Gottlieb had not yet moved.

No life is easy to the person who lives it; but Manfred Gottlieb had never thought of himself as having had a particularly hard

130

life either. There were too many people who had had lives too much like his own for him to think of himself as having been marked out for hardship; and if he had come to South Africa at the age of sixteen, an immigrant Jew, a stranger, unable to speak the language, and with barely a penny in his pocket, so had thousands of others like himself who had proceeded to lead the best lives that they could, as he had done. And Gottlieb knew too what would have happened to him had his parents not brought him away from Europe.

Buying and selling, buying and selling – Gottlieb had been buying and selling ever since his arrival in South Africa; and one of the reasons for the success of Fink & Gottlieb Ltd. was that both he and Fink knew a surprising amount about the innumerable articles which they offered to their customers. And about a great many others which they did not sell. Gottlieb could go into a butcher-shop and pick out for himself without hesitation the choicest cut (or the best value for a particular sum of money) from any number of slabs, haunches and joints of meat on display, for Gottlieb had spent a year of his life learning to be a butcher. But then, as a country storekeeper, among other occupations, what had Gottlieb not bought and sold, so that itemization became even for himself impossible? A store in the country was still the best training of all for buying and selling just about everything any human being ever wanted to buy or sell, and there was not a province in the country in which Gottlieb had not worked as a country storekeeper, and in two of the four provinces he had actually been owner or part-owner of the store. A Jew from Lithuania in those earlier days saved a hundred pounds and offered to become partner with another; and if he had no money at all he could always get an assistantship, and hope that one day he would have a hundred pounds saved up.

But Gottlieb had stayed in none of these places he had worked in: always he had moved on, for in none of them had he done really well, in none of them had he been free from financial anxiety and from an anxiety of another kind of which he was to free himself only after his arrival in Lyndhurst and his eventual success there with Fink. It was an anxiety, a pressure upon him, that for Gottlieb was associated with his boyhood in the old country, and with the lives of his parents. Gottlieb felt that his parents had sacrificed their lives for his own, in bringing him to the new country; and it was for them too, and not only for himself or his own family that he had had to win for himself, in the harsh African sunlight that hid nothing above the sand, his place, his certainty, his establishment. That was the duty that had been placed upon him, and it was by that duty that he had lived. So always, dissatisfied, he had moved on, from the country to Johannesburg and from Johannesburg back to the country, and then to Johannesburg once more, until in his partnership with Fink, modest though it had always been, Gottlieb had found more what was like a fulfilment of his duty than any other he had known.

'Never before have I been so cheeky! Is that what I told myself? For a diamond? Such a quiet conservative fellow – is that what I told myself?' Gottlieb's voice was loud in the quiet house, and through the open living room door he heard Riva stir in her bed at the sound. He lowered his voice, but still he muttered aloud. 'What have I ever had in my life except what I grabbed and held on to with both hands and made a plan for, at once? For God's sake, I have always been cheeky! But for better things, for better things.'

When he at last went to his bedroom that night, Gottlieb reached into the wardrobe and took out the little box of diamonds. He held it clenched in his fist, and brought it to his ear; he heard the box creak as it began to give way under the pressure of his hand. 'You will see, I will try to be cheeky for a better thing. I will try not to be frightened, if the worst comes for me.' Gottlieb brought his hand down; he opened his fist and looked at the box of diamonds in his hand, where it lay, a little squashed, a little bent. Then Gottlieb put the box back in its place in the wardrobe, for now, if the worst came, he would need it.

The next morning again the telephone rang early, and again Gottlieb answered it. Fink's youngest daughter, Althea, was phoning from Lyndhurst railway station.

'I'll come and fetch you,' Gottlieb said to her.

'No – it's all right. I'll stay at the hotel. There's no need for you to bother.'

'Is this a fine time for politeness?' Gottlieb asked.

There was a silence at the other end of the wire.

Then the young woman asked, 'How is he?'

'You must ask the doctor and the matron. You had my wire.'

'Yes ... but –'

'I'm coming to fetch you. You will stay with us.'

'Thank you.'

When Gottlieb arrived Althea was waiting on the pavement outside the station, with her suitcase next to her on the ground; she was the centre of the close attention of several railway idlers in peaked caps who sat on luggage trolleys outside the booking office. She extended one loose, gloved hand to Gottlieb. 'Mr Gottlieb,' she said. 'How are you?' Even after a night on the train from Johannesburg she was, to Gottlieb's Lyndhurst eyes, so smart, so poised, so urban, that in spite of himself he fussed a little unnecessarily over the handshaking, over getting her case into the back seat of the car. She was wearing a dark green tailored suit that fitted smoothly over her small hips and set off well her dark hair and clear, pale skin. Her legs were light, almost powdered in appearance, in their fine stockings, and her shoes were small, flat, made of black suede – the shoes impressed Gottlieb with their casualness;

they made her smartness seem the result of no special effort but something everyday, habitual, taken for granted.

Only when they were both in the car did she ask: 'And how is Daddy?'

'You had my telegram.'

'But –'

'But?'

The girl said placatingly, leaning forward and turning in the seat to face Gottlieb, 'Is he just the same?'

'As far as I know – yes.'

'Oh.'

They sat in silence until they reached the Gottliebs' house. When she saw Althea tears rolled from Riva's large, open eyes. 'You look so well,' she said, embracing the girl. 'Your poor, poor father. Such a thing to happen to a man who did no harm to anyone.' The girl submitted to Riva's embrace, bringing one gloved hand up to Riva's shoulder.

'Come, my dear, I'll show you to your room,' Riva said, and took Althea down the passage, Gottlieb following with her suitcase, Benjamin and Sylvia looking on from the kitchen.

'It's such a long time since you were here,' Riva said reproachfully, in the bedroom.

'It is,' Althea replied, seeming not to notice the reproach.

Gottlieb and Riva left her to tidy herself before breakfast. 'She's so smart,' Riva said to her husband, in the breakfast room. 'Her suit … and did you see her handbag?'

'I saw everything. Even the rouge on her cheeks.'

'So, she shouldn't wear rouge? She's a young girl, she's entitled.'

'For sure she's entitled. But if my father was lying in the hospital with critical injuries I wouldn't be thinking of the rouge on my cheeks.'

'Life goes on,' Mrs Gottlieb said. 'Your father passed away too.'

'For God's sake, who in the whole world is talking of such a thing as passing away? No one. Only you. Why do you talk of such things?'

Althea came into the room, and Gottlieb turned to the window. He did not know how much she had heard of what he and Riva had been saying to one another. He did not care very much either.

Althea did not take at all after her father, except that she, too, was small. She was dark-haired, with a pale, smooth skin: her hair was parted in the middle and her forehead was clear, her sharp little nose seeming to lean out of her face; and when she spoke her words engaged her lips in much small compressed action. She and Riva talked in a desultory way through breakfast – of their families, of Irvine whom Althea had last seen by accident in a bioscope in Johannesburg, of Althea's small daughter.

'When are your sisters coming down?' Gottlieb asked.

Althea hesitated, and attempted a smile, with her lips together: 'They sent me down first, to find out how Daddy was.'

'To find out if he's bad enough to make it worthwhile for them to come too?' Gottlieb asked, with a kind of hostile, jogging emphasis on each word.

Althea did not reply.

On his way to the office, Gottlieb dropped her at the hospital. 'Phone me up when they tell you to go,' he said.

'I can take a taxi.'

'Phone me up!' Gottlieb commanded rudely.

When he came back Gottlieb found her at the top of the steps at the hospital entrance. She had been waiting with her handbag clasped tightly in both hands in front of her stomach, as if it could protect her.

'Now your sisters will come down?'

135

'Oh yes.' She climbed into the car with a movement like that of a child on all fours. 'They'll have to come down now. I'm going to phone them up straight away.'

Gottlieb did not tell her that they should have been down already; he simply drove her home in silence. Going back once again to the office, on an impulse Gottlieb turned his car towards the hospital, and drove up the hospital's main drive, round the centre island of grass and flowers, and parked the car in front of the main door. A sign announced that only doctors' cars should be parked there, and when he saw the sign Gottlieb left the car where it was, put the handbrake on, put the car in gear, and locked the doors. Then he went up the steps.

But now he was not allowed into Fink's ward. He wandered into the matron's office, and asked her, 'How are things?'

'Not good,' the matron replied. 'Not good at all.'

Passionately Gottlieb said, 'Fink will surprise you, matron.' Puzzled, the woman looked at him, and Gottlieb said: 'Fink is a man of surprises. He is like that. I promise you, Fink will surprise you. All my life since I've known him Fink has been giving me surprises. So why should he stop now?' Shaking his head, muttering, Gottlieb left the office before the woman could rise from her chair.

The next morning brought Fink's two remaining daughters, Lynda, and Claire, who came with her husband. Claire was the one Gottlieb decided he liked best, because she reminded him of her father: she had the same dwindling face, the same straight, soft, fairish hair. Lynda looked more like Althea, and Gottlieb liked her less. But he found that he had little to say to any of them. They were all strange to him, now that they were adult, well-dressed, concerned about children he hardly knew, married to men that he had hardly seen since the wedding ceremonies; now that they spoke English not merely as their mother tongue, as they had always done, but even with an accent that he recognized as different from the drawl that he heard about him in the streets of Lyndhurst. They spoke like Johannesburgers, with higher-pitched voices and shorter vowels; and they spoke for the most part to each other.

The morning after brought the husbands of Lynda and Althea: Gottlieb complained to Riva that as for the husbands, he couldn't tell one husband apart from the next. To him they were all big, well-dressed, embarrassed, South African-born young men who on their arrival smoked cigarettes in his lounge, talking subduedly to one another. There were too many people now for them all to stay with the Gottliebs, and one family went into the King's Hotel, another into the Diamond. The men had nothing to do, so they came into Gottlieb's office and wandered out of it again; they drank tea with Riva and their wives. The sisters talked together, and in the evening they took their husbands to visit former schoolfellows who had grown up with them, but had not, as they had, escaped from the forlorn little mining town. The girls even shopped a bit, having nothing else to do, having only an hotel room in which to sit. Religiously each phoned up her parents-in-law in Johannesburg at night, and spent three minutes, six minutes, nine minutes, inquiring about the children she had left behind.

One day passed, a second, and the husbands became more restive about the work they had abandoned; the sisters became more anxious about their children, and spent more time on the telephone. The husbands conferred together, and separately, with their wives and sisters-in-law; the medical husband conferred with the local doctor who was handling Fink's case. At the end of the second day there was talk of flying a specialist down from Johannesburg, but the idea was dropped.

The husbands flew away in a body on the third morning, leaving their wives behind. Althea and Lynda quarrelled suddenly about who should have come down in the first place, about the words that Althea had used when she had telephoned them to come down; then all three wept together for their own folly in quarrelling at such a time. One night a parent-in-law reported a little boy sick with what looked like tonsilitis, and the little boy's mother, Claire, decided that it was impossible for her to stay on any longer: she was just hanging around, she said, and she could be in Johannesburg with her sick child instead of just hanging around, like this. Both her sisters said that if she could not stay nor could they; they agreed that someone should stay, but none of them could see that she should be the one who would have to stay. They decided that if there was no change by the next day they would all leave, and one would come down the very next weekend, if nothing had happened in the meantime to bring them all down again. But they could not agree which one of them should come down the next weekend, until Althea said that she would come down and honestly she thought it a pretty poor show the way they were all carrying on. Then they wept again. They spent the last evening waiting in Riva's lounge, all three of them, until they could go to bed. There was no change in Fink's condition the next morning, and they left by the mid-morning plane.

Then every evening until the weekend each of them phoned the Gottliebs, and Riva told them, 'No change. The doctor says there's no change.' Riva asked Gottlieb, 'For how long can there be no change?' and Gottlieb replied angrily, 'For longer perhaps than suits Fink's daughters.' The weekend came, and Althea spent the weekend with the Gottliebs and left on the Monday morning's plane. 'Goodbye to you,' was Gottlieb's only word of farewell to her.

Riva had to rebuke Gottlieb for the rudeness of his behaviour to the girls. 'It's hard for them,' she said. 'They've got other responsibilities. They're doing their best. They're doing their duty.'

'I know, I know.'

Gottlieb still went to the hospital every morning and evening; he saw Fink every day in the coma, and it seemed to him so deep, to have made such a change so to have silenced Fink, that he could not believe that Fink could ever come out of it – though to Fink's daughters he said angrily, as if they were trying to deny his words, 'He'll give you a surprise. He has a life of his own. He does things no one can expect.' Gottlieb could see that Fink's daughters did not know what to make of his words or the tone of voice in which they were said: the daughters seemed a little frightened of him and at the same time a little contemptuous, as if he were a man about whom it did not matter if they could not understand his words or the tone of his voice; and Gottlieb did not try to explain himself. To Fink, in the isolation and the silence of the ward amid the meaningless reverberating noises of the hospital building, Gottlieb said, 'If you only knew! What would you think of me then? What would you tell me?'

Almost every day he phoned the police to ask if they knew any more about what man it was who had attacked Fink, but the information they had or gave him was scanty. A waiter at the hotel had reported that earlier on the evening of the attack he had seen Fink in conversation with a young man he had never seen before, and the waiter had described the stranger to the police. Mr Joffe, the proprietor of the hotel, reported that Mr Fink had said to him, just before going out later that evening – very late, after closing time – 'I am just going to get some fresh air – perhaps a stroll will help me to sleep,' for Mr Fink had seemed worried, Mr Joffe had said. More than that the police did not know, or would not tell Gottlieb.

Gottlieb never asked the matron how Fink was doing; he went for his information straight to Fink's doctor, and listened carefully, with a bowed head, to what the doctor had to say to him. But in the ward he said to Fink, 'I can't stand it, Fink. I must know what I have done.' And at other times he said, 'I am sorry a thousand times, believe that. Oh, Fink – I am trying, believe that too.' How much Gottlieb said aloud he did not know, for Fink could not tell him. 'I am tied up in what I have done,' Gottlieb said to him. 'But I will break out, for you, for me, or else there is nothing.'

To Riva, Gottlieb said, 'Unless I do something it's like my life that is lying there silent. Because Fink was just such a man as me, only better.'

'What are you talking about?' Riva implored him. 'What can you do?'

'I have done my worst,' Gottlieb cried. 'And that is my punishment. Poor Fink, poor man, and I was so busy and now when I want to hear him he can tell me nothing.'

'It is terrible,' Riva said, thinking not only of what her husband had just said, but also of the sounds she heard from his bed at night, when he lay in sleep with his arms heavily folded on his chest, the only life in him seeming to be the hoarse unrecognizable groans that were so profound that they seemed to come from under a depth of water, from the very bottom of himself. Nor would she have been reassured by her husband's words had she heard him telling Fink, in guilt and remorse, 'I am trying to break out, Fink. You will see.'

10

The next days were hard for Gottlieb, as hard as any he had yet gone through. He had waited, hoping that Fink might recover consciousness or that the police might find the man who had committed the crime. But Fink still lay comatose; and the police were still at a loss to know who had struck him down. So on his own Gottlieb went once again to all the places he had visited with so much pride and excitement a few weeks before. He went without pride and without excitement now: he felt only shame when he saw around him again the scenes where he had enacted the dishonesties and follies that had led to the present pain, the present guilt. From bar to bar and hotel to hotel and in and out of the few private residences Gottlieb dragged himself, in a kind of pilgrimage which, because it was unsuccessful, was no expiation of what he had done.

The evenings were warm, dust-scented, still; Lyndhurst seemed familiar to Gottlieb, and peaceful; within the wide stretches of the town only he had to move from place to place, asking, searching, moving on again. Fans whirred, voices called, faces he had seen before glistened in electric lights; but Gottlieb did not wave his hand when hands were waved at him, or smile when he was smiled at. He asked his interlocutors if they knew of a man named Groenewald, and he described Groenewald's appearance; when the vague and negatory answers were given to him he got up and left. But he was long enough with each person of whom he asked his question to see on every face the lines drawn by evasiveness and equivocation, the smiles that uneasiness strained at the corners of the lips; he saw the gestures of suspicion and resentment that accompanied them; he heard in each voice the tones of self-doubt and fear. And when Gottlieb remembered how he had gone among these people, he knew that if they had refused to have anything to do with him it had not been because he had been so much unlike them. He too had been evasive and equivocal, doubtful and suspicious, fearful, uneasy; there had been nothing to choose between himself and these people; and Gottlieb despised himself for it in a way he did not despise them. For he had deceived himself about them, and about himself: his actions had never been heroic, independent, remarkable; they had been conceived in shabby dishonesty, and had issued at best in shabby deeds amid shabby surroundings, and at worst in the guilt that drove him now.

Gottlieb did not know what he would do if he found Groenewald, but the only alternative open to him if he should fail to find the man was so frightening that for as long as he could he made his inquiries, wherever he could. But he had no more success in this search than he had had in the last. There was no one who would admit to knowing the man that Gottlieb described, though a few people offered him other Groenewalds – elderly Groenewalds, female Groenewalds, half-caste Groenewalds.

When Fink's daughters told Gottlieb that they were thinking of putting a notice in the paper announcing a reward to anyone who came forward and gave information which would lead to the discovery of the man who had made the attack, Gottlieb gave himself three more days in which to find Groenewald. If he failed, then – Gottlieb told himself, making an ugly joke at his own expense – he would come forward to claim his reward.

Those three days were desperate. Gottlieb could not be in the streets when he was in the King's Hotel, nor could he be in either the King's or the Diamond or in twenty other places when he was in the Comet; and when he was in one street there were so many others that he was missing. For the only hope left to Gottlieb now was that he would see the man by chance; and that was more a symptom of despair than it was a hope. Whether it was hope or despair, it was violent, and kept Gottlieb moving in a frenzy about the town. When he drove his car he looked incessantly from side to side and in the mirror; when he walked he quickened his pace at the sight of every straight, grey-suited back he saw; he stood at the entrance to public places and looked to see if the man were there, and he returned to each place as soon as he could after having been to as many other places as he had been able to. He waited in the Market Square, under the few neon signs, among all the cars parked in rows while their owners were watching the bioscope, and when each of the town's three cinemas ended its show he was in the foyer searching among the blinking pale faces that emerged. He saw people looking curiously at him, and he did not care; he knew that his behaviour and his appearance were arousing comment, and he did not care. He felt ill, overweight; he sweated too freely and stumbled too easily; his suits were rumpled and his collars askew; his hands shook at the end of his gestures, as if making threats and supplications of their own at himself. And when he hailed a man in the street, angrily, at the top of his voice, and then found that he had the wrong man he hardly apologized: the strangers were left amazed at the faces Gottlieb pulled at them, the way he stamped his feet, muttered, shook his head and went off hastily, as if there were nothing less precious to him than his temper or his health.

In all this time Gottlieb hardly went into the office, which was left to Miss Scholtz to manage. Gottlieb was grateful to

Miss Scholtz for being capable enough to look after what routine business there was, and he appreciated the anxiety she showed for Mr Fink. He was struck that with her too this anxiety seemed to have in it the elements of guilt, as if her own obvious firmness of body were something of which she felt ashamed, now that Mr Fink was so critically ill in the hospital. And that was how Miss Scholtz felt! Then how should Gottlieb feel? What should Gottlieb do? So his calls on the office never lasted long; he left it after barely reading the correspondence that came in, and giving Miss Scholtz a few incoherent instructions. Sometimes he returned to the office to rest, when he sat there alone and silent; on other days he did not even do that.

Riva he did not speak to, except sometimes to say a few comforting words to her, as incoherent as those he uttered to Miss Scholtz. But on the fourth morning of the time he had set himself since his talk with Fink's daughters, Gottlieb said to Riva, 'My duty to Fink is plain. I will not say what I am going to do, because you will worry and I have no idea what is going to happen. If it is bad you will know soon enough; if it is good perhaps we will laugh about it later. I have no choice, Riva, and if the worst comes, then I hope you will understand, and perhaps Irvine too. We pay for what we do, and I am no exception.'

'I don't understand, Manfred. What are you talking about?'

A little stiffly Gottlieb kissed her on the cheek. He left her staring after him, with her hand to the cheek he had kissed.

Still it was hard, bitterly hard, and when he came to the Lyndhurst Central Police Station, Gottlieb found that he could not get out of his car. In front of the police station Gottlieb rested for a moment. Then, with deliberate slowness, he drove on again. He did not know where he was going, but he let the car drift along the street, as if he might simply continue along it, out of the town, and to the northbound road beyond. There, in the veld he would be nobody and nothing; he would be a car with a trail of dust behind it, a flashing of metal and glass in front of it, something for the piccanins along the road to shout and wave at, for the horses along the wire to hear coming and to flee from with their heads shaking and their manes lifting and dropping, for the inhabitants of the *dorps* to stare after as his car bounced through their rutted, wide streets.

Gottlieb let the car go down the Johannesburg Road; but he knew that he was not going to go over the railway crossing where the houses ended, and on to the road payed out like a ribbon over the clear veld. And as he let the car drift on, Gottlieb could not help remembering that this was not the first time he had gone to a police station, though it was the first time he had feared to go. So many times a native in his employ had got drunk, or been caught without a pass; so many times the telephone had rung in the morning and a deep Afrikaans voice at the other end of the line had said: 'Good morning, Mr Gottlieb, we picked up a kaffir last night for not having a proper pass. He says he works for you, so if you could come along with his work permit and identify him then we can just let him go.' On these occasions Gottlieb had driven down to the police station, and when the door of the cell was opened behind the charge office, and the sunlight and the two white men came in, the native that Gottlieb had come to release had scrambled up from the floor to the yell of the policeman. '*Opstaan!* Kaffir, here's your baas come to help you. Next time it's six months for you.' And Gottlieb would have to say no more than a word. 'Yes, he does work for me.' When Gottlieb would step out of the shadow of the cell, the sun would be so warm upon him that it would feel as if his neck was scarfed, his hands were gloved, in sunshine.

Gottlieb turned at the corner, and as he did so he saw the trick that he had played upon himself by letting the car come as far down the road as it had. For there, within convenient distance from the Lyndhurst Central Police Station was the Lyndhurst Central Prison. In this prison Gottlieb had never been, for those locked up for one night were not sent here, and he had never been called to this place. But on this morning he had come to it nevertheless.

The prison had no door, no entrance at all that Gottlieb could see, from where he was, as he leaned across the seat to see better through the passenger's window. The door to the prison must have been around the other side, and also around the other side there must have been some break, some gate, in the tall barbed-wire fence that ran directly in front of Gottlieb, parallel to the road into which he had turned. A hedge behind the barbed wire was supposed to hide the prison grounds from view, but no hedge grew thickly in Lyndhurst, and the soil from which this one had to grow was particularly thin-looking, whitish, sandy. Within the grounds every inch of the soil had been worked over: even now, as Gottlieb looked, he saw a party of barefoot native convicts in their red blouses and dirty white shorts working with spades and pitchforks in the beds of dark-green vegetables. To the side of the prisoners a warder leaned against his heavy black rifle as if it were a stick to support him. There were no trees in the prison grounds, no flowers, only the rows of low, dark vegetables and the turned-over furrows in the pale soil, all stretching towards the prison, whose wall was in shadow, though the sun was beginning to clamber in rays over its red roof. And then, on the other side of the building, there ran the line of the farther fence, and beyond that again there was the clean straight glint of the railway lines. So the convicts at night – the native convicts in their half of the building and the white convicts in their half – could hear at night the hissing and jolting of the passing trains, their whistle as they approached the Johannesburg Road level crossing, their departure in the distance over the Koranna Pan. Gottlieb wondered what it must be like to lie in a cell at night and hear the trains beginning their journeys across the wide spaces of the veld that the whistling and scurry of wheels heard from a distance made more imminent even to himself, lying in his comfortable bed with his bedroom window open to the sky. Gottlieb wondered what it must be like, and the wonder drove out for a moment his fear at how close he seemed to be to finding out.

The fear came back, and this time the trembling seemed to start in his stomach, and to move outwards from there to his arms, that were stretched forward to hold the steering-wheel. He could feel the trembling run lightly along the back of his neck, as if he were being touched there, and his head started to shake a little, uncontrollably. There were men Gottlieb had seen whose heads always trembled like that. Gottlieb looked again at the prison building – from where he was now sitting, upright in the driver's seat, he could see only the roof, and that was trembling too. Then Gottlieb saw that it was the light of the sun that, as it rose over the building, was melting the straight line of the roof, and making it shudder in the clear morning air.

Gottlieb could wait no longer, for every moment that passed made it harder yet for him to carry out his decision. He started the car, turned back along the Johannesburg Road, and this time when he stopped at the police station he did not pause, but climbed out and slammed the door behind him. He began walking slowly across the street towards the charge office – a small brick building, with the bulk of the administrative offices heavy behind it. Gottlieb watched only his own shadow moving in front of him, and when he stepped on to the pavement he saw his shadow rise before him and then decline into a little hollow, in which a tree was planted – the hollow being for the water deposited in it once a week. The shadow began to climb the trunk of the tree: for all the water it received the tree was not much taller than Gottlieb, and his fingertips would have met had he put them around its black, dry, flaking trunk. But the trunk was so hard and sapless that if he had it would have scratched his hands.

And Gottlieb realized that with his eyes wide open and his hands swinging in front of him, he was walking right into the tree; and he swerved and ducked to avoid its lowest branches. When he reached the wall of the charge office he had to lean against it; he had to rest; he had to wait until the trembling of his head and his hands had subsided, and he could feel again some strength in his legs. The wall seemed firm against his back, and to help him steady himself Gottlieb rubbed one hand hard against the rough bricks. The pain did help; he looked at his palm, where the small scratches stood up against the yellow, used skin of his hand. Then a car passed, and Gottlieb stooped as if to do up a shoelace – both his shoelaces were knotted, but he would not let himself be seen leaning in weakness against the wall of a police charge office. He fumbled with the shoelace, touching it, seeing the eyeholes through which the lace ran, and the wrinkled leather of the upper. He groaned when the car had passed, and he had to straighten himself again. But he saw another shadow at his feet now – not his own – and Gottlieb looked up to see Groenewald standing above him. Gottlieb was still bent as he spoke. 'Murderer,' Gottlieb said, 'Assassin – what are you doing here? Are they on your track already?'

'No,' Groenewald said. 'But they are on yours.' Groenewald began to walk away casually. He said: 'I'll be waiting for you around that corner.'

Gottlieb watched him go. 'It's better so,' he called after Groenewald's retreating back. 'I have been looking for you. I will meet you man to man. I am not afraid.'

Groenewald did not turn or change his pace, but walked on, over the grey sand, his shadow black before him in the strong sunlight.

11

What had happened to Groenewald in the time since Gottlieb had last seen him was important enough to Groenewald, but it was not what Gottlieb thought it to be. For one thing, Groenewald believed that he had fallen in love, and for another he had had a disagreement with Conroy. Both his falling in love and his disagreement with Conroy were interdependent, for he had fallen in love with Miss Scholtz, and had disagreed with Conroy about Fink and Gottlieb.

Groenewald's own inclinations being so strongly what they were, he had been convinced by Gottlieb's words, coming so soon after Riva's, that if either of the partners were guilty of I.D.B. it was Fink, not Gottlieb. But this was not the only conviction with which Groenewald had left Gottlieb's office. He had also been convinced that he had seen Miss Scholtz before. And so he had, for she lived near the New Temperance Hotel, and Groenewald had passed her house many times on the walks he took when his loneliness and depression drove him out of the hotel to walk aimlessly in the streets nearby. On these strolls he had heard the noises made by Miss Scholtz's brothers, and those she made as she tried to keep them in order; he had watched her cuffing and chasing them in her front garden, and he had discreetly admired her persistence from where he stood on the opposite side of the street. Where he had stood, indeed, for as long as he possibly could each time – not

149

only in admiration of Miss Scholtz but in simple envy of the cheerfully communal hubbub that arose from her house.

The evening of the same day on which he had called at the offices of Fink & Gottlieb Ltd. Groenewald visited the Diamond Hotel. As he had hoped – after hearing from Riva Gottlieb about Mr Fink's way of life – he found Mr Fink in the lounge of the hotel, and in a casual and companionable way, he sat down with Mr Fink and had a little chat with him. They talked only of the weather and the state of business and the amusements that Lyndhurst offered in the evenings, for Groenewald believed he would have much time in which to do his work on Mr Fink. Fink seemed to Groenewald a harmless old man, but in his determination to work alone, for his own success, Groenewald was not prepared to forgive Fink on that account. For about a half-hour they chatted, among the battered armchairs and the stained wooden tables of the hotel lounge, while Groenewald drank a whisky and soda which an observant waiter brought to him; and then Groenewald bade Fink a courteous good evening, and took his departure. But he went only as far as the hotel foyer, where he closeted himself in one of the telephone booths. Though he had hoped to do no more than to make Fink's acquaintance at this meeting, and though he had succeeded in doing this, Groenewald's work was not yet over for the evening.

There were three Scholtzes listed in the book; Groenewald was not sure of the name of the street in which lived the Scholtz he was after, so he tried the one at the head of the list. A man answered the call and said no, his wife did not work for Fink & Gottlieb Ltd., and what the hell was it to Groenewald anyway. But when his second call was answered by a small muffled voice that said hullo three times and then lapsed into complete silence, Groenewald knew that he had the right number.

'Is your sister there? Please, I want to speak to her.'

The boy at the other end of the wire breathed heavily, but did not speak. Behind the breathing Groenewald could hear the tiny sound of a radio playing music, and other voices.

'Call your sister for me, please.'

The breathing grew even thicker, and then the telephone clattered loudly and a somewhat stronger and older voice said above the protests of a smaller one, 'Yes, is that Jimmy?'

'No,' Groenewald said, 'I want to speak to Miss Scholtz. Is that your sister?'

There was a high snort of laughter from the other end. The voice said, 'How can I be my own sister?' Another snort of laughter was interrupted by the faint sounds of altercation, followed by yet another clatter. 'No, give it to me, it's Jimmy,' a voice said desperately, but a third voice spoke to Groenewald. It was a woman's voice. 'Yes, Fink & Gottlieb Ltd. No – ach – Maisie Scholtz speaking.'

'Is that Miss Scholtz?'

'Yes.'

Business with pleasure, Groenewald had told himself, was what he might be able to combine in his call on Miss Scholtz; but it was the hope of pleasure and not of business that made the black earpiece a little moist against Groenewald's ear, as he pressed it closer and went into the little speech he had prepared. 'Miss Scholtz, I don't know if you remember me at all, but I was in the office this afternoon, where I saw you. My name's Dirk Groenewald, and I was speaking to Mr Gottlieb on a business matter when you came in – I don't know if you remember me at all, but I was ...' Immediately Groenewald knew that he had said this before, and he struggled to recover lost ground, 'Well, I was,' he said firmly.

'Yes?'

Groenewald's speech had deserted him. 'Do you remember me?' he said.

'Yes.'

'You do?'

'Yes.'

'Well –' Groenewald said with relief. He waited for Miss Scholtz to say something, but spoke again when she did not. 'I remembered you, you see. I've seen you sometimes, so it was funny seeing you again like that, in the office and everything. I mean I've seen you around – I live just around the corner from you.'

'You know where I live?'

'Yes,' Groenewald assured her, 'I do.'

Miss Scholtz's voice was quieter, less eager. 'Oh,' she said. Groenewald waited again; and in the pause he heard the radio again, and the distant raised voices.

'What's the matter?' he asked.

'Well, what do you want?'

Her voice was so brusque that in his surprise Groenewald could only repeat more urgently his last question. 'What's the matter? Please?'

'If you know where I live then why have you phoned me up?' the girl asked, and at the anger and desperation of her voice, above all the other sounds of the house, Groenewald clutched even harder at the receiver.

'Hell,' he said, 'what makes you talk like that? You should see where I live,' he said, understanding suddenly and feeling a responsibility at once. 'It's terrible where I live. You've got a nice place there. Any place is nice when you're not on your own all the time, like I am.'

'Are you on your own all the time?'

'All the time. I'm new in Lyndhurst, really. But don't get the wrong idea, please, that isn't why I'm phoning, honestly. It was just that seeing you, and remembering you, it was funny, and I thought that perhaps you wouldn't mind if I phoned like this.'

Again he waited.

'I don't mind,' Miss Scholtz said.

'You don't?' Groenewald leaned against the side of the booth. 'Then perhaps you wouldn't mind too much if I came round to see you? Would you?'

'No,' Miss Scholtz said, and though her voice was cautious the word was all that Groenewald needed.

'Then I will,' he said. 'Just you watch. I'll be coming round to see you, you wait and see if I don't. I mean, when I remembered you and saw you in the office – and you remembered me too, you said you did. So why shouldn't I come and see you? There's no reason at all, that's what I thought.' He said carefully: 'Thank you very much. You've been very kind to me, remembering me, and letting me speak to you like this, and letting me come round too. I appreciate it.'

Miss Scholtz's voice was still cautious, but very polite. 'Not at all,' she said. 'Don't mention it.'

Duty with pleasure, Groenewald told himself, that was what he was doing, combining duty with pleasure. Conroy had told him to find out all he could about Gottlieb, and what better way was there of doing this than by seeing Gottlieb's secretary as often as she let him? Especially as she was also Fink's secretary, and it was Fink that he would have been after, had not Fink been taken to the hospital the next day and had he not lain there all the days after. Conroy did not know it was Fink that Groenewald would have been after – and Fink that he would be after again, when the old man came out of the hospital – but Conroy did not know everything in the world.

The thought of the things that Conroy did not know was one that never failed to sustain Groenewald in the days that followed. Conroy ignorant was Conroy wrong – wrong about Groenewald, who did so many things that Conroy knew nothing about.

Conroy did not know what a privilege it was for Groenewald to sit – after all that time in the New Temperance Hotel and the streets of Lyndhurst – at a supper table with Maisie Scholtz and her family, and to eat food that Maisie had prepared, and to help Maisie keep order among her brothers by telling them about the circuses and the rugby matches he had seen and the towns he had visited and the buck he had shot on his uncle's farm. Conroy did not know how illuminating it was to discuss politics and the state of the world with Miss Scholtz's bent old father, who agreed with everything Groenewald said. And Conroy had no idea at all what it was like to be with a girl like Maisie. In a town where Groenewald had known only loneliness, subterfuge, and ignorance, where his only delight had been the prospect of lonely, independent action, where he still, with increasing unhappiness, passed himself off as an official of the Rural Roads Board, Groenewald met Maisie Scholtz who had a large family and no subterfuges at all, whose hopes and angers and pleasures were always so near to the surface that to Groenewald she seemed continually to put herself in danger, to expose herself to attack and disappointment; and also, as continually, to provoke protection. And to Groenewald there was no action more independent, less like any Conroy might have envisaged for him, than putting an arm around Maisie's broad waist, turning her body towards his, and kissing her lips with his own.

Only the second evening he saw her he did this, in a park, whose trees were too small and thin to hide what they were doing from anyone who might have passed or been sitting nearby. But they seemed to be on their own, and the only sounds close around them were the insects chirping in the warm air and the sounds they themselves made as their breath came faster, their clothing rustled, and their feet scraped on the sand under the bench. Her lips seemed small to Groenewald as he kissed them, and – the word came to him, with a sense of poignance – so neat that he was afraid for a moment that he might have bruised them with his kiss. He had not thought of neatness before in connection with Maisie Scholtz, and he was

154

THE PRICE OF DIAMONDS

surprised, and tender to her. And he was grateful too that when they drew apart she did not giggle, or accuse him of being fresh, or ask him what he thought he was up to on just the second night he had known her. Instead, after a long silence, she asked him if he was cross with her.

Cross with her! Groenewald protested violently against the idea that he might be. Why should he be cross with her?

'I don't know. I thought perhaps you were.'

'But why – ? I *couldn't* be cross with you.'

'Even when I'm like what I am?'

'And what's wrong with that?'

'Sometimes I think – everything,' Maisie said, and laughed a little fearfully.

'There's nothing wrong with you,' Groenewald assured her. 'You're pretty, and I like you, and I like your family, and your clothes are very pretty. Look at this dress – that's a nice dress,' Groenewald said, touching Maisie's yellow print frock at the knee.

Miss Scholtz too took the dress between her fingers, above his hand. 'It's old,' she said, but she was pleased, and their hands met, and then their lips again.

Later Miss Scholtz was anxious that he might think that she was like this with anyone who came to see her. Groenewald assured her that he knew she was not. 'This is different,' he said.

'It is,' she agreed. 'I'm not like this.'

Groenewald dared himself to say, 'Only with me,' and Maisie did not deny it.

Along the road outside the park few cars passed, and the sounds that came through the darkness were the more meaningless for the clarity with which a distant voice called, or a dog barked, or a car hooted. There were few lights that could be seen, and barely one was raised higher than another by any building or rise in the ground. With Maisie Scholtz in his arms

Lyndhurst seemed to Groenewald a different place to what it had before: sandiness and flatness now seemed a charm, emptiness an opportunity. .

In the days that followed the one thing that troubled Groenewald was Maisie's loyalty to both Fink and Gottlieb. This was something that had come up early, for on the first evening, when they had been laughing at some joke he had made, Maisie had suddenly grown grave and said, 'Here we are laughing, and just think about poor Mr Fink.' Since then she had said much the same thing many times, though the activity that prompted her to the thought was not always that of laughter. 'Yes, it's tough,' Groenewald had said the first time; but later he had realized that this was not enough to satisfy either Miss Scholtz or himself. She would be satisfied only with more emphatic expressions of regret, even grief; and he would be satisfied only if Miss Scholtz lost her loyalty to them both, or at least to Mr Fink. One problem, indeed, with regard to Fink and Gottlieb Maisie had spared him, and that was when Groenewald had tried discreetly to warn her against letting Gottlieb know that they were seeing each other. Maisie had replied that she wouldn't dream of bothering Mr Gottlieb with the details of her private life – especially as they were of this kind – now that he was so worried about Mr Fink. Maisie had added that she herself felt bad enough about the way they carried on, while poor Mr Fink lay so critically ill in the hospital; and thus even in sparing him one problem, Maisie succeeded in reminding Groenewald of the other.

Groenewald attacked Fink and Gottlieb because they were Jews; but Miss Scholtz said she didn't care what other people said about the Jews, or whether other Jews deserved the things that other people said about them, but she knew Mr Fink and Mr Gottlieb well enough, and what she thought was that it was a pity that there weren't more people like them, whether they were Jews or Christians or Chinamen or anything else. Then

Groenewald attacked them because, he said, they were crooked businessmen. He said that he had called at the office to make an inquiry for a friend of his, who was a shopkeeper in the country, and Gottlieb, like a real black-marketeer, had quoted him on the particular article – of which there was a scarcity – twice as much as any other firm had in the town of Lyndhurst. Miss Scholtz replied that the article Fink & Gottlieb were offering was probably twice as good in that case, and the scarcity had nothing to do with it. Groenewald said that Fink and Gottlieb were underpaying her; but Maisie was able to prove – by comparing her salary with those of some other girls she knew – that they were not. He said that from some of the things Maisie had told him about them he could see that their manners weren't really very good; but Maisie said that they were gentlemen all the same.

In fact, Maisie said ultimately – after Groenewald had also tried mockery, threats, and dark hints, in tones that varied from the loud and bullying to the small and wheedling – she didn't know why Groenewald kept on and on about Mr Fink and Mr Gottlieb, or what business it was of his anyway, but in the first place he ought to be ashamed of himself for talking like that about a man who was lying so critically ill in the hospital, and about that man's partner who was so worried he just wouldn't sit still for a moment and was absolutely wearing himself out just with his anxiety; and in the second place Mr Fink and Mr Gottlieb had been as good as gold to her in all the years she had been in the office, long before she had ever heard of Mr Groenewald, and she wasn't going to turn her back on them just because he came and said a few mean things about them. What was the matter with him anyway, she asked. Was he jealous? Did he think she flirted with Mr Fink and Mr Gottlieb? Or was he jealous because they were making more money than he was? He shouldn't think she hadn't noticed, Maisie said, that the only place he ever took her to was that measly old park, which cost him nothing. And if he was jealous, Maisie asked, why didn't he leave his old Rural Roads Board or whatever it was, and do something for himself, like Mr Fink and Mr Gottlieb had?

The only quarrels which Groenewald had with Maisie were on the subject of Fink and Gottlieb, and Groenewald did not enjoy them. He enjoyed even less the evening that he had been forced to spend alone after Maisie's outburst, which had ended with her simply telling him to go away. After confronting once again the *objets d'art* in the parlour of the New Temperance Hotel, and studying at even greater length the swollen, shining, bruise-like plaster of the ceiling above his bed, Groenewald went to see Miss Scholtz late that same night, and apologized to her for having spoken to her the way he had. It was even later before Groenewald returned again to the New Temperance Hotel; and in the subsequent evenings and lunch-hours they spent together Groenewald did not say a word against Fink and Gottlieb, though he silently said many against Conroy.

Groenewald did not know what to do about Conroy and the case of Fink and Gottlieb, until one afternoon Miss Scholtz tearfully told him that from the way people were speaking it did not seem likely that Mr Fink would ever recover from his injuries. This she had heard, she said, from Mrs Gottlieb, who had called at the office one day, and who had given her husband as the authority for her words. 'The head is a delicate thing,' Mrs Gottlieb had quoted him to Maisie; and also, giving again her husband as the authority for her words Mrs Gottlieb had said, 'He is not a young man any more and we must be prepared for the worst,' and, most hopeless of all, 'The whole world is talking of him passing away.' Miss Scholtz admitted to Groenewald that she herself had not heard Mr Gottlieb use such phrases about Mr Fink; he had always spoken a little more cheerfully to her than that; but she supposed that was just his way of cheering her up, in the best way he could. There could surely be no one who knew better than Mrs Gottlieb how Mr Gottlieb really felt, Maisie said; and presumably he wouldn't feel like that if he hadn't been warned by the doctors. It was terrible, Maisie said; it was unfair and terrible and she did not know what to do about it.

'It is terrible,' Groenewald agreed, but his heart was suddenly lighter. 'He isn't expected to recover, you say?'

'Well, that's what Mr Gottlieb says. And he must know.' Maisie began to cry.

'Shame, poor old man,' Groenewald said. 'Poor old chap.' He shook his head and lowered it, because he was afraid that otherwise she might have seen him smile. Then he took Maisie in his arms. 'I know how you feel, my poor Maisie.' The fact that Fink had been attacked for no reason that anyone knew of was to Groenewald conclusive proof of the accuracy of his guess that the old man had been mixed up in I.D.B.; and he would tell that to Conroy too; but to Maisie he said, 'Don't cry, Maisie. There's nothing we can do about it … Such a harmless old bloke, and such a thing to happen to him.' And he patted her back and held her head.

He and Maisie had the habit of walking to the park after supper, when it was really dark, for Groenewald did not much care to go out before then, and there was nowhere else he felt they could go. On this evening Groenewald had to persuade her to come, for she said that after hearing about Mr Fink she didn't really feel like it. But Groenewald's mood was so good, and he pressed her so fondly to come, that she could not withstand him. They walked with their arms around one another's waist, and though as they walked Groenewald felt that Maisie was just a little too large (not in herself, as it were, but in relation to him), he was nevertheless content. And so too, a little later, was Maisie.

159

Professionally, Groenewald had not been kept very busy during this time. He had reported regularly to Conroy; but from these reports Conroy had seemed to demand little more than an assurance from Groenewald that he was still in the town and still active. Conroy had said, long before, that he knew what Groenewald had to do often took a long time to develop and mature, and, though he expected results he did not expect them immediately. And as Conroy had also given Groenewald the task of approaching and establishing relationships with another gentleman and his family and friends in Lyndhurst, Groenewald had been able to get by, in the interim, with saying very little about either Fink or Gottlieb. Only lately had Groenewald begun to feel that his delay in speaking had grown altogether too great.

After hearing Miss Scholtz's news about Mr Fink, however, Groenewald felt that he was in a position, at last, to present a full report on Fink and Gottlieb – a report which he hoped would close the case. And once that had been accomplished, Groenewald intended telling Maisie, under a vow of secrecy, what his business in the town really was. Because the case would have been closed there would be no need for him to mention that he had been conducting his business in connection with Fink and Gottlieb; and Groenewald looked forward to the excitement he was sure Maisie would show when she found out that he was not an official on the miserable old Rural Roads Board, but a detective. Groenewald was much less happy than he had once been about being a detective; but being a detective was, he assured himself, better than being an official on the Rural Roads Board. Or at any rate, Maisie might think so.

So Groenewald made an appointment to see Conroy, and went once again, as he had done so often before, to the administrative building behind the Lyndhurst Central Police Station. As Conroy had done so often before, he kept

Groenewald waiting, and when Conroy came in he did not apologize for being late. His greeting was: 'So? What have you got to tell me? Sit down.'

Conroy had seated himself behind his desk, and Groenewald accepted the abrupt invitation which had been extended to him. 'I think I do have something to tell you, Mr Conroy.'

'You've been told not to come here unless you did. What is it?'

'It's about Mr Gottlieb, Mr Conroy.'

'Yes.'

'I don't think he's the man we want.'

Conroy looked up. 'Is that what you think?'

Conroy's tone was not encouraging, but it never had been; so Groenewald produced the few sheets of paper on which he had written down the results of his interviews with Mrs Gottlieb, and some of the results of some of his interviews with Miss Scholtz, and the one with Gottlieb. He had faked the dates a little on these reports, for he did not dare to show Conroy that he had gone straight to Gottlieb, on the very first day of his investigation, nor did he say that in his talk with Gottlieb he had come so directly to the point. In his report he claimed that he had passed himself as someone about to open a store in the country, who had only towards the end of the talk showed any interest in trading of a different kind; and Gottlieb, he reported, had shown no interest in this at all for himself but instead had referred him, in terms of strongest disapproval, to the partner, Fink. The second part of the report dealt with Fink, and Groenewald attempted to summarize both parts of the report, verbally, for Conroy.

He exaggerated particularly his success with Fink. 'Of course I had only one interview with him, before this thing happened, that put him into hospital; but it was a very promising one, when you remember what his own partner said about him, and Mrs Gottlieb too.'

'And Miss Scholtz?'

'No, not Miss Scholtz. She didn't say anything about him, except that she liked him, and so on.' Groenewald hastened away from this to the story which he felt to be safer for his purposes. 'I just sat with Mr Fink that evening, and we sort of talked about various things, and then I tried to lead him on to the kind of topic which interests you and me; I said something about making easy money, and he said that that's always a good thing to do, and I said that in some towns it was easier than in others, and he agreed. I didn't want to push things too hard, because this was just a first talk, so this time I just said that it seemed to me that Lyndhurst was probably one of those towns. And he said that it was, if you knew your way about it. So I said that after all these years he must know his way about all right, and he said that I'd be surprised. And so we went on talking, this way and that, and always he was saying that he knew a thing or two, and there were plenty of opportunities in Lyndhurst if a man only kept his eyes open. I said I was trying to do that, and he asked me to let him know how I got on. So I was pretty pleased with the way it went, especially after hearing what the others said about him, and about how careless and reckless he was. I could see it for myself – a man who would talk like that to a complete stranger, and in Lyndhurst too, must be pretty careless. I was just thinking that it wouldn't be too hard for us to trap this one, like you've told me we would do. He would have been in the bag, I'm sure.'

Conroy said: 'You're sure?'

'Well, pretty sure. I mean, that was what I was hoping, at any rate. But now of course it's no good. It's a hell of a disappointment for me – he would have been my first, and everything like that. The same thing that put him in the hospital is the thing that's saved him from us – isn't that strange? – especially when you think of the way he was put in the hospital. You can see that I've tried to put two and two together; I think we can guess why he was attacked in that way. Of course,' Groenewald added, 'none of this is evidence yet, and now it seems that he's so badly injured that he isn't expected to recover. I've been making inquiries, and it seems that's what the doctors are saying about him; they're expecting him to – to – well, just pass away, any time now.'

'So,' Conroy said at last, leaning back; and in the man's glasses Groenewald saw a tiny reflection of himself swing up suddenly – his hands in his lap and his head held anxiously forward.

'It's all in there,' Groenewald said, pointing at the papers he had laid on Conroy's desk, and at which Conroy had not yet looked. 'I suppose you'll find that I've done some wrong things, but this is the first time, I mean, I've never done something like this before, or presented a report on it. And I'm sorry I couldn't bring more back; but I might have been able to if that thing hadn't happened to that old Fink. That just finished it off. And I mean, you were right to send me after old Gottlieb; I can see how things got mixed up between them – they're both old men, and they're partners, and the same kind, and so on. And Gottlieb *knew*, all right, that his partner was up to some kind of monkey business; and he didn't inform us, which puts him into the same class too, but that isn't anything we can hold against him, when we've got nothing to hold against Fink.'

Groenewald knew that the interview wasn't going as it should have. The strength of his determination to strike even this much of a blow for himself had dissipated; and his loyalty to Maisie seemed of little account, in this bare office, under Conroy's greenish gaze. He struggled on for a little longer. 'Isn't it a funny business, this one?' he asked, conversationally. 'Two old Jew-boys like that – harmless-looking old blokes – getting mixed up in such a business. It makes you think. Well, it makes me think, that's what I mean.' Groenewald's straying hand pointed apologetically and unconsciously at himself; he looked down and saw it, and with care, almost as if it belonged

163

to someone else, he put his hand in his lap and looked once again at Conroy, 'You know –'

'All right,' Conroy interrupted him. 'I've heard enough. There's only one thing that puzzles me, Groenewald. If all this is what you thought, why didn't you tell it to me the day after Fink was attacked? Why have you waited all this time before talking?'

Groenewald could not explain that at first he had wanted to keep the case of Fink to himself; nor could he explain the problem which his friendship with Maisie Scholtz had introduced; he could only say, 'Well, I was waiting – I thought I might be able – well, what I thought was –'

'What's the matter, Groenewald? Have you had a quarrel with your friend Maisie Scholtz?' Conroy leaned forward, coming closer to Groenewald. 'Is that it? Am I right?'

It was a delicate moment for Groenewald. But he had staked so much on Conroy's being wrong that when Conroy repeated the question, 'Am I right?' Groenewald answered him almost instinctively, and not with the truth.

'Yes,' Groenewald said, and nodded. 'You are right.'

Conroy said, 'So now you've broken with her you don't care if the case remains open or closed?'

Groenewald shook his head in reply to this question.

'And for the sake of Maisie Scholtz you were prepared to delay letting me have information which you considered important?'

Groenewald nodded again, his chin close to his chest.

'You're no good,' Conroy said, without passion. 'You've bungled it. There's nothing good about you except the way you look.'

Groenewald did not speak; he sat as if he were trying to hide himself behind the top of his own head.

'As for your important information, it's just your luck that it isn't important at all. It's true that we don't know why Mr Fink was attacked, but we do know that it's got nothing at all to do with my department. We've tested Mr Fink several times in the past, and we've never got anything out of him. Not a thing. He didn't want to hear our stories, even though we'd get these reports now and then about the way he was talking. But Fink knew the difference between talking and doing. It was that fat fool, his partner, Gottlieb, who didn't know the difference; and now all you've done is warn him. There's something happened that's made him lay off; I didn't know what it was, but now I think it's you, Groenewald.'

'But –'

'Shut up. Listen to me. You're weak and you're idle, and you're not to be trusted. What were you doing all this time with that Scholtz girl? Do you think we wouldn't know about something like that? Is that what I brought you to Lyndhurst for, to go and take a girl into a park, for God's sake?' Still Conroy spoke without passion; and his severity and uprightness seemed worse to Groenewald than anger and a raised voice would have been. 'Well, you won't be able to do it for much longer. And let's hope they'll send me someone better next time. What's the matter with you people?' Conroy asked, speaking quietly, hardly opening his mouth at all, staring steadily in front of him. 'I've had people like you before – you're worse than most, but not so much worse than some of the others I've had. There's so few of you who'll do what you're told, but sooner or later you start running after girls, or drinking, or getting ideas of your own.'

Conroy waited, but Groenewald was silent, and did not lift his head. As evenly as before, Conroy spoke again. 'If you hadn't made such a fool of yourself with that girl, Groenewald, I can tell you that I'd have had quite another suspicion about your reasons for trying to shift the blame on to Fink, and then holding back information so that the case could remain open. That would have left you free to try and do a deal on your own with Gottlieb, wouldn't it? It's all right – you don't have to look at me like that – I know you haven't been dealing with Gottlieb.

We've been watching you, and I suppose that's the one thing you haven't done. It's probably not your honesty but your stupidity that saved you from that – you really believe that Gottlieb had nothing to do with the I.D.B. You really believe it, hey? You think you know better than me what's going on in this town? Then I'll tell you how we knew about Gottlieb, and you listen to me, Groenewald. And for your sake remember what I tell you.'

And Groenewald listened; and when Conroy had done he said, 'Let that be a warning to you if you ever come back to Lyndhurst. Believe me, it won't be as a detective, in any branch, I'll see to that; and I'm putting in a report that isn't going to do you much good in Cape Town either, and I hope they'll act on what I tell them. You can call downstairs at three, they'll have your rail warrant ready for you.' Conroy looked away, and the interview was over.

Groenewald was dazed, angry, incredulous; he hardly noticed the sunlight when he stepped outside, for within him there was a stronger heat, in his stomach and behind his eyes, as if he might be sick, or cry. He hurried away, to get away from the building and out of the yard, where uniformed men glanced at him indifferently as he passed and native convicts were sweeping and sweeping the dust. Beyond the yard entrance Groenewald saw the street, and he almost ran towards it.

At the entrance he found Gottlieb crouching curiously, as if in prayer. Groenewald did not know why Gottlieb had come; but Groenewald knew that he was innocent of the accusations Gottlieb hissed at him. And then in his anger and bewilderment Groenewald knew too that here was his chance to strike that blow for himself, that here was his last chance to prove Conroy wrong.

12

When Lyndhurst was no more than some dark and irregular bumps on the horizon behind them Gottlieb pulled up under a clump of thorn-trees, so that the car was just off the road and half-hidden from it. Several times Groenewald had looked back, but no car had followed theirs.

'Anyone who passed would think that you've brought a girl here,' Groenewald said. He had not spoken before, since he had climbed into the car, and nor had Gottlieb.

It was fiercely hot, and where the sunlight fell above the dashboard of the car the metal glowed as if it were molten. Near them there was nothing but the road and a wire fence; beyond, as far as the eye could see, was the pallid scrub, tufted irregularly with darker bushes – a waste that had for grandeur only its own disordered width. And in all the strong light and hot black shade there was no sound but that of the invisible hard-shelled insects.

Yet Gottlieb looked round once, as if to make quite sure that they were alone. Then he took from the pocket of his suit the small box of diamonds, and held it towards Groenewald. 'You know what this is?' Gottlieb shook the box, so that the stones within it rattled. 'Do you know now?' Gottlieb's hand clenched tightly over the box. 'Do you want it? Then do to me what you did to Fink! You will not get it until you have.' And Gottlieb brandished his fist in front of Groenewald's face, waiting for Groenewald to strike.

'What's the matter?' Gottlieb jeered, when Groenewald did not move. 'Are you frightened all of a sudden? Are you a man when it is a dark street on a dark night with Mr Fink, but a coward when it is in the daylight? You prefer to come creeping from behind with a club in your hand? There is no one here; why should you be afraid? Or are you frightened that I will hit back? I will try, believe me, but you are a young man and I am an old one. So begin!' Gottlieb shouted, and suddenly flung himself across the seat to grab at Groenewald's neck. But Groenewald was quicker, and more expert. He held Gottlieb's arm, pinioned, across his chest; and though Gottlieb struggled with his free hand Groenewald managed to open the door of the car, and shoving Gottlieb away from himself, he jumped out of the car. He slammed the door behind him.

'No!' Gottlieb shouted. 'You will not run away! You will face me. You tried to kill one man, here is another! You want diamonds, you murderer, I have them for you.' In his rage Gottlieb was beating his hands against the steering-wheel, and Groenewald watched him through the window of the car.

'Please, Mr Gottlieb,' Groenewald said. 'I did nothing to Mr Fink. I'm a policeman.'

'Poor Fink,' Gottlieb cried. 'Cheated, lied to, robbed – and then hit on the head by a man I sent! All my fault, all my blame, all my guilt from the very beginning!' Gottlieb's flailing hands found the hooter of the car. Gross, drunken, injured, insupportable, the sound of the hooter blared wildly across the veld.

'I'm a policeman,' Groenewald yelled, sticking his head through the window of the car. 'Can't you hear me? I'm a policeman.'

'A policeman? I'll call a policeman to carry you away when I'm finished with you!' And Gottlieb lunged at Groenewald's head.

Groenewald banged his head as he pulled it back. 'Why don't you listen? *I'm* a policeman!'

Gottlieb was wrestling with the door handle on Groenewald's side. He thrust his sweating, distorted face through the window. 'What's that?' he demanded. 'I'll kill you,' he shouted.

'I'm a policeman. Here –' Groenewald felt in the inside pocket of his suit, and pulled out a wallet with a transparent plastic pouch for the card he showed Gottlieb. 'Now can you see? Do you believe me now? I tell you that I'm a policeman.'

Gottlieb felt his heart beat two fierce strokes against his chest, and then it seemed to hold off. 'You did not attack Mr Fink?'

'No. Why should I? I'm a policeman. We were trying to trap you, for I.D.B., Mr Gottlieb,' Groenewald said. Then he said: 'And now it looks as though we've succeeded.'

Gottlieb could feel his heart beating again as if it were the only organ in his empty body. His chin rested against the bottom of the window; his cheek, his mouth were pushed askew by the side of the frame.

'I was going to the police –' Gottlieb said eventually, the words coming with difficulty through his twisted mouth. 'It comes to the same thing in the end.'

Groenewald stared for a moment at the wallet in his hand. Then he put it in his pocket. 'Well, I don't know about that,' he said, and climbed back into the car.

'So Conroy's been after you for a long time,' Groenewald told Gottlieb, after he had explained how he had come to Gottlieb's office. 'He probably still is, now.'

'But how did he know? How did he find out about me, when I had *done* nothing – nothing for him to know?'

'Christ,' Groenewald said. 'With all those blokes phoning him up, and even writing to him – of course he knew there was something going on.'

'Which blokes?'

'The gang. The crowd. The boys.'

'Which gang?'

'The I.D.B. gang. Who do you think?'

'Which I.D.B. gang?' Gottlieb cried.

'I can't remember their names. Wait, there was a bloke Cloete, and an Indian, Bannerjee, and who else? I think there were one or two others. Talk about honour among thieves! There's no honour among them, that's for sure.'

'And does he know these people?'

'Doesn't he know them! He depends on them. He'd never get anywhere if it weren't for them, he practically said so. You see, if there's one thing these I.D.B. people don't like at all, not one little bit, it's new people coming into their business. The fewer of them there are in the I.D.B. the more they can get for their parcels, you understand, from the buyers in Johannesburg. So when you first came round talking about diamonds, they got in touch with Conroy straight away.'

Groenewald tried to cheer Gottlieb up: 'They had nothing against you, it's just that they want to keep the business for themselves. Whenever a party like you tries to start up, Conroy hears about it from them, and then sends someone to find out how far the party is prepared to go. If he's prepared to go too far, then it's all up with him, I can tell you.'

'You hear from these people?' Gottlieb asked again, incredulously.

'He does, all the time,' Groenewald said. 'They know each other, and Conroy knows them, the old ones. But just let anyone new try to start up, and they're the first to write or phone. They've got nothing to lose, the old ones. They know Conroy knows who they are; they know he watches them all the time, and sets traps for them, and all that sort of thing. The business can't be any more dangerous for them than it is already, and they've got to see that they get well paid for it. They can't have just anybody coming in and spoiling their market. And Conroy's as glad of their help as they are to give it to him. So the new ones – with both sides against them – ?' Groenewald shook his head.

Then Groenewald said, as he had earlier, that it was just his job. That he had nothing against Gottlieb personally. That he did what Conroy told him to do. That a bloke had to do what his boss told him to do, even if a bloke didn't enjoy it. And he certainly hadn't enjoyed it. He would have said more if Gottlieb hadn't interrupted bluntly. 'And why do you tell me these things?'

'You don't seem to realize, Mr Gottlieb, that I'm saving your neck,' Groenewald replied with promptitude, as if he had been waiting for just that question. 'There's nothing to stop me from taking you back right now, and settling you, once and for all.'

Groenewald frowned at Gottlieb, but he was friendly again, and jerked his neck clear of his collar to show that he was relaxing again, after his previous moment's severity. 'I must say, I don't understand it. A man like you, Mr Gottlieb, doing such a silly thing. It doesn't make sense. You don't need the money.' Groenewald looked carefully around Gottlieb's car; he seemed to appraise Gottlieb's suit, even his wedding ring. 'A man like you has got more money than he can – float in,' Groenewald said, offering the suggestion respectfully. 'In business –' he shook his head. 'That's where the money is. In private business. A self-employed man must make more money than any other kind of man, if you ask me. I've been thinking about it. You know, a bloke gets older and then he starts thinking about the kind of living a man can earn. There's no money in being a policeman, that's one thing I can tell you straight off. It's not a profession for a bloke who wants to do well in the world. Even a farmer makes more money than a policeman, if he's any kind of a farmer at all. I'm not talking about the wool farmers, because they're just millionaires. But there's other kinds of farmers. Milk, it's also good, and the mealie farmers!' Groenewald whistled at the thought of the mealie farmers. 'And that's what I plan to be. This job's not for me. A kind of a farmer. Pigs. You can start with pigs on just a small scale, you don't need so much capital for pigs.'

With a solemn, snub-nosed face, Groenewald essayed his first joke. 'You wouldn't be much good for a customer for me when I'm in the pigs, would you, Mr Gottlieb? It's lucky not everybody thinks like you people, isn't it? Because then where would the pig farmers be?'

Groenewald waited for Gottlieb to smile: if he was disappointed that Gottlieb's pursed mouth and frowning brow did not relax into a smile, he did not show it. But the pause drew his attention back to Gottlieb and away from his agricultural fantasies. 'So much money a man like you must have,' he mused.

'I see,' Gottlieb said without bitterness.

'I thought you would,' Groenewald said warmly. 'You know when I left Conroy's office I was thinking about things I'd never thought of before, I can tell you. I mean, who's Conroy to talk like that – ? He's always been saying things about me – on and on, until – well, when I bumped into you I wanted to help you. Why not? – that's what I thought. So now –' Groenewald hesitated and pulled at his jacket cuffs briskly – 'I talk to you straight, like one businessman to another.'

'Ah,' Gottlieb said.

'Yes,' Groenewald said proudly. 'Like a businessman, and no mistakes.'

'And how often have you done this before?'

'Never!' Groenewald was shocked at the suggestion. 'I've never had a chance, anyway. And I never wanted to either. It's this business with Conroy and the diamonds, that's what's got me so mixed up. Burglars – all right, you know where you are with burglars. But I.D.B.?' Groenewald shook his head. 'Pigs is more my line.'

Gottlieb stared out of the window of the car. But outside it was too hot, there was too much light, he was too exhausted to meet the glare. He put his hand to his forehead. 'And now I suppose you want your reward?' he asked.

Groenewald ducked his head.

'What do you want? The diamonds?'

Groenewald smiled, and Gottlieb asked: 'Do you think I'm joking?' The smile contracted a little, expanded, contracted again: Groenewald did not know whether Gottlieb was joking or not. 'Well?' Gottlieb asked.

'Mr Gottlieb, what would I do with the diamonds?'

'I don't know. You should.'

'What I know, Mr Gottlieb, is that maybe it's easy getting a parcel if you go down the river; but once you've got the diamonds you've also got a hell of a job getting rid of them again.' Groenewald's voice acquired an injured, disappointed edge. 'That wouldn't be a reward for me, Mr Gottlieb; it would be a *punishment*. No, Mr Gottlieb, that's not how a sport talks.'

'How does a sport talk?'

'A sport says, Mr Gottlieb, how about – two hundred pounds?'

'Perhaps these diamonds are worth more than two hundred pounds.'

'Not to me, Mr Gottlieb. Two hundred pounds is what I want, and then I'll go away, and I'll say to anyone who asks me that Mr Gottlieb is a sport.'

'I see,' Gottlieb said. He waited; then he said slowly, 'There is only one thing you have not taken into account, Mr

Groenewald.' He covered his eyes with his hand. 'I will not be blackmailed,' Gottlieb said. 'I will drive us both back to the police station, if that is what you want; but I will not be blackmailed.' He turned to Groenewald, and dropped his hand, but still he spoke quietly. 'A few weeks ago, perhaps yes; when I was jumping around like a madman, when I was a lost man through my own folly – just swinging loose – then I might have been blackmailed. But I have had enough of being loose and lost,' Gottlieb said. 'I am not going to lose myself again. I am not going to be blackmailed. For nothing; for no one.'

And Groenewald suddenly and petulantly flung himself against the seat of the car. 'Ah Christ!' he exclaimed, 'I can't turn you in, and now just look what happens when I try to make something out of it. Everything goes wrong,' Groenewald complained. 'What *chance* is there for a bloke if this happens to him when he tries to do something on his own?'

'I'm very sorry,' Gottlieb said politely.

'That's no help to me. I was *trying*, that's what I was doing, and you just say you won't be blackmailed, you won't be blackmailed, over and over again – as if *I* don't matter at all! You just think about yourself all the time, that's the trouble with you. Why won't you be blackmailed? You've got no consideration for others, that's your trouble. You've *got* to be blackmailed,' Groenewald shouted at Gottlieb. 'I won't let you get away with this. I can't turn you in, but that doesn't mean you can treat me like dirt.'

'What's that?' Gottlieb asked. 'What do you say? You say you can't turn me in?'

'No, I can't.'

'Why not?'

'Because of Maisie. Now do you understand? And is that *fair*? I ask you?'

'Maisie? What are you talking about? Who's Maisie? Are you a madman, Groenewald?'

Groenewald was settled dejectedly into the corner of the seat. 'No,' he said.

'No what?'

'I'm not a madman. Except I feel like one right now,' Groenewald added indignantly, and then slumped again in his seat. 'All right,' he said, 'take me back to town. But not to the police station, I'm not turning you in. Just let me get away from you, that's all.'

'But I demand to know! I have a right to know. You can't tell me that you aren't going to turn me in, and then just sit there as if everything's finished. What is this? What kind of a way is that to talk? I tell you to turn me in, and then you say no. Is that what you say? Then you must tell me why you say no, or else – or else – I'll turn you in,' Gottlieb threatened, shaking his finger at Groenewald. 'So help me God, I will.'

'I've told you already. It's because of Maisie.'

'What Maisie? Where Maisie? Whose Maisie?'

'Your Maisie.'

'I have no Maisie.'

Their tempers were both roused; the heat, the strain, the confusion had made them irritable as dogs. Gottlieb tore his collar open. 'Now speak quietly,' Gottlieb said, speaking quietly himself, with a great effort. 'Tell me, please, what is this Maisie you keep on talking about?'

'The Maisie who works in your office.'

'You mean Miss Scholtz?'

'That's what I said.'

'That is not what you said!' Gottlieb flared. But he fought to bring himself under control. 'Tell me, please, what the hell has Miss Scholtz got to do with all this?' By the end of his sentence Gottlieb was shouting again; but Groenewald did not meet this anger with his own.

'I want to marry her,' he said.

'So? For God's sake – so?'

'What do you think she'll think of me if I turn you in?'

Gottlieb leaned against the seat, and they both lay back, exhausted suddenly. 'Would she care?' Gottlieb asked, turning his head to look at Groenewald.

'Of course. And a lot, too. And she'd think I'd just been using her, which would be worst of all. And that's why I can't turn you in. And that's why I tried to blackmail you, because I can't go on being a policeman after this. I want to do something on my own. Well – with Maisie, too. On our own. And that's –'

Gottlieb interrupted him. 'You silly boy,' he said. But he could not continue. 'Why didn't you tell me –?' He gestured, and then let his arm fall. 'And Fink?' he asked.

'I've got nothing to do with him.'

'Do you know how he was hurt?'

'No. But it had nothing to do with diamonds, or I.D.B., or anything like that. That's what Conroy says, and he should know.'

'If only he should be spared!' Gottlieb said, turning away. 'I can meet him now. I have done what I could.' Gottlieb saw Groenewald looking at him, and he roused himself. 'I am sorry, I'm speaking to myself. It's a bad habit that I have. Come, Mr Groenewald,' Gottlieb said. 'I will help you and Miss Scholtz, if you will not turn me in.'

And Gottlieb drove Groenewald back to the town, and dropped him on the outskirts because Groenewald said it was safer that way.

13

'That I should be talking to you again!'

Fink merely nodded his greeting, lying back with the pillows puffed up on either side of his head.

Gottlieb took a pace from one side of the bed to the other, and a pace back again. He turned and looked abruptly at Fink, as if in fear that Fink might have disappeared in the moment he had not been watched. Then Gottlieb put his head to one side, and looked at Fink from that angle.

Twice Gottlieb ran his hand over his bald head, and stepped to the side of the bed nearest the door. He plucked at his nose, breathing into his fingers with little spurts, as if he were blowing his nose. 'That I should be talking again to you, Fink!'

Under the bedclothes Fink stirred a little. 'Didn't you think you would?' he asked.

The first day Fink had been in the hospital his hand had seemed very red to Gottlieb, where it had lain against the hospital's white sheet. Now Fink's hands looked almost yellow. 'What an idea!' Gottlieb said too loudly, suddenly, looking up with a jerk of his head. 'Of course I knew I would. It's just fine that it should have happened today, that's all I meant.'

Fink was silent.

'Ever since the day of the accident I've been waiting for just this day, and now it's happened. And what do I find, Fink? I have nothing to say to you. Or too much to say to you.'

Gottlieb smiled at himself, and plucked again at his nose. 'For this I've been waiting, Fink.'

Fink asked, 'So what do you feel?'

'What do *I* feel?' Gottlieb straightened himself from the foot of the bed. 'What does it matter how I feel? It is how you are feeling that is important. How are you, Fink – tell me?'

Fink's mouth and throat worked for a moment, but it was not to answer Gottlieb's question. It was to ask another of Gottlieb, who was again leaning over the foot of the bed, in his anxiety to catch Fink's words.

'Was it worth waiting for?'

Gottlieb looked in astonishment around the ward, as though seeking from it an explanation of the question Fink had asked. In distress Gottlieb said, 'It was worth waiting for a hundred years. Why do you ask such a question of me, Fink?'

'A hundred years,' Fink repeated slowly, his gaze moving about the smooth white ceiling above him. 'Who lives so long?'

Gottlieb had been told that on no account was he to tire or excite the patient, and Gottlieb was taking this order seriously, for he did not wish his visits to be forbidden. So he did not reply to Fink's last question; and Fink did not speak again; and then it was time for Gottlieb to go.

Afterwards Gottlieb said to Riva: 'It looks like it will take years for Fink to recover his strength. Imagine a whisper from Fink!'

But to Fink, two days later, at his next visit, Gottlieb said, 'In a few days' time you will be out of here and jumping around as good as ever, you mark my words.'

'The doctor doesn't say so,' Fink said. His voice was as weak as before, little more than a whisper.

'The doctor!' Gottlieb exclaimed scornfully. 'He's a good fellow, he tries hard, I'm not saying anything against him. But he doesn't know everything. You should have heard the things he was saying –'

Gottlieb could have bitten off his tongue, for Fink asked immediately, 'What was he saying about me?'

'Nothing. Rubbish. I don't know what he was saying about you.'

'Gottlieb, you do. You were going to tell me.'

'Well –' Gottlieb admitted, with a wholehearted gesture of discomfort towards this point in front of him, that point to the left, a third to the right, 'I remember a couple of the things he was saying, but not very clearly, you know, Fink. Things were a bit mixed-up, and all sorts of people were saying all sorts of things at different times –'

'But the doctor?'

'The doctor – yes – what about the doctor?' Gottlieb asked, all alert willed stupidity.

'What did he say about me?'

'He said that you had a nasty knock. And that's true, isn't it? You can see for yourself that you had a nasty knock.'

'And did he think it would finish me off?'

'No! No one ever thought such a thing. Who has been putting such ideas into your head? Everyone was quite sure that you would soon be well again.'

'Were you?'

'I was the surest of all that you would soon be well again.'

'Were you?'

'I tell you I was.'

'Do you tell me the truth?'

'For sure.'

'I don't believe you, Gottlieb.'

'Why not?' Gottlieb asked, almost with a touch of his old anger in his voice. 'Is it pleasanter not to believe me?'

Fink seemed to consider this for some time. He lay on his back, as he lay always when Gottlieb came to see him; his nose started more sharply than ever before from his face and pointed straight towards the ceiling, on which his gaze seemed always to be set. He looked from point to point on its smooth white surface. 'I don't know,' he said. 'Perhaps it is wiser.'

After a silence Gottlieb said: 'Business is good.'

'Good,' Fink replied without stirring, clearly not interested in business.

'When you are quite better again,' Gottlieb said, 'the first thing I must do is to take a long trip into the country. I couldn't go all this time, and a man can't do everything on the telephone.'

Fink did not reply to this; in the silence Gottlieb heard the distant sounds of the hospital, and the nearer passing of feet and complaint of wheels in the corridor just outside the ward. Then, with a feeling of surprise, Gottlieb remembered that Fink too could hear these sounds now.

'Fink,' Gottlieb said cheerfully, 'this hospital is a terrible noisy place.'

'Is it?'

'Fink!' Gottlieb exclaimed, before asking carefully: 'Can't you hear the noises?'

'I'm not deaf.'

'Ha-ha! How can you be such a thing as deaf when we are talking together so nicely?'

'I don't know,' Fink replied.

To Riva, Gottlieb said: 'He's had a nasty knock on the head. He is still a little mixed-up. What else can be expected so soon? How can there be no after-effects, with such a knock like he had? He will soon be quite well again, and then perhaps he won't talk so strangely.'

Riva was prompt to say: 'I hope it won't have any *lasting* effects.'

'Ach!' Gottlieb cried out. 'You are always the one to say such terrible things. What makes you say them? Why do you let them come into your head, and then straight out of your mouth?'

'I don't know,' Riva said apologetically, regarding her husband, whose worried tone of voice and heavily frowning brow were precisely what had put the idea into her head. 'They just do, sometimes.'

'You must try,' Gottlieb said absently. 'You must think first before you talk.' But Gottlieb knew that he too was guilty of a lack of thought and insight. When he had looked forward to Fink's recovery it had always been in anticipation of something direct, simple, speedy, that would immediately bring them together again; he hadn't thought that it might be slow – and for Fink at least – harsh, even painful. Gottlieb's pleasure in Fink's recovery, and Gottlieb's repentance for the crimes he had committed against Fink, were not all that mattered.

So Gottlieb watched what he said the next time he went to see Fink, and did not allow the conversation to turn to anything at all closely connected with Fink's present state – not the hospital nor its noises, not the matron, nor the attack that had brought Fink to the hospital – none of these. Instead he tried hard to be of help to Fink in a simpler way: he talked about the weather; he brought along a newspaper, and he read to Fink a couple of items which he judged were harmless and would not excite Fink. 'Here's a remarkable thing,' Gottlieb said. 'Here's a cat that walked twenty-five miles from Lyndhurst to Dors River. Here's a photograph of the cat.' Gottlieb folded the newspaper so that Fink could see the photograph and extended the paper to him. 'Twenty-five miles. It's a long way for a cat to walk.'

'It's a long way for Gottlieb to walk,' Fink replied crookedly, and Gottlieb laughed with an amusement he did not altogether feel.

'It is a long way. And at my age too. How tired I'd be by the time I reached Dors River!' Gottlieb laughed too heartily again. 'Yes, that cat is clever.' He thrust the newspaper away from himself with an expression of disgust. 'A girl they've elected

Miss Citrus Fruits! Such an ugly girl! In a swimming costume!'
He brought the newspaper back to him and began folding it so
that Fink would be able to see the picture of Miss Citrus Fruits.
'A fright!' he assured Fink; but when he held the newspaper up
Fink could not be persuaded to look at it.

'I believe you,' Fink said, his gaze on the ceiling, and Gottlieb
had no choice but to take the newspaper away.

The next time Gottlieb came to see Fink he again confined
himself to trivialities in which he was not interested, and which
he could not pretend to himself interested Fink. 'Slow but sure,'
Gottlieb told himself 'is the way to recovery.' It was easy for
Gottlieb to conduct these visits, for Fink did not initiate a single
remark, and hardly responded to those that Gottlieb made.
'What do you want of the man?' Gottlieb asked himself. 'It's a
big thing that has happened to him, and at his age too. He was
nearly a dead man.'

Fink's daughters were coming down regularly from
Johannesburg to see their father, and from them Gottlieb
inquired eagerly, 'And how do you find your father?' When
they told him that they thought he was getting on just fine,
Gottlieb wondered, for it did not seem to him that Fink was
getting on so well. From the doctor Gottlieb could learn only
that Fink was getting on as well as could be expected, under the
circumstances. 'Under the circumstances' – Gottlieb repeated
the phrase, but he could get no comfort from it. For the
circumstances, as he said to the doctor, were terrible; and to
Gottlieb they had to include now Fink's apathy and listlessness,
the way Fink – his face so small and yet so haggard – lay staring
upwards from his hospital bed as if he did not think there
would be a day when he would have to get out of the bed.
Gottlieb made all allowances for his own shortsightedness in
expecting anything else immediately, yet he could not but be
alarmed at Fink's continuing indifference to what was brought
to him, to all outside himself.

And this was from a man whom Gottlieb more than ever before believed to be a hero. Fink knew neither the people who had attacked him, nor the man in whose defence he had incurred the injury, and yet when Gottlieb heard the details of the attack – like everyone else who heard them, like anyone in South Africa who heard the details of any such incident – he did not feel the event to have been accidental, trivial, haphazard. Nor were the guilts and fears that it stirred in him the less personal for being so widely shared. Fink had been able to give the police an account of how he had come by his injury: on his late walk in a dark and unfrequented side street he had seen two white hooligans seize for no reason at all a passing kaffir and begin to beat him up. 'Catch the kaffir,' Fink could remember them crying, as they had pulled the man off his bicycle. And Fink could remember going up to them and shouting at them to leave the poor kaffir alone, and he could remember too the native taking advantage of the interruption to run away. More than that Fink could not remember, though he knew what must have happened. The hooligans had turned on him – in all like likelihood meaning to give him no more than a shove for being an interfering old man – and they had run away in fright when they had seen how hard he had cracked his head on the corner of the kerb, and how lifelessly he had then lain. And the native, of course, in the way of a native, had been too frightened to come forward to the police to give evidence. The police now were searching for the two men, and for the native too.

What Fink had done was heroic, Gottlieb felt – knowing how easy it would have been to look the other way, how customary indeed it was to look the other way when such things happened. But now it was a different kind of heroism that Fink had to show – and Gottlieb grieved that Fink seemed unwilling to make the effort.

'But does he say things to you?' Gottlieb asked Althea Fink. 'I mean, before you say things to him?'

Althea had to think hard before she could answer the question.

'I don't know, we just talk about all sorts of things.'

'And does he argue about anything?'

'Oh no! What is there for him to argue about?'

'I don't know,' Gottlieb replied. 'And that seems to me just the trouble. He always used to be such a fierce man. Look how he was injured! He was always ready for an argument about anything, even rubbish.'

'With you, perhaps,' Althea said, in her precise, small-girl's voice.

Gottlieb nodded, and retreated, taking no offence.

Then one day Gottlieb came into Fink's room and found Fink lying upside down on the bed, on top of the bedclothes, his head near the bottom of the bed and his bare yellow feet pointing up from the pillows.

'Fink,' Gottlieb exclaimed, 'what are you doing? Why are you lying like that, so strangely?'

Fink was staring up at the ceiling, as Gottlieb always found him.

'I wanted a change of view,' Fink said.

Gottlieb stared wonderingly at the white, flawless, unmarked ceiling of the ward. He stared at it for a long time, trying to see what there was on it or about it that Fink found so fascinating. There was nothing at all that Gottlieb could see: not even any cracks or stains that might to a man lying in bed all day assume shapes and contours of meaning. The ceiling was bald and blank and white, neutral, lifeless.

'Won't the nurses mind what you are doing?' Gottlieb asked, for want of a better reason for the alarm he had felt at finding Fink upside down.

Fink did not reply. He stared up, and Gottlieb too stared again at the ceiling overhead.

'What do you see there, that you're always looking at?' Gottlieb asked.

'Where?'

'In the ceiling.'

'Nothing,' Fink replied.

'Then why do you look at it so much? Especially when you have a visitor, and can look at me?'

Fink did not respond to the invitation.

'Because it is simpler this way,' he said.

Gottlieb stood dismayed, near the door of the ward. 'Please, Fink,' he said, and in his dismay there was nothing he could do but to speak frankly to Fink, as if he were a man who could be spoken to sensibly, and would have insight into his own condition. 'What is the matter?' Gottlieb asked Fink. 'Why do you not want to talk to me, Fink? Why do you treat me in this way, like a stranger? There is nothing that I do that seems to be of any interest or meaning to you, Fink. I have been coming with fruit and flowers and newspapers; but that is nothing. I have tried talking to you about the business and other interesting things; but that is also nothing. I have come here as often as they let me; but that also is nothing.' Gottlieb paused; almost hopefully he suggested: 'Perhaps you are different with others, Fink. I would be glad to hear that you are, for your sake, for you mustn't think that I complain for mine. Are you different with the daughters?'

Fink stared at the ceiling.

So Gottlieb raised his voice. 'Then that is also nothing. What is the matter, Fink? What is it that you want? What do I do wrong now? I have been wrong – and I would speak to you about that too – if that is what you want. I am trying to think only of you, Fink, please believe that.'

Fink replied indifferently, 'Do what you like, Gottlieb,' and Gottlieb threw up his hands in despair.

To the doctor Gottlieb admitted: 'It's got me beat. Perhaps it would be better if I didn't go to see him. Perhaps he wants to be left alone in peace and loneliness to recover. And then perhaps I will be able to talk to him again.'

Gottlieb decided that he would not go to see Fink for two whole weeks; and he told Fink's daughters why he was not going to the hospital. None of them seemed to think that their father would much miss Gottlieb's visits; but Gottlieb prayed that he would. And they seemed content that their father should be listless. 'He's not a young man,' they said severely, and Gottlieb could feel their eyes on his own bald head.

'If this is how he is always going to be,' Riva Gottlieb said to her husband, after hearing from him for the tenth time an account of Fink's indifference, after seeing her husband enact for her, on the living room sofa, the way Fink lay staring in silence at the ceiling, 'perhaps we will one day say that it might have been better for him if he had never recovered.'

The depths of Gottlieb's fear that this might be so – a fear for which he had given ample justification in his enactment of Fink's listlessness – could be gauged only by the furiously angry stare that he directed at her from under the heaviest of his frowns. 'Always calamities,' he accused her. 'Only calamities.'

'I'm sorry, Manfred, but I must say what I see.'

'Where do you see it? Where? Where?'

And Riva Gottlieb did not seem to know.

Two weeks is a long time; and the two weeks were almost over before Althea stepped with her small gait through the door of Gottlieb's office, and told Gottlieb that she had something important to discuss with him, if he could spare the time to hear her.

'For you I can always spare the time,' Gottlieb said gallantly.

'I don't know where to begin,' Althea said with a little laugh, after she had taken her chair. 'The others said I should be the one to speak to you. They seem to think that I'm the one who knows you best.' The expression on Althea's face disclaimed this distinction; and so did her next words. 'I said that one of them should, but they wouldn't, they've sent me.'

'Wherever you begin will be all right,' Gottlieb said.

A frown like a ripple began to form itself on Althea's clear brow, but it was washed away by another, lighter confession. 'I don't know anything about business.'

'How could you?' Gottlieb asked, still patient and gallant. 'You have never had anything to do with it.'

'No,' Althea said, looking around the office with which she had never had anything to do.

'No,' Gottlieb agreed.

'Well – we've been talking together. I mean me, and Claire and Lynda. We had to, you know, under the circumstances.'

'Terrible circumstances,' Gottlieb said.

'Yes. And especially once we could see that – that – since we could see that Daddy was going to recover,' Althea said, carefully circuitous, but with one straight glance at Gottlieb. 'We began to wonder what would be the best for him when he actually comes out of the hospital.'

'A long holiday,' Gottlieb said.

'Oh yes, certainly a long holiday. But we were wondering if we shouldn't – well, if we shouldn't do more than that. All this has given us a chance to think things over very carefully –'.

'Oh yes?' Gottlieb said.

'Sooner or later we would have had to, but this has really made us consider – oh – all about Daddy and everything.'

'I can see that, yes.'

Althea laughed off what she was going to say before she had said it. 'Then I suppose it doesn't come to you as such a surprise, what we're going to suggest. I mean, there's only one thing we could have been thinking about, isn't there?'

'And that is?'

'We've been wondering if it wouldn't be best for Daddy to leave Lyndhurst and come to live with us in Johannesburg.' Quickly, as if in fear that Gottlieb might interrupt, though he had shown no sign of doing so, Althea went on: 'It does seem

187

the best idea. There's Daddy lying in hospital, and there's all of us in Johannesburg who want to do something for him – it makes sense, doesn't it? Better sense than him staying on here by himself, living in that awful hotel, coming –' She broke off suddenly.

'Here,' Gottlieb said.

'Yes.'

'And you think it would be better for him if he didn't?'

'Well – yes, we do.'

'And have you told your father what you think?'

'Actually,' Althea said, with an air of candour that Gottlieb found appealing in the light of what she then said, 'we haven't.' But she added: 'We thought we should say something about it to you first. You've been Daddy's partner for so long, and everything – we thought –' She broke off, but it was only to continue in another direction. 'What we wondered is what you would think about it all. I mean, you know Daddy so well, and I'm sure you're as anxious as we are that whatever is best should be done for Daddy. I know what we're suggesting is a very big thing, and means turning everything upside down, and that must be hard for you, but if it's the best thing for Daddy, we know that you'd agree to it.' As a consolation, Althea offered, 'And we thought that perhaps Daddy could still take an interest in the business and still come down to Lyndhurst every now and again ...'

'You want me to agree to it?' Gottlieb asked. 'Before you've spoken to your father about it?'

Althea's candour held her upright in her chair, held her face lifted earnestly towards Gottlieb. 'We knew you'd understand. Because we thought you'd want to help us do the best for him.'

Gottlieb believed he knew what kind of an assault was being made on him; cautiously, for the moment, he agreed to no more than, 'Only the best is good enough for your father, I suppose.'

'So we are in agreement.'

'As far as that goes.'

'You can't think that the Diamond Hotel is best for an old, sick man,' Althea said, laughing at the idea that anyone might.

'No.' Gottlieb was still cautious, despite the laugh. 'Not necessarily the best. I believe the food was disagreeing with your father.'

This triviality made Althea impatient. 'It's everything, it's not just the food. You must understand how important this is.' With a gesture of confession and appeal, Althea admitted at last: 'We thought Daddy would listen to us more if – well – if you were saying the same thing.'

'Ah! I understand. The man is to be given no alternative. I agree and you agree, so he will have to go.'

Althea blinked twice at this; then it was clear that she decided it would be better to keep the peace. 'That's a hard way of putting it,' she said, and laughed a little. 'You did say you wanted the best for him.'

'I did, yes, and that is what I want.'

The girl cried out suddenly – her brow crumpling, her mouth pulling down on either side, so that her face was ugly, hooked – 'Mr Gottlieb, you must tell Daddy to come away. It's your duty. I don't know what all this horrible talk is about, but you'll be responsible if Daddy –' Her voice cracked, as if she was about to cry; but she bit at the gloved hand that she had brought to her mouth. 'The others said that I shouldn't say anything about it, but I can't help it –' She did begin to cry. 'Daddy's got nothing to do with diamonds. We aren't going to let Daddy stay in this town. You started it all and you've got to help us.'

Before Gottlieb could speak she got up and ran out of the office.

'Althea!' Gottlieb shouted. 'Althea!'

But now she was at the door that led to the street. He could not follow her, to make a scene in the street.

189

'Althea!' he called again from the door.

But she ran on as if she did not hear him, towards the car she had parked down the road. He saw her get into it, and he saw the car pull violently away from the pavement. It went straight down the road, past the Legemco offices, and then straight on, until another car came between, and Gottlieb could see Althea's no longer.

Gottlieb saw one or two passers-by looking curiously at him, and hastily he went back into the office.

'Poor girl,' Gottlieb said aloud, waving his hands distractedly. 'That Fink must have been talking. Why does he talk to upset the girls? What use is that?' Gottlieb scratched at his brow, then slapped at it hard a few times. 'It must be worrying him all this time, what has happened to his diamonds. It is preying on his mind, after such a knock on the head.'

When Gottlieb remembered what he had done to Fink for the sake of those diamonds he had to sit down, for that was the posture of shame. Ever since Fink had recovered consciousness Gottlieb had intended telling him the story of the diamonds – complete, with all its evasions, errors, lies, and the last desperate attempt at restitution that had led him to his meeting with Groenewald. 'Now they want to take him away – and I have a story that will make him go,' Gottlieb said aloud. 'This is the time, there can be no more delays.' He had not told Fink before because he had been instructed to avoid exciting the patient; and also because he had thought that Fink was depressed enough without hearing a tale of his partner's deceit and treachery. 'So now he hears it just when the daughters are pulling him to go. And then goodbye Fink and Gottlieb Limited.'

When Gottlieb was able to get up from his chair – which was some time after he had said his provisional farewell to his business and partnership – he drove home and took the packet of diamonds out of its place in the wardrobe, and slipped it into his pocket. He felt the packet against his thigh as he walked to the car, as he drove to the hospital, as he walked down the hospital corridor towards Fink's ward. But they seemed no weight at all, these diamonds – no more weight than the disregarded fluff and scraps of paper and the pins and fallen shirt-buttons and the dust that collect in a man's pocket as he goes every day about his business.

So Gottlieb went again to the hospital, and this time when he came into the ward he found Fink, dressed in a grey dressing gown and a muffler around his neck, sitting comfortably in an armchair. Fink stood up without difficulty and extended a hand to Gottlieb.

'I see you make steady progress,' said Gottlieb.

'Yes, why not? And how are you?'

'I am the same as I've always been, you know.'

'And Riva?'

'The same too.'

Fink nodded, Fink smiled, Fink indicated with a gesture that Gottlieb should take the chair and that he would sit on the bed. He hoisted himself on to the bed and sat there with his legs dangling over the side, his yellow and white striped pyjamas showing beyond the end of the dressing gown. His feet were in soft leather slippers that fell loose from his heels and that he worked back into position with a movement of his toes. In appearance, Fink now seemed as well as he had been before the accident, though paler: his eyes were as sharp, his eyebrows still started upwards in a bristle of reproof an almost insect-like fierceness. 'So?' Fink said. 'You have come, hey? Yes,' Fink said. 'It is a long time since I last saw you. I think you are a little older in the way you look, Gottlieb, if you don't mind me saying so.'

'It's possible,' Gottlieb said.

Gottlieb did not know how to begin what he had to say. So he made a general remark about his visit. 'I am not calling here just on a personal matter, Fink. It is in a business capacity that I am calling. I am here because of the affairs of Fink & Gottlieb Ltd., Manufacturers' Representatives, and not because of the affairs of Manfred Gottlieb. Except' – honesty forced Gottlieb to add – 'so far as Manfred Gottlieb is involved with Fink & Gottlieb Ltd. And that' – honesty forced Gottlieb to add further – 'is a terrible lot, Fink.'

Gottlieb found that he had nothing to say except simply to tell Fink: 'Your daughter Althea was in the office this morning, Fink, and I had a talk with her. She was speaking for her sisters too. They want you to go to Johannesburg with them, when you come out of hospital. Not for a holiday, but to live. I wouldn't speak before them if they hadn't said something that involves me too much for me to be silent.'

Gottlieb paused and wiped his forehead, though the room in the hospital was cool, air-conditioned.

'They want this, Fink,' Gottlieb went on, 'partly because of the accident – they believe you will want more looking after than before. But also, Fink,' Gottlieb said gravely, 'it is because you have given them such a big fright by telling them of what you were doing with the diamonds. What exactly you told them I don't know, but they think you are in danger. I also have something to tell about these diamonds,' Gottlieb said, after a pause, but with a steady voice. 'I know that you are in no danger, Fink. But I do not tell you this to influence you to stay, because what I have to tell you will not make you feel friendly to me. I tell it to you just so that certain things may be straight between us.'

Gottlieb put his hand into his pocket and brought out the packet of diamonds. 'This is what I must show you, Fink.'

He tossed the packet on to the bed, and Fink looked down at the little box where it lay, next to him, on the blanket.

'What is this?' Fink asked.

'That is what I must tell you about, Fink, if you will let me.'

When Gottlieb had done, Fink, who had sat quite still throughout the story, picked up the little box and opened it, and looked inside before closing it again and handing it quietly back to Gottlieb. 'So that is what you came to tell me?' Fink said. 'At last.'

'Yes,' Gottlieb said, 'that is what I had to tell you.' Only then did he look up. 'You say *at last*. So you have known all the time?'

Fink nodded.

'I thought so often,' Gottlieb said. 'Sometimes more, sometimes less.' Gottlieb turned his head away. 'So you heard me boast and knew I was boasting; you heard me tell you lies, and you knew I was telling lies?'

'Yes,' Fink said. 'I knew.' Then he was silent; but Gottlieb did not look at him until Fink said, 'I have been waiting for a long time to hear your story, Gottlieb. You see, I also have something to tell you about these diamonds; and I want you to listen to me.' After another pause, Fink began slowly. 'When I first found out that the diamonds had come into your possession, and when I saw that you were going to keep them secret from me – I was amazed, Gottlieb, I was betrayed by what I saw of your nature. You remember how first I was angry, and I shouted at you? It was then that I was waiting to see if you were a real partner to me, or just a – just –'

Gottlieb could listen no longer. 'Fink, I am sorry,' he interrupted. 'I am not a partner, I'm a rascal. Forgive me, Fink.'

But Fink went on. 'And then I thought that this friend of mine, this partner of fifteen years' standing tells lies and cheats and keeps secrets for a handful of diamonds –! Then I stopped swearing; I was filled with silence, I had nothing to say to him.'

'Fink, forgive me. Forgive me for my lies and secrets and cheating!'

So softly that Gottlieb had to lean forward to catch the words, Fink said, 'Gottlieb, have you not thought that perhaps I should ask you to forgive me?'

'Fink – ?'

'Where was I better than you, Gottlieb? Why did I leave you to go further and deeper into your lies and foolishness and danger? Was that the action of a friend? No, Gottlieb, no – it was the action of a man who knows only his own pride, who wants only to be top dog, who thinks to himself in his desperation, "Aha, I will get that Gottlieb in the end, by silence – I will fool him by pretending to know nothing when I know everything – it will be a good joke, a good trick, ha-ha!" What kind of a man is that, Gottlieb, who carries such jokes and tricks in his heart? Do you think I have learned nothing from this knock on the head, from being brought here like a dead man, to lie in a coma for so long, and then to wake and stare at the ceiling, only at the ceiling, where there is nothing? You learned, you tell me, from my knock on the head. Do you think I wouldn't have leaned too? When all around us there is nothing in the world except what we make, Fink was busy making such jokes and such tricks … That is why I tell you, Gottlieb, I am a man to be forgiven, not a man that you should ask forgiveness from.'

Fink had spoken slowly, with little gestures of his hands; now he fell silent, and sat still. The lace curtain across the window of the ward billowed inwards on a breeze, and then sank flat again, as if it had been pressed by a hand. Outside in the driveway a car crushed the gravel beneath its tyres, the sound growing louder and then more faint as it circled away. Fink sat staring at his hands in his lap, as if ashamed to look up.

Gottlieb's voice shook when he said: 'Fink, you do yourself an injustice. You are a gentleman, Fink, for saying such things;

but what I did was worse, and what you have said is not all true. You forget a certain afternoon, Fink, when you *did* try to tackle me on the subject of your diamonds, when you *did* try to save me from what I was doing. And then I lied to you, outright, like a rascal, with no shame. How could you do anything but wash your hands of me, after a rebuff and a lie like that?'

Fink's head began to shake slowly from side to side. Soon his body shook too, rocking gently. 'You make it worse for me, Gottlieb, remembering that time. It's true that you lied to me, and I knew that you lied. But what I was going to ask you was a lie too. There was a lie in my heart even then. I was going to ask you about a parcel of diamonds that was supposed to have come for me and that didn't come – yes, I was going to ask that. In my pride, in my determination not to let Gottlieb think that he was the only one who could do brave things, that was the question I had ready for you. Gottlieb, that was a lie I had ready for you, as much as the one you told me. I have met your treachery, Gottlieb, with my own kind, and your deceit with my own kind. Gottlieb, those diamonds aren't mine. I have nothing to do with them. I don't know where they come from.'

In Gottlieb's ears there was the sound of blood flowing; Gottlieb felt himself flowing with it, in weakness, in dissolution; before he closed his eyes even the walls of the ward seemed to soften, to yield a little, to lean back from him. But in his hand Gottlieb held something that wasn't his, and he fought as though upstream, wearily, to open his eyes. He looked at the little box in his hand, and with an effort he lifted the flap of the box. The stones were in a huddle – small, yellow stones, one of which shone with a little light that was gone from it as Gottlieb's hand shook.

'Then for God's sake how did you know I had them?' Gottlieb shouted.

195

'From the same place, I expect, that the girls know,' Fink said. 'I have not said a word to them.'

'Then who told them?' Gottlieb cried. 'Who – ?'

But before Fink could speak Gottlieb answered his own question, slumping in his chair, speaking quietly, without doubt and without anger. 'Riva.'

'She told me that very first morning that I came back from Johannesburg,' Fink said. 'Poor Riva. She told me how worried she was, and how she had to speak first, even though you had ordered her not to. And even to Riva I told my lies. I told her not to worry about the diamonds, that I was looking after them – and this was after I had seen that you were keeping them to yourself. When you did not tell me, and when you started teasing me, then it was not difficult for me to guess what you were up to, whose diamonds you thought they were, after all my talk. After all my talk! My pride stood up; and my pride became me – me – me –' As he said the word Fink tapped himself on the chest, and again harder, and harder yet, and Gottlieb could not bear to see it.

'Fink!' He grabbed at Fink's arm, but Fink jerked out of his grasp.

'Now you know me for what I am, Gottlieb – not just a liar and a keeper of silences, but on top of all that a big talker who is ashamed to admit that he is nothing but a big talker. And now you know why I have been ashamed to look at you since I've been here. For fifteen years I have talked diamonds, and in all those years I have been frightened to touch one. In all those years you have been shouting at me that I am nothing but a boaster; and now, after all that time, you know at last, Gottlieb, that you are right.' Fink's voice failed; he sat small, hunched, his hands pressed between his knees and his head moving down, still farther down.

And Gottlieb came closer gently, and spoke quietly. 'I know nothing of the kind, Fink. And if you want to touch diamonds, here they are.' He held out his hand to Fink. Fink looked at the box in the outstretched hand.

'I don't know what to do with them, Gottlieb,' Fink said.

Gottlieb thrust them into his hand. 'It's because you don't need them,' Gottlieb cried triumphantly. 'Fink, we are finished with them! Believe me, this is the truth. You can keep them, you can throw them away – now, now, Fink; if you look into your heart you will know that they mean nothing to you. We are done with them, both of us. We have what is dearer and harder than diamonds, Fink.'

When Fink at last dropped the box on the floor and looked up at Gottlieb with a smile, it was a moment for an embrace, at least for a clasp of hands. But neither of them could manage anything so sensational; and then the moment was over.

A little later Gottlieb asked wonderingly, 'Then for God's sake, who do the diamonds belong to?' and Fink could not answer him. Fink, who was now lying on his bed, resting after the exertions he had just been through, suggested that if Gottlieb wanted to find the person for whom the stones had been intended he might try One Hundred and Eleven, Old Mine Street, or Eleven, New Mine Street.

'Or One Hundred and Eleven, New Mine Street.'

'Or Thirteen, Old Mine Street, just next to our place.'

Gottlieb smiled. 'Do you think I am going to do any such foolish thing?'

'I hope not.'

Gottlieb weighed the packet of stones in his hand. 'They have been abandoned – the people must have decided that the danger of following up such a small parcel is worth more than the stones are worth. So now they belong to no one, no one at all.'

'What are you going to do with them, Gottlieb?'

Gottlieb considered for a moment. Then, smiling again, he answered Fink. 'Throw them away, with pleasure. In a place I have just thought of, where they will never look to find them.'

14

As the days passed towards the day when Fink was due to come out of the hospital, the weather grew steadily hotter. There was as yet little change in the look of the sky, little change in the hour of the sun's rising or setting, little indication of the grass or leaf above the sand of the town that one season was ending and another beginning, yet now the heat each day came upon the town with the sun's first ray and slackened reluctantly from it only when the last light was gone from the iron rooftops and the dusty leaves of the tallest trees.

But Gottlieb had spent too many summers in Lyndhurst and was too busy to take much notice of the weather. There was so much for him to do in the office, which he was running almost single-handed – Miss Scholtz, for reasons of which she made no secret, being abstracted, inefficient, and generally too pleased with herself and what she described as her old man-friend to care much about the work in the office. The gentleman in question was in Cape Town, where he was arranging his discharge from the police force, with a view subsequently to becoming a pig farmer; and Miss Scholtz heard from him frequently, and in the office read many times over each letter she received from him. When she had thanked Gottlieb for the help he was giving them in setting up the piggery, Gottlieb had confessed to her – though it had been unpleasant for him – that he had been mixed up in a shady business and that

Groenewald had helped him a shady way. Gottlieb felt this confession and warning to Miss Scholtz to be his duty; but apparently Miss Scholtz knew all about it: she seemed to have forgiven Groenewald his deception of her, and to be positively proud of his deception of his superiors. 'He did it for me,' she told Gottlieb, 'and then I knew he really loved me.' Her own boldness silenced her for a moment, but she went on: 'He was scared that I'd have fixed him if he didn't help you. And I would have.' Miss Scholtz's face softened at the thought of what was before her as she said, 'Now I won't.' And there was nothing for Gottlieb to do but to wish her luck.

And when Gottlieb came home from work he found Riva complaining so unhappily of the heat that one evening it was arranged that she should go to Johannesburg for a few weeks, where she would be able to get away from the heat, do some shopping, and see Irvine. The date for her departure was fixed for a few days after Fink was to come out of the hospital, and Gottlieb told her, 'In the meantime you must try to manage,' and Riva was comforted. Riva had not yet got over the fact that Gottlieb had let her know in such a *quiet* voice that he knew she had been talking to all sorts of people about the diamonds; and Riva now assured Gottlieb that the way he managed was an inspiration to her. 'So it should be,' Gottlieb told her without severity, and to his surprise almost with a kind of belief that so it might be.

Fink's daughters were still coming and going, staying for nights with the Gottliebs. Gottlieb still did not have very much to say to them, but he was trying hard to be polite and attentive – the more so because Fink had told them so many white lies about the diamonds that now the girls, convinced that their father had never been in any danger, had turned against Riva for alarming them unnecessarily with her stories. Not that they said anything to Riva about it: soon they were to believe that they had never attached any credence at all to her stories, the whole affair of their father and the diamonds becoming a joke among themselves, another example of the small-town alarms and gossipings and credulities which flourished in a place like Lyndhurst, and from which they, by virtue of being Johannesburgers, were immune. And they had accepted their father's decision to stay in Lyndhurst. 'So they aren't nagging,' Gottlieb said to Fink, when he went to see him in the hospital, which he did every day now, and Fink replied, 'Certainly not. They are good girls and come often to see their poor father.' When Gottlieb sighed and said, 'Yes,' then Fink told Gottlieb to mark his words that Irvine would be coming down with Riva when she returned from her holiday, because he was a good boy too. 'I hope so,' Gottlieb said. 'I think he is a busy, but good boy.'

A room in the Gottliebs' house was prepared for Fink, for the night he would spend there, before going down to the Cape for the first few weeks of his long holiday. While he was at the Cape he would stay with Lynda and her family, in a cottage they had hired near Muizenberg. Then he would go to Johannesburg, and there he would stay first with Althea and then with Claire. Only then would he return to Lyndhurst, by which time, everyone hoped, his health would be entirely restored. That is, Gottlieb added, for as long as either he, or Fink, could really expect, at their age in years.

Early on the morning that Fink was to come out of the hospital Gottlieb stood alone on the observation platform of Lyndhurst's largest abandoned diamond mine.

With a flick of his wrist Gottlieb flung the little packet of diamonds over the fence in front of him. The box fell on just the other side of the fence, and for a moment it seemed that it would lie where it had fallen; but the slope was too steep, and the box began to roll away from Gottlieb, slowly at first, but gathering speed. As it rolled it set other small stones moving;

the box and the stones rolled on, indistinguishably, and from them there rose some whitish dust, which hung like a trail in the air to show where the disturbance was making its way. The movement was tiny against one of the naked narrowing walls of the mine: a little clattering and a little dust, in a vast arena of silence and motionless sunlight.

But by the time the dust settled Gottlieb had already hurried away, to join the others who were meeting his partner.

Dan Jacobson

The Confessions of Josef Baisz

Josef Baisz is as remarkable a creation as the imaginary country, Sarmeda, in which he lives. Throughout his career – whether as soldier, scholar, husband, murderer or kidnapper – he is driven by the overwhelming urge to subvert and destroy. A man of peculiar genius, this desire spurs him on to 'greater' things until he finally arrives at the inevitable and yet crushingly unexpected denouement of the tale which he himself narrates.

The Evidence of Love

Kenneth Makeer – intelligent, South African and black – travels to London to study law where he meets a fellow South African – a white girl – whom he eventually marries. Yet mixed marriages are outlawed in the Union, and so when they return home they come face to face with racial intolerance and hatred at its most brutal.

This is a passionate, harrowing and dramatic story which hurtles towards its ugly and untimely conclusion.

'It is scrupulously well written. It is very much the sort of novel that counts' *Guardian*

'An admirable writer has written another admirable book' *Spectator*

Dan Jacobson

Her Story

Celia Dinan died some two hundred years ago – back in the twenty-first century. As her life is rediscovered it becomes apparent that she is the author of a powerful and passionate tale – a tale which only she could have written but which 'everywoman' will painfully acknowledge as her own.

The Rape of Tamar

Dan Jacobson retells the age-old biblical story of the rape of King David's daughter by her brother, Amnon. Out of this material he creates a tragic and sardonically humorous novel, wholly modern in spirit and yet true to the time in which it is set. On first publication *The Rape of Tamar* was hailed as a masterpiece.

Dan Jacobson

The Trap and A Dance in the Sun

The Trap and *A Dance in the Sun* bring together Jacobson's initial two novels – stories of racial confrontation and social injustice on the South African veld. In *The Trap*, relations between the white farmers and their black workers are brought on to a sinister and harrowing conclusion whilst *A Dance in the Sun* sees two young innocent bystanders becoming embroiled in a long-standing family saga. These stories have retained their freshness and their power to move the reader.

'This author is stylish, he tells everything in simple words, but his undertones are subtle…it is quite masterly' *Observer*

The Wonder-Worker

As events switch between London and Switzerland, Jacobson introduces us to a host of vivid and extraordinary characters. Most notable amongst these is London-born Timothy Fogel, a child with the wilful belief that he has been endowed with special powers. As events unfold it becomes apparent that this belief has cataclysmic implications for all involved. *The Wonder-Worker* is a remarkable and evocative novel about obsession, passion and the extraordinary power of the human imagination.

OTHER TITLES BY DAN JACOBSON AVAILABLE DIRECT FROM HOUSE OF STRATUS

Quantity		£	$(US)	$(CAN)	€
☐	THE BEGINNERS	7.99	12.99	19.95	13.00
☐	THE CONFESSIONS OF JOSEF BAISZ	7.99	12.99	19.95	13.00
☐	THE EVIDENCE OF LOVE	7.99	12.99	19.95	13.00
☐	HER STORY	7.99	12.99	19.95	13.00
☐	INKLINGS: SELECTED STORIES	7.99	12.99	19.95	13.00
☐	THE RAPE OF TAMAR	7.99	12.99	19.95	13.00
☐	THE STORY OF THE STORIES	7.99	12.99	19.95	13.00
☐	THE TRAP AND A DANCE IN THE SUN	7.99	12.99	19.95	13.00
☐	THE WONDER-WORKER	7.99	12.99	19.95	13.00

ALL HOUSE OF STRATUS BOOKS ARE AVAILABLE FROM GOOD BOOKSHOPS OR DIRECT FROM THE PUBLISHER:

Internet: www.houseofstratus.com including author interviews, reviews, features.

Email: sales@houseofstratus.com please quote author, title, and credit card details.

Hotline: UK ONLY: 0800 169 1780, please quote author, title and credit card details.
INTERNATIONAL: +44 (0) 20 7494 6400, please quote author, title, and credit card details.

Send to: House of Stratus Sales Department
24c Old Burlington Street
London
W1X 1RL
UK

Please allow for postage costs charged per order plus an amount per book as set out in the tables below:

	£(Sterling)	$(US)	$(CAN)	€(Euros)
Cost per order				
UK	2.00	3.00	4.50	3.30
Europe	3.00	4.50	6.75	5.00
North America	3.00	4.50	6.75	5.00
Rest of World	3.00	4.50	6.75	5.00
Additional cost per book				
UK	0.50	0.75	1.15	0.85
Europe	1.00	1.50	2.30	1.70
North America	2.00	3.00	4.60	3.40
Rest of World	2.50	3.75	5.75	4.25

PLEASE SEND CHEQUE, POSTAL ORDER (STERLING ONLY), EUROCHEQUE, OR INTERNATIONAL MONEY ORDER (PLEASE CIRCLE METHOD OF PAYMENT YOU WISH TO USE)
MAKE PAYABLE TO: STRATUS HOLDINGS plc

Cost of book(s): _____ Example: 3 x books at £6.99 each: £20.97

Cost of order: _____ Example: £2.00 (Delivery to UK address)

Additional cost per book: _____ Example: 3 x £0.50: £1.50

Order total including postage: _____ Example: £24.47

Please tick currency you wish to use and add total amount of order:

☐ £ (Sterling)   ☐ $ (US)   ☐ $ (CAN)   ☐ € (EUROS)

VISA, MASTERCARD, SWITCH, AMEX, SOLO, JCB:

☐ ☐ ☐ ☐ ☐ ☐ ☐ ☐ ☐ ☐ ☐ ☐ ☐ ☐ ☐ ☐ ☐ ☐ ☐ ☐

Issue number (Switch only):

☐ ☐ ☐

Start Date: ☐☐ / ☐☐   **Expiry Date:** ☐☐ / ☐☐

Signature: _____

NAME: _____

ADDRESS: _____

_____

POSTCODE: _____

Please allow 28 days for delivery.

Prices subject to change without notice.
Please tick box if you do not wish to receive any additional information. ☐

House of Stratus publishes many other titles in this genre; please check our website (**www.houseofstratus.com**) for more details.